NOMAN

William Nicholson

NOMAN

THE THIRD BOOK
OF THE
NOBLE WARRIORS

HARCOURT, INC.
Orlando   Austin   New York   San Diego   London

www.HarcourtBooks.com

First published in Great Britain in 2007 by Egmont Books Ltd.
First U.S. edition 2008

Library of Congress Cataloging-in-Publication Data
Nicholson, William.
Noman/William Nicholson.
p.   cm.—(The noble warriors; bk. 3)
Summary: Seeker, who is obsessed with his increasingly perilous
quest to kill the last of the old ones, finds that his mission has placed
him at odds with a new leader who preaches peace and joy.
[1. Self-realization—Fiction.   2. Conduct of life—Fiction.
3. Faith—Fiction.   4. Fantasy.]   I. Title.
PZ7.N5548No   2008
[Fic]—dc22   2007011209
ISBN 978-0-15-206005-3

Text set in Bembo
U.S. edition designed by Cathy Riggs

First U.S. Edition

A C E G H F D B

Printed in the United States of America

❖ CONTENTS ❖

THE FIRST STAGE
OF THE
EXPERIMENT

OBSERVATION

*As I slept, I dreamed that all men and
women long to live in peace; but when I woke I
saw that the world is ruled by fear. Fear makes men
cruel. Cruelty breeds hatred. Anger feeds on anger, and
misery gives birth to misery down the generations.*

*I saw how men and women turn to their gods
for protection. I saw their hunger to believe their gods
are strong, and their dread of the gods of others. I saw
how gods drive men into wars, and the wars of the
believers are the most merciless conflicts of all.*

Then I asked myself: must it always be so?

⊰ 1 ⊱

The Hunter

HIS PREY WOULD NOT ESCAPE HIM NOW.

Seeker climbed the narrow mountain track at a steady pace, following in the agile footsteps of his guide. Ahead and above them loomed the steep face of the mountainside, a fractured wall of rock that rose and broke and rose again—like a giant's staircase.

"There," said his guide, pointing, breathing hard with the exertion of the climb. "You see where the track comes to an end?"

Seeker looked, and saw that the rock face above was scored by regular lines.

"Is it a wall?"

"That's the way into the cave."

They continued up the zigzag track, and as they came closer, he saw it clearly. The wall was made of blocks of the same stone that formed the mountain, laid flush with the mountain's side—but this was the work of men.

"They're in there?"

"That they are," said his guide. "But once the mountain men close the door, there's no one can breach it." He spoke in the peevish tones of one who suspects he is not believed. "I told you you'd have a wasted journey."

"I see no door."

"No one sees it. But it's there."

They climbed on, and so at last reached the shelf of rock where the track ended. Here rose the wall, each block as high as a man and as wide as a man's arms can reach. They were set tight, one against the next, and cut clean into the mountainside. High above, in the third row of blocks, a horizontal line of small circular holes had been drilled through the stone to admit light and air.

Seeker studied the fortification. He felt the cracks between the blocks with his fingers, and pushed with his hands against each block in turn. It seemed impossible that one of these massive stones could swing open.

"Now you see for yourself," said the guide. "You wouldn't believe me. But you asked me to lead you to the cave, and I've done as you asked."

He rubbed his hands together, anxious to receive his payment and go.

"Can they hear us?" said Seeker. "Do they know we're here?"

"Oh, they know. They'll have been watching us since we left the valley."

"If I call to them, would they hear me?"

The guide became agitated.

"Best not to anger them. We should go back now."

"I'm not going back."

"But there's no use in it," whined the guide. "These old ones you seek, they'll have paid well. The mountain men keep their bargains."

"And so do I," said Seeker.

He stood back from the high wall, as far as the narrow shelf allowed, and called in a loud voice.

"Mountain men! Open your doors! I mean you no harm!"

"No!" cried the guide, frantically waving his arms. "No! They'll stone us! Leave them be! We must go!"

Seeker turned to the guide and spoke to him quietly.

"You go, my friend. My business is here."

The guide shuffled his feet and rubbed his hands together and looked at the ground.

"And my payment?"

"I have no money."

"No money? But you promised me payment! Am I to be cheated?"

Seeker touched his cheeks.

"I will pay you as I promised."

He held the guide's face lightly between his palms.

"I give you peace."

The guide became very still. Then he gave a small shudder and looked up at Seeker with shy, uncertain eyes.

In place of the shrill whine, there came a soft whisper. "Thank you," he said.

Seeker withdrew his hands. The guide looked round

him, blinking, as if he had just woken from sleep. Then he stretched all his body, reaching his arms out wide, and sighed deeply. Then he smiled.

"Thank you," he said again.

With that, he set off back down the track. Seeker watched him on his way. Then he turned back to the high rock wall.

"Open your doors!" he cried. "Or I'll break them down!"

From deep within the rock he heard the sound of mocking laughter.

"So be it."

He let his arms fall to his sides, and he closed his eyes. He felt his own weight on the warm ground. He felt the pressure of his bare feet on the mountain rock. Deep below he felt the slow stirring of the mountain's lir. He drew two long steady breaths and drove down and down until he touched the heart of that great slumbering power. Then steadily, surely, irresistibly, he drew it up into himself, making of himself a channel for the force of the mountain range.

All things are connected. All power is one power.

He opened his eyes and raised both arms. He stretched his arms out before him and summoned the lir to flow down his arms to his fingertips. He touched his two forefingers together.

A bolt of pure force struck the rock wall. The wall shuddered under the impact. Dust rose from the lines of mortar. The shuddering intensified, and the great stone blocks began to part. Seeker held his ground, arms out-reached, streaming power into the shivering wall. Now the stones were rattling against each other like teeth. One high block cracked with a sound like a hammer blow, then fell crashing and tumbling down the mountainside. There followed a deep grinding roar. The lower blocks began to bulge outwards as if pushed from within, opening up gaping cracks. The tall square-cut stones were rocking, moving, advancing like limbless giants. One block in the lower line staggered and fell. With a rending crash the rest came toppling down, one on another, amid a gush of debris and stone dust.

Seeker lowered his arms and waited for the dust to settle.

"Send out the old ones!" he cried. "I have no quarrel with anyone else."

There was no answer. From far below came the rattle of falling fragments, bouncing down the mountainside to the valley floor.

The broken outline of the cave mouth now became visible. Seeker stepped into the shadowy space. The walls and roof were those of a natural cave, which narrowed as it penetrated deeper into the mountain. The only light came from the opening. Within, all was darkness.

Seeker felt no fear, and no weariness. The destruction of the last two savanters was his mission and his obsession. Until it was accomplished, he had no other life. But now he had hunted them to the end. There would be a kill, and a kill.

And afterwards? Peace, if allowed. Rest, if deserved. Love, if given. And a home on the quiet side of the world.

He strode into the dark tunnel. As he went, the light behind him grew fainter and the only sounds he could hear were his own footsteps. The tunnel narrowed and twisted and turned. He began to feel his way with outstretched hands. The light dwindled, then was gone. He advanced in utter blackness. No longer guided by sight, he concentrated his attention on the sounds round him.

Nothing moved, but the sounds were changing. The passage was becoming wider. He sensed space opening up on either side of him. He came to a stop.

Now, his footfalls silent, he heard the faint sound of men breathing.

"You can't hurt me." He spoke his warning into the blackness. "Don't make me hurt you."

There came a soft stirring in the still air. Seeker's hyperacute senses traced the source: invisible arms reaching up, preparing to strike. Then came the rush of sudden motion, the hiss of hurled missiles. Too turbulent for spikes. They were throwing stones.

He stood still and flooded his body with force. The stones struck him and fell harmlessly to the ground. When the last missile had rattled into silence, he spoke to his attackers, saying again, "You can't hurt me."

There came a cry of fury, and the unseen mountain men fell on him from all sides. Seeker stood rooted as the mountain itself while his attackers dashed themselves against him like waves against a cliff. Every blow they struck made him stronger and left them weaker.

"What sort of devil is this?" they cried in terror.

A spark flickered. A candle flame swelled into brightness. An older man held the candle high. By its light Seeker saw the mountain men who had attacked him, lying groaning and helpless on the ground.

A rapid scan of the cave told him that the ones he hunted were not here.

"Where are the old ones?" he said.

"We promised them protection." The man with the candle spoke in a voice full of bitterness. "They paid well."

"Did they pay a price worth dying for?"

The mountain man broke into a harsh laugh.

"They offered us eternal life," he said. "And now you come to kill us."

"I've no quarrel with you," said Seeker. "Just tell me where they are."

"Deeper in," said the mountain man, handing Seeker the candle. "Follow the cave."

Seeker set off, holding the candle before him. The tunnel narrowed once more as it cut deeper and deeper into the mountain. In one place it opened out into a larger chamber, where there were signs of the life lived here—clay pots of water, rolls of bedding—but Seeker saw no other people. Evidently the savanters had retreated to the innermost reaches of the great cave.

The candle flame began to flicker. A little farther down the twisting tunnel, and it flickered more violently. Then

came a rush of air and the candle went out. In the sudden
darkness, Seeker felt wind on his face. Ahead, he caught a
glimpse of a faint light.

Filled now with fear, he hurried forward. As he went,
the light grew. He rounded a bend in the tunnel, and there
before him was the bright glare of a disc of sky. He raced
down the last stretch of tunnel and found himself emerging into open air.

He was on the far side of the mountain.

Bitter with disappointment, angry with himself for not
having anticipated such an obvious possibility, he scanned
the scene before him. A broad road ran down the mountain to a gorge. A bridge carried the road across the gorge
to the flanks of the next mountain on the far side. And
there, toiling up the distant slope, was a wagon drawn by
two horses.

Seeker strained his eyes to see. On the flat bed of the
wagon lay two white-canopied litters of the kind used to
carry the dead. The wagon was making good progress and
was far away. The savanters had escaped him again.

Now as he studied the terrain, Seeker saw that the fleeing savanters had taken another precaution to slow down
his pursuit. The timber bridge that spanned the gorge was
anchored by ropes on either side. The ropes on the far side
had been cut. The main span was still attached on his side
of the gorge, but the roadway now swayed untethered in
the wind, tilting down at a steep angle.

He looked up again and watched the wagon crest the
far peak and disappear out of sight. He lifted his gaze to

the sky to gauge the position of the declining sun. The wagon was heading east.

He loped down the road to the broken bridge, and from there he made a rapid survey of the gorge that cut off his pursuit. The savanters had planned their escape well. The sides of the gorge were vertical and very deep. Without the bridge in place it was impassable.

For a few wild moments he considered whether he could jump it, but he knew the gap was too wide. He stared at the far side of the gorge. He lifted his eyes to the steep mountain slopes that rose above it. Then he had an idea.

"If I can't get myself to the far side," he said, "I'll have to get the far side to me."

It was a crazy idea. It would take time. But he had the power.

Once again he planted his feet square on the rock, then merged his own life force with the life force of the mountain. Once again he hurled his unstoppable power at the rock face. But this time it was the far side of the gorge that he struck. His blows cracked open the rock and caused it to fall away in a shower of fragments, down and down to the dry riverbed far below. Again and again he struck, driving jagged fissures into the slopes above the gorge, and ever larger sections of the mountain broke loose and slithered down into the smoking depths.

Never relenting, hammer blow after hammer blow, through the afternoon hours as the sun sank in the sky, he pounded the mountain into rubble, and the rubble piled up higher and higher in the gorge. So at last the time came when he could scramble down below the broken bridge and make his way through the swirl of dust over the newly made mound of debris to the other side.

From here he was on his road. Half a day had been lost; but the hunt was on again.

"You won't escape me," he said aloud, as if the savanters could hear him. "You'll never escape me."

At the top of the pass, he paused to study the land ahead. The road wound its way down the mountain to a desert valley studded with rock formations. Beyond the valley rose a further line of hills, much lower than the mountain range on which he stood. Beyond the hills, he could make out a wide plain; and in the far distance, a forest. He searched long and hard for the wagon and at last saw it making its way between the columns of rock in the desert valley below.

The road looped back and forth down the mountain's broad descending flank. Seeker took the direct route, springing from loop to loop, landing each time on the flat road, steadying himself for the next jump. In this way, making up for lost time, he found himself in the valley as the sun was setting.

From here he could see the wagon clearly. It was now climbing the slope of the far hills. In the still evening air, he could hear the tramp of the horses' hooves, and the creaking of the wagon wheels, and the thin high cry of the driver urging on the weary horses: "Tuk–tuk–tuk!"

He was so focused on his prey that he barely noticed the curious features of the valley through which he was passing. It was dominated by a soaring massif called the Scar, a lone crag whose sheer sides rose up from the sandy ground like a castle in the sea. Beyond the Scar stood hundreds of towering sandstone tines, jagged needles of rock, which cast before them long shadows, bruise blue on the hot amber of the desert land. Seeker strode on, now lost in the shadow of one of these natural columns, now emerging suddenly golden into the slanting sunlight, throwing before him like an avenging arm his own long purple shadow.

As the setting sun touched the ridge of the Scar, some instinct told Seeker to pause and look back. The sun's final descent was rapid. The burning disc dwindled to a dome, a streak, a gleam, and it was gone. Then all at once a spark sprang to life on the upper wall of the Scar, and without warning, a shaft of brilliant light streamed out over the valley. There followed another and another, and then a curtain of light burst through a narrow cut in the crag. As the angle of the sun's rays changed second by second, so the beams of light came and went, and the Scar glittered like a colossal lantern. Cracks and fissures in the sandstone, invisible to the eye of the traveller, were penetrated by the brilliant light and turned into lancets of crimson and gold. The long beams lit up the tines in the valley, picking out one here, one there, as the rest of the land slipped into soft twilight.

Seeker saw the streams of dazzling light and was overwhelmed with awe. The crag was glowing as if it were alive. Only a trick of the setting sun, but all at once the whole world was charged with light. At any moment now, it seemed to him, the very earth on which he stood might shiver and crack and send forth from its secret depths rays of glory, as if it were a second sun.

What is this place? I must come back.

Then, as abruptly as it had begun, the dazzling display was over. The sun sank below the mountain horizon, and darkness flowed over the valley like sleep.

Seeker set off again, moving more rapidly now to make up for lost time. The wagon was out of sight over the crest of the hill. Beyond the line of hills lay the plains; beyond the plains, the great forest. Somewhere between here and there he would meet the savanters for one last time.

Then it would be over.

⹥ 2 ⹤

A Kiss at Last

MORNING STAR LAY ON HER BACK ON THE WARM EARTH and gazed up at the sky. Not a cloud broke the blazing blue of the summer morning. The branch of a tree overhead shielded her from the burn of the sun; its leaves stunted and already beginning to wither. No rain had fallen for six months. Even the grass was dying.

I must tell him, she thought to herself.

She heard shouts from the river below and, turning her head, looked down the bank to the cluster of men and boys gathered there. Two were standing ankle deep in the brown water, one with his head bowed, the other wielding a razor. As she watched she saw the razor slick neatly over the bowed head, and the last thick hank of hair plop into the water.

"Now get your stripes," said the man with the razor.

The shaved man looked up, grinning, uncertain, and

felt his bare scalp with both hands. Morning Star was struck by a deep sadness. Now this youth would have his head and face and neck painted with black-and-yellow stripes, and the Tigers would be one man stronger. Already they formed the biggest single band in the spiker army.

I must tell him today.

He wouldn't believe her, but still she must tell him. He was in danger. But when she told him, what would he do? What could he do? The Wildman's sudden rages had grown more frequent in recent months, and he could be murderous when roused. Only she could restrain him. Only she had some degree of influence over him, and even that was waning.

No time to lose. Go to him now.

Morning Star rose to her feet and turned towards the great camp. Every day it grew bigger. New bands of spikers came from far and wide, drawn by the Wildman's ever-growing prestige, and pitched their tents and threw up makeshift shanties. They dug fire pits and latrines, tethered their bullocks, and set their children loose to run about the alleyways. No one knew any more how large the spiker army had become; but it covered the land all the way from Spikertown to the swamps.

She walked back down the packed earth of the camp's main street, passing a platoon of armed men loping out to one of the training grounds. As they went by, red-faced and sweating, a gaggle of small boys punched the air and cried, "Wildman! Wildman! Wildman!"

So much training. So much cheering. What else could an army do when there was no enemy left to fight?

Turn in on itself, thought Morning Star. Fight itself.

A scarfed woman came out of a tent and ran to overtake her. She tugged at her sleeve.

"Little mother, help me. My husband's a good man, but he beats me. When he's drunk, he beats me."

She drew back the scarf and showed the bruises on her face.

"One day he'll kill me, little mother," she whispered. "But he's a good man."

Morning Star touched the woman's wounded cheek.

"Tell him I'm watching," she said. "Tell him I see everything he does."

"Oh, I will, little mother!" The woman was filled with joy. "He won't hurt me while you're watching! Oh, thank you, thank you!"

Morning Star continued on her way. She no longer tried to tell the people that she was no different from them. It had begun with the Wildman, who called her "the spirit of the spikers." From there the rumors had multiplied. Now she was looked on with reverence, as something between a lucky charm and a god.

A band of Tigers was approaching. They walked with an easy roll of the hips, filling the roadway from side to side, so that she had to step out of the way to let them pass. They looked about them with bold, insolent stares, inviting challenge. Their colors were easy to read. They wanted action.

Ahead she saw the high canopies of the command tent; not so much a tent as a long open-sided space formed by rows of poles, over which were stretched sailcloth awnings.

In this shade, on benches or on cushions among tables and water vats, gathered the chiefs of the spiker army. Here she would find the Wildman, each day quieter than the last, moving more slowly, speaking more softly, his gaze taking in everything and nothing. He was still wild, still beautiful, still unpredictable in his anger; but these days he felt so far away.

Now, she promised herself. Tell him now.

Snakey was prowling up and down, his eyes bright in his striped black-and-yellow face, stabbing the air with his hands.

"March on Radiance! What's to stop us?"

"What do we want with Radiance?"

The Wildman lay stretched out on the ground, his back supported by a mound of cushions. He was eating nuts from a bowl by his side, cracking them with his teeth, dropping the shells into a growing pile on the dry earth floor.

"Spiker rule!" exclaimed Snakey. "Spiker power!"

A growl of assent sounded from the Tigers gathered behind him.

"You want to rule Radiance, Snakey?"

Snakey stopped prowling and turned on his friend.

"You got an army here, Chick. Lot of itchy blades. Lot of hungry mouths. How long do we sit here and cook in the sun?"

"Till I say we go."

"Used to be you were the one in front and the rest of us running to keep up."

"No call for running till you know where you want to go."

The Wildman's slow speech frustrated Snakey. He squatted down before him and boxed his friend's arms with light jabs of his fists. He was only playing. He wanted true attention.

"Don't matter where we go," he said. "Let's go! Let's move!" He stabbed one hand at the bright light of the street. "Look out there! The women are planting corn between the tents. We're turning into farmers!"

The Tigers laughed at that. Farmers were soft, peaceable, helpless. Their only purpose was to grow food for spikers to rob.

"We go when I say we go," said the Wildman.

Snakey sprang up at that, offended, and strode off. His men followed. The Wildman didn't seem to notice that they'd gone.

Morning Star met Snakey on his way out as she entered the command tent.

"Heya, Star," said Snakey.

"Heya, Snakey."

"Wake him up for me." Snakey nodded back towards the Wildman. "Too hot to be doing nothing."

Morning Star dipped herself a cup of water from one of the vats. The Wildman lay on his cushions and cracked nuts and gazed at nothing.

Now, said Morning Star to herself. Now.

"I was down by the river," she said.

The Wildman went on cracking nuts.

"Watched the boys shaving heads, painting faces."

Still he didn't turn to look at her. But he was listening.

"Someone has to say it," she said.

"What?"

"Too many Tigers, Wildman. Can't go on like this."

"Don't see why not."

"Yes, you do."

He put another nut in his mouth and cracked it and spat out the shell. He did it all slowly, as if in a dream. So Morning Star found the courage to say what she knew, so that he would wake up.

"He means to kill you," she said.

He turned to her with empty eyes.

"Who?"

"Snakey."

"Snakey?" he said. "No. You're wrong there, Star."

"I can see his colors," she said, speaking low. "I'm not wrong. He's going to kill you."

"No," said the Wildman, shaking his head. "Snakey won't kill me. Snakey loves me."

Suddenly he woke from his dream and his eyes flashed with anger.

"Why do you say that? What's Snakey ever done to you? Are you jealous?"

"No, no—"

"You want me to have no friends but you?"

"No—"

"You want to have no one love me but you?"

This was far worse than anything she had prepared herself to face. His words wounded her and shamed her. She turned away, unable to speak.

"Snakey watched over me when I was five years old!"
Now he was shouting, out of control. "Snakey was father
and mother to me! Snakey saved my life every single day!
What have you ever done for me?"

There was nothing she could say. All she wanted to do
now was to get away without crying in front of him.

"You say you love me. Well, I don't want your kind
of love!"

She kept her head averted and waved one hand to say,
Yes, I understand; no more. She left him there, forcing herself not to run, feeling a stinging in her eyes.

Outside the command tent the sudden brightness of the
sunlight dazzled her. She shielded her eyes with one hand
and faced the ground. As she did so, the ground turned
dark. Frightened, she looked up and saw the same darkness everywhere, as if night had descended. The tents lining the street were black masses, past which walked gray
people, casting black shadows. Beyond the great camp the
hills were gray, beneath a leaden sky. All color had been
drained from the world.

She closed her eyes and leaned against a tent pole,
breathing rapidly.

I'm losing control of the colors. I'm going mad.

When she opened her eyes again the world had returned to its proper hues. Morning Star gave herself a
shake and walked away rapidly across the camp. When she
was sure she was far enough away not to be seen, she let
the tears come.

"This can't go on," she told herself.

———

Once Morning Star had left, the Wildman's mood changed. His anger faded, and he found himself consumed with restlessness. He stamped up and down the shaded length of the command tent, and kicked away the pile of cushions on which he had been sitting, and trod with one bare foot on the little heap of nutshells, and shouted out loud at the stab of pain.

Then he strode away down the main street towards the river.

As he walked, buried doubts began to surface. All round him was the great army he had called into being. Not just the fighting men: the women, the children, the cart oxen and the milk cows, the huts and the wagons, the cats and the dogs and the rats, an entire seething city sprung out of nowhere. For what? He had dreamed of becoming a warlord like Noman, the only living man to come face-to-face with the All and Only. But the god he had believed in was dead. The Nomana were dispersed. And he was left alone, powerful but purposeless, a warlord without a war. Snakey urged him to march on Radiance, but there was no army in Radiance. The axers had melted away after the disappearance of their priest-king. Radiance was given over to bandits and looters. There was no glory to be won there; only the messy business of imposing order and policing the streets. The Wildman was a bandit, not a policeman.

Snakey said, Let's go! Let's move! But where?

On the high bank above the river, the Wildman came to a stop and looked down at the scene below. A group of men were painting black-and-yellow stripes over newly shaved heads. More recruits for Snakey's Tigers.

He watched the upraised faces as the paint transformed the young men into some other kind of creature, something pitiless and frightening. The stripes created a powerful bond. The Tigers were the finest fighters in his army. But were they his, or Snakey's?

Snakey loves me.

Suppose Snakey were to make a challenge to his leadership. Would the bands loyal to him be strong enough to defeat the Tigers?

He shook his head angrily. This was the work of Morning Star. She had infected his mind with doubt. But he was proud of the Tigers. He had always looked on them as his surest line of defense.

Now, watching the new recruits swagger in their striking new markings, he saw the Tigers for the first time as an army within his army, and he knew that their power must not be allowed to grow any stronger. Morning Star was wrong about Snakey, he was sure of that. Snakey would never turn on him. But there might rise up other chiefs within the Tigers with ambitions that were harder to control.

What should he do?

The answer lay before him. It was the shaved heads and the painted stripes that made the Tigers. Scrub off the paint. Let the hair grow back. No more private army. He, the Wildman, united all spikers under his leadership. That alone must be the source of their pride and their strength.

The decision made, he felt a wave of new resolve flow through him. For weeks—he could admit it now—he had been becalmed, like a sailing ship at sea when the wind has died. Nothing had interested him. Nothing had given him pleasure. Even now he had no idea where he should go, or what he should do with his great army. But he had an immediate challenge before him, one that he was sure would meet resistance, and the Wildman liked opposition.

"No," said Snakey.

"I'm the chief, Snakey." The Wildman stood before him, his eyes glittering. "I give the order. You have to obey."

"It's a bad order, Chick. Nobody obeys a bad order."

"Then you answer to me."

Snakey held his painted head high with defiance. On either side the chiefs of the bands looked on in utter silence. All understood that suddenly, out of nowhere, a battle for supremacy had exploded into the open.

"Our stripes are our pride," said Snakey. "You don't take our pride."

"There's only one chief."

"You're the chief. When did I say different?"

"Then, you obey."

"Not this time, Chick."

Morning Star, standing unnoticed at the back, could see from Snakey's colors that he had come to the meeting ready to fight. Even now he was working himself up for the conflict. His colors pulsed a deep fierce red, and he rose up and down on the balls of his feet, tensing every muscle in his body, for action. He was a bigger man than the Wildman, and hardened by long years of bandit fighting; but he had no chance. The Wildman had been trained as a Noble Warrior.

"You mean to fight me, Snakey?"

"Man-to-man. No tricks."

"Any way you want."

"Call it."

"Now."

So quickly it had begun. Neither man moved for a moment. They stood some five paces apart, watching each other, sensing each other's intentions. Morning Star, looking from one to the other, realized that the Wildman still did not believe that this was a fight to the death. He was not afraid enough, and so not angry enough.

Snakey turned and walked away. His back was to the Wildman, presenting an easy target. The Wildman made no move to attack.

"You breaking?"

"No break," replied Snakey. "The fight's on."

He walked out into the blazing brightness of the street, and down the bronzed earth road to the far end, where he came to a stand. The more public the encounter, the more pride was at stake. On the street, you fought to the end. No mercy, no surrender.

The Wildman followed more slowly. He made his stand facing Snakey. A hundred paces between them, and their shadows sharp on the dirt.

"You don't want to do this, Snakey."

"I'm doing it, Chick."

Spikers came crowding from all sides to line the long

street, the Tigers massing on the south side, armed and ready. When the Wildman saw this, he understood that everything that was happening had been planned. But still he could not believe that Snakey wanted to kill him.

"Don't do this, Wildman," shouted Morning Star.

"You started it," replied the Wildman. "Now I'm going to finish it."

Morning Star knew what would happen now. She didn't want to see it, but couldn't leave. So she stood still and silent in the sun, like everyone else in the ever-growing crowd, and waited for the storm to break.

The Wildman was the first to move. He set off at a slow deliberate pace down the street towards Snakey. His lean golden arms swung by his sides, his silver bracelets jangling and glinting in the sunlight. He carried no weapons. His eyes shone.

"Chuck-chuck-chicken," he murmured as he walked. "Here comes the Wildman."

Snakey drew his spike and moved it from hand to hand. He could throw with his left as well as his right. One spike, one throw. Then it would be bare hands.

The Wildman kept on walking, twenty paces away now, closing in. Snakey crouched, bouncing on his long wiry legs, still passing his spike from hand to hand.

"No tricks, Chick," he said.

"Just you and me, Snakey."

On he came. No way of knowing what strike he was planning. The way he was walking he looked as if he had in mind to walk on by.

"Heya!" he called softly. "Do you lo-ove me?"

Snakey sprang. With one bound, he halved the distance between them, and as he sprang, he hurled his spike. Not at the Wildman, but up, spinning over his head, forcing him to look up—and as he looked up, Snakey struck, hands in a double fist, punch powering deep into the Wildman's belly. And the Wildman was down.

The spike fell to the ground, impaled itself in the dirt, and Snakey seized it. The Wildman lay buckled on the road, winded, struggling for breath, seeing only the patch of earth before his eyes. But onto that patch of earth fell the shadow of the spike as it descended, and with a violent convulsion of his body he twisted aside, and the spike smashed into the ground. Snakey had struck with so much force that he couldn't pull the spike out again. The Wildman rolled and looked up, saw Snakey black against the glare of the sky, and knew the blow had been intended to kill.

So Star was right.

The certainty released him. No more doubt. Now it was kill or be killed.

"Hey-a-aa!"

With a ripple of pure force he was up on his feet and one hand was jabbing, jabbing, nothing too serious, just to keep his opponent on his back foot. Then two swift steps in close to a full-body hold, each now holding the other, and Snakey squeezing him, aiming to crack his ribs in his strong arms. But the Wildman had him where he wanted him, and his hands felt for his black-and-yellow striped neck.

Once he had his neck he had his life. This was what he knew how to do, no tricks, man-to-man. There in the street for all to see, in the burning mid-afternoon sun, he gripped and gripped and felt Snakey's arms go limp round him, and a savage exultation flooded his senses. From somewhere far away he heard Morning Star's voice calling, "No, Wildman! No!" but the joy in his heart answered, *Yes, Wildman! Yes!* and he squeezed the life from the one who had tried to kill him, his challenger, his enemy, his childhood friend.

Such a silence at the end. Nothing moving now. With difficulty he cracked open his hands and the thing dropped to the ground, and the silence covered it. No joy now. Only exhaustion, and something deeper than exhaustion. The Wildman sank to his knees. There was Snakey staring up at him, only he didn't see him, because he was dead.

And I might as well be dead too, thought the Wildman as he slid into the silence.

It was dark, and Morning Star was standing by his side, illuminated by the soft light of a candle.

"Night already?"

"Almost morning."

"I've slept long."

"You emptied yourself," she said. "You had to sleep."

"What did I do?"

"You took a life."

He remembered then. Snakey loved him. Snakey tried to kill him.

"Seems you were right."

"Wish I hadn't been."

Her voice was different. She sounded as if something had broken in her.

"Had to do it, Star."

She was silent for a moment. He looked up at her and smiled. He liked to see her familiar face. He was used to having her watch him. But she was not watching him now. Her eyes were gazing into the shadows.

"I'm going to go away," she said.

That was what had changed. She had stopped needing him. The Wildman had never known how much she had needed him until it stopped.

"Don't go."

She shook her head, very slightly. The decision was made. Inside herself, she had already left.

"You're the spirit of the spikers, Star. You're the little mother. Can't do it without you."

"You don't need me, Wildman. You don't need anyone."

"Don't go today. Today's not a good day."

"Like you always say," she said, "people do what they have to do."

She rose to her feet.

"I only stayed this long to say good-bye."

Through the opening of the tent the Wildman saw his friend and self-appointed bodyguard, Pico, asleep on a rug. Beyond him the Caspian called Sky, who was only ever ridden by Morning Star or himself.

"You'll take Sky?"

"No. I'll take nothing."

That was the Nomana way: to possess nothing, to build no lasting home. To love no one person above all others.

A great ache opened up in the Wildman. He wanted to say to her that the bond between them, between himself and her and Seeker, was all they had. He wanted to tell her that he missed the old days. He wanted to tell her that he hadn't meant to kill Snakey, and didn't want to be the leader of an army, and no longer knew where to lead them. But he said none of it. Partly it was pride. But also he knew it would make no difference. People did what they had to do.

"Take care on the road, Star. Dangerous times."

She stooped down and kissed his cheek; a kiss at last. She had wanted to kiss him for so long, but now that she did, what had once seemed so big had become little. Only a pressure of the lips.

"Till we meet again, Wildman."

⊰ 3 ⊱

Lost Children

MORNING STAR LEFT THE SPIKER CAMP BEFORE THE SUN rose, while the new day was still cooled by the night. She had no direction to go; but she walked fast, simply wanting to be gone.

As she walked, her mind was full of what she was leaving, and of the momentous fact that she was leaving. For so many months she had allowed herself to be filled by her passion for the Wildman, and now, as quickly as it had come, it had gone. She felt as if she had woken from a dream. Now she could admit to herself that she had been unhappy for all that time. She had no place in the spiker army. She was not their little mother. She had stayed in the camp only to be close to the Wildman. That closeness had been necessary to her, but it had not made her happy. Most days he had not even noticed her existence. Over the months she had shrunk in size, it seemed to her, until she had reached the point of invisibility, or of not existing at all. That was why she had had to go. To exist once more.

That, and the killing. It had shocked her deeply. In those terrible last moments, she had looked at the Wild-man and seen on his face and in his colors, in the pulsing reds shivering into orange, a terrible ecstasy of killing joy.

She didn't blame him. If she blamed anyone, she blamed herself: for not speaking sooner, for not knowing the Wildman better, for provoking the fight—in sum, for see-ing too much and doing too little. Her gift had brought no good to anyone. Better that she go.

As the sun rose and cast her shadow long and thin be-fore her, it struck her that this was how her mother must have felt, all those years ago, when she had run away from her husband and child to escape the darkness.

Am I running away from the darkness?

She followed the road into a dip in the land, at the bottom of which was a stream lined with willow trees. The stream had dried up, leaving its stony bed exposed to the light of the new day. At the point where the road in-tersected the stream, three large smooth boulders lay in a line: stepping-stones to carry travellers over the water, now beached by the drought. On the middle one of the three stepping-stones sat a small boy, his head in his hands, weeping.

As the child became aware of her approach, he stopped snivelling. He peeped at her between his fingers. She ad-vanced slowly, not wanting to frighten him.

"Can I help you?" she said.

"Lost," he replied.

He was indescribably dirty. She guessed he was about six years old, but he was wearing the clothing of a grown man. The sleeves and waist and leggings were hitched up and tied with string.

"Who are your people?"

"Don't know."

"How did you get lost?"

"Don't know."

He had stopped crying. His grimy cheeks were well smeared by the rubbing of his hands, but there was no sign of tears. His aura was a feeble muddy orange.

He jumped off his boulder and held out one dirty little hand for her to take.

"You look after me," he said.

It was more a demand than a request. He had a sharp little face and long matted brown hair that kept falling across his eyes. Morning Star took his hand and felt the immediate tenacious clamp of his grip.

"Come along," he said.

He tugged at her, so she came along. They crossed the stream to the other side, then left the road to follow a faint path. For a lost child he seemed to be in a remarkable hurry.

"Where are we going?"

"Along," he said.

She established his name, which as far as she could tell was Burny, but he did not ask for hers. He struck her as being very nervous. Nothing odd about that, given that he was a lost child, but it felt somehow out of place, or unexplained.

The boy must have sensed her hesitation, because all at once he started to talk.

"So I'm lost and you found me," he informed her. "I'm a lost child crying and that, and here we are, coming along."

"Yes," said Morning Star, rather taken aback. "Here we are."

"And you're holding my hand and that, and I'm the poor little kiddy you found lost and crying—"

It seemed to strike him then that he wasn't crying, so he offered a few token whines as if to round out the picture. They had now left the road and the stream and the willows behind and were approaching a section of the old ruined wall that had once formed the boundary of a long-forgotten kingdom. Where their path met the heaps of fallen stones, the way had been cleared so that travellers could pass unobstructed. On either side the remains of the wall rose up in broken mounds.

Morning Star came to a stop. The child jerked on her arm, but she didn't move.

"You'd better tell me, Burny."

He started to cry. This time actual tears flowed.

"I'm just a poor little kiddy," he wailed. "You found me lost and crying. You got to look after me." He gave a violent tug on her hand. "You got to come along. Just over there."

"What's just over there, Burny?"

"It's not fair," he wailed. "I said the words. I did the crying. It's not fair."

"You did it all very well," said Morning Star soothingly. "No one could have done it better."

"There," said the boy, looking round and raising his voice. "Lady says I done it right, so it's not my fault."

Morning Star looked towards the tumbled mounds of stones.

"I think you might as well come out," she said.

So out they came. There were three of them, a boy of about thirteen and two girls, one big and one little. They were all as ill-dressed and dirty as Burny, and had the same pinched, hard look on their underfed faces. They carried knives.

"You boggy baby!" said the boy. "Trust you to make a muck."

"Didn't!" cried Burny. "Lady says I done it right!"

"Don't need boggy babies in the band."

"I said the words! I did the crying!"

"Let him be," said the big girl, a sullen-faced ten-year-old. "We got work to do."

The children were closing in on Morning Star, forming a circle round her. They held their knives in their hands and fixed their eyes on her legs and arms.

"If you mean to rob me," she said, "I've got nothing."

"Everyone got something."

"The clothes I'm wearing. That's all."

"They'll do."

Now they were very close. Morning Star looked from

face to face, seeing there the tense energy focused only on the deed, not on her. They were more like young wolves than children.

But they were children.

"All right," she said. "You can have my clothes."

She let go of Burny's hand, and making only slow movements, she unwound her badan. She drew her tunic over her head and laid it on the ground before her. The two girls started to snicker. She shrugged off the vest she wore beneath, and she laid that too on the ground. The snickering stopped.

Now she was naked from the waist up, and the bandit children were staring at her in absolute silence. In particular the one she took to be the leader, the big boy, was staring with his mouth open.

She began to untie her breeches.

"Stop!" cried the sullen-faced girl. "This is stupid."

She turned on the boy in a sudden fury.

"What you gooping at, Hem?"

The boy jumped as if she had smacked him.

"Nothing."

The two little children looked to their leaders.

"Do we cut her? Do we do it?"

"No," said the girl. "We don't want her boggy clothes."

Burny ran to the sullen girl and pulled at her arm.

"Libbet!" he cried. "Libbet! I did it right, didn't I? It's not my fault. I never made a muck."

"Don't matter now," said Libbet.

Morning Star put her clothes on again. Hem, the big boy, was trying not to stare at her and failing. His colors were quite different from the others. All round him hovered the gray blue of helpless yearning.

Throughout the entire confrontation, Morning Star had felt no fear. It hadn't been necessary to use her strength to defend herself. But now it was over, she found she wanted to help these wild children; and for that, she needed to command their respect.

"Look at me, all of you," she said.

They all looked at her but for the one called Libbet.

"You too, Libbet."

Libbet glanced round, full of scorn.

"If you think—"

It only needed that one moment of eye contact. The angry words died on her lips. Morning Star held them all, touching them with the smallest tremor of the power that was in her, not wanting to crush them or awe them, only to make them understand that she could protect them.

Then she sat down on one of the mounds of rubble and spread her arms wide.

"Come to me," she said.

They came, their knives still in their hands, and crowded into her embrace. They didn't jostle or quarrel, but each one strained to be as close to her as possible; Libbet too, and Hem. They huddled round her in the early morning sun, and felt her warmth and power, and nuzzled her body with their dirty faces as if she were their mother.

"We can all help each other," she said to them, stroking their bony backs and their knotted hair. "Let's all be good to each other."

After this they took her back to their den, which was no more than a burrow in a nearby bush. Here they had stored the fruits of their robberies: some old empire gold shillings, some clothes, some travel packs. They robbed for food, which they ate there and then. The rest was of little use to them.

"When did you last eat?"

"Yesterday," said Libbet.

"What time yesterday?"

"'Bout now."

"So you're hungry again."

"Always hungry," said Libbet with a shrug.

"Me too."

"You can share what we get," said Hem.

"Thank you," said Morning Star. "But this doesn't seem the best place to get food. I'm on my way to my home village. Why don't you come with me?"

"We stay clear of villages," said Hem.

"They chase us!" chimed in the little girl, who was called Deedy. "They put dogs on us!"

"I'll tell them not to," said Morning Star. "But you'll have to stop attacking people."

"Then, how are we to live?"

"We'll find a way."

"What makes you so clever?" said Libbet in a surly tone.

"I'm a Noble Warrior," said Morning Star, drawing her badan over her head.

They all gasped at that.

"A real hoodie?"

"Yes."

"I heard they was gone," said Hem. "I heard their castle was smashed to muck."

"They've gone from one place. Now they're every place."

"So, you're a hoodie." Libbet was taking in this information, and it pleased her. It made it all right that she had given in to her. "I'll come along with you if you want."

That was all it took. Burny and Deedy clamored to come with her too, and Hem shrugged as if to say that he cared very little either way.

Burny chose to take this outcome as a personal triumph.

"I found her!" he said to anyone who would listen. "I said the words. I did the crying. I got us the hoodie lady."

Morning Star was glad of their company on the road. They quarrelled with each other and endlessly demanded her attention, and that stopped her from thinking about herself. Libbet scolded and chivvied them, graceless but caring in her way, and Hem acted the man, strutting ahead of their little procession and scowling at others they encountered on the road.

When they reached one of the many rivers that watered the fertile plain, Morning Star proposed that they all take a wash. The river was low, but clear water was flowing in midstream, and it was shallow enough for even the smallest to stand up in. The little ones regarded washing as a water game, all the more welcome after a long morning tramping the sunbaked road. They stripped themselves naked and hurled themselves into the river, then set about an activity they called washing but which more closely resembled fighting.

"Let's wash Burny! Grab him! Wash him!"

"Yow! Ow! Let me go!"

Libbet washed herself more sedately, sitting on the riverbank, stripping off sections of her clothing one at a time. Hem did not wash at all.

Morning Star was aware that he watched her, while doing his best to make out he was doing nothing of the sort. She could still see the look on his face and the color of his aura when he had seen her stripped before them. She had thought about it since and had come to the conclusion that Hem had been struck with admiration. Morning Star was far from vain about her personal appearance, but the colors never lied. This led her to a further conclusion that was new to her. She was no beauty, of that she was sure. But perhaps—just possibly—she had a beautiful body.

Hem was only a boy, but he was a boy forced by hardship to grow up young. He was a boy becoming a man. He was awkward and shy and aggressive and suspicious of everyone, but in his unguarded eyes she had caught the first ever reflection of herself as a woman who might be desirable to a man. She was not a little mother to Hem.

"Not going to wash, Hem?"

"What for?" he muttered. "The muck comes back."

They didn't eat all that day, and were dull with hunger by the time they reached the village. Morning Star led her

ragged little troop past the familiar landmarks of her childhood towards her family home. Here was the timber
bridge over the stream, and here the long stone on which
the village women beat the wet clothes on washday. Here
was the bakehouse with its great oven, where once she had
seen a whole pig being roasted. Here was the fork in the
road, with its bench made of a felled tree, where there was
always one of the old people sitting watching the world
go by. But there was no one on the bench this late afternoon. There was no one to be seen anywhere. There were
chickens scratching in the dirt in front of the houses, and
a cat asleep in a warm patch of late sunlight; but their
owners were out of sight.

It had always been a quiet village. Hill people kept
themselves to themselves. Perhaps it was market day in the
town by the river.

Morning Star reached the last house, which was her
own house and was set apart from the rest, its back to the
stream. Barely a trickle was flowing between the brown
and yellow grasses. The neat verge in front of the house
was bald. No rain here, either.

The door stood open.

Morning Star half expected Amik to come bounding
out to greet her, or little Lamb. Not so little any more.
Lamb must be fully grown.

"Is this it?" said Libbet.

"This is my home."

"Just so long as there's something to eat."

Morning Star called ahead into the house, not wanting
to arrive entirely unannounced.

"Papa! Mama!"

No sound from within.

She entered. The main room was empty. Her father's papers and pen and ink were neatly laid out before an open book. Everything was as it had always been, but the occupants were gone.

The children came crowding in after her. Practiced thieves, they soon found the food store and started snatching for the victuals.

"No! Put it down!" she ordered them. "You can't just grab what you like."

"Why not?"

"Because we have to share. That way it's fair."

Under their suspicious gaze she divided up the sheep cheese and the bread and honey.

"Libbet got more than me!"

"I didn't!"

But they were hungry and would rather eat than argue. The food was soon gone. Before Morning Star could stop them, the children had run out of the house and into a neighboring house, scavenging for more to eat. She followed behind.

"Creepy place," said Hem. "Ghost village."

"It's not a ghost village," said Morning Star.

"So where's everybody?"

"Out. Working."

"Children, too?"

He was right. It had never been like this. Every house the children raided was deserted; but everywhere there were signs of recent life. The people seemed to have left, but there was no evidence of any struggle. In one house there was even a meal laid for two, complete with a full bottle of apple brandy that had been uncorked but not poured. Somewhere between the drawing of the cork and the raising of the bottle something had happened, and the meal had been abandoned.

In the smallest and poorest of the cottages, tucked away behind the bakehouse, lived a crippled lady known as Nanna. She had never left her single room in all the years Morning Star had known her—receiving charity and companionship from those villagers who chose to call on her at her home. Surely Nanna could not have left.

Morning Star sought out her cottage and found the door open here, too. But as soon as she stepped inside she knew the house was not empty.

"Nanna?"

She peered into the gloom of the interior. A rustling came from the box bed. A white face rose up from the pillows to peer at her.

"It's me. Morning Star."

"They've gone," said Nanna in a thin trembly voice. "They said to go with them. But I have my trouble, you see."

"Where have they gone, Nanna?"

"Oh, I don't know where, dear. They've gone with the happy people."

❊ 4 ❊

Death on Horseback

CARESSA WATCHED FROM THE DOORWAY OF THE FARM-house as the horsemen made their way up the track. This time she counted twelve of them. This time, she knew, they would not leave until they had got what they wanted.

She took up a short sword and strapped it into her belt on her left side. On her right side she fixed a quiver of slender throwing spikes. She had no plan, no certainty that she would use the weapons. She only knew that she would not stand by and do nothing while they humiliated a help-less man.

The riders were nearer now. In the lead was Sasha Jahan, the eldest of Amroth Jahan's three sons. He glared from side to side as he rode, as if the sight of the aban-doned farm was a personal affront: the gates of the pens swinging on broken hinges, the doors to the outbuildings kicked in by looters, the giant weeds standing like sentries across the cracked earth.

Caressa had brought the Great Jahan here as the fierce short spring had driven out the last of winter, and here she had watched over him as he had aged and sickened before her eyes. He laughed as loudly as ever, and shouted as much, but his body dwindled day by day. They never spoke of it. They made no plans for the future. When his sons had come to him before and asked him to name one of them as his successor, he had burst into a mighty rage and slashed at them with his whip; the same silver-handled whip that must be passed on to the next Great Jahan of the Orlan nation.

And now he was weaker still; and they were back.

The horsemen stopped at the broken fence and dismounted. They spoke together briefly, in low voices. Then the three sons approached Caressa in the farmhouse door.

"We've come to talk with my father," said Sasha Jahan. He spoke abruptly and did not meet Caressa's eyes.

"He doesn't want to see you," Caressa replied.

"We'll see him," said Sasha grimly. "Whether he wants it or not."

Caressa's black eyes flashed with anger.

"Who are you to give orders to the Jahan of Jahans?"

"Who are you to stand in my way? What business is this of yours? You're no Orlan. What is it you want with a feeble old man?"

Caressa stared at him with contempt.

"I saw your father when he was the leader of ten thousand men. I saw him take on each one of you and drag you down into the dirt. And you call him a feeble old man! Have you forgotten so soon?"

"No," said Sasha Jahan bitterly. "I've not forgotten. I've not forgotten how he laughed at me, and called me a lumpish fool, and rolled his eyes when I spoke. I've not forgotten how he beat me when I offended him, and made me fear him, and made me hate him. No, I've not forgotten."

A silence followed this outburst. Then Alva Jahan spoke.

"What my brother says is true."

Caressa looked from one to the other.

"So now that he can no longer defend himself, you come for your revenge?"

"No," said Sabin, the youngest brother. "We come to ask him to name his successor. The Orlan nation must have a leader again."

"And if he refuses?"

"What's it to you?" exclaimed Sasha. "He's twice your age, and always drunk, and no beauty, and sick. What's he got left to give you?"

"He gives me nothing," said Caressa proudly. "But he has honored me with his love. I saw him when he was great. I would rather have nothing and the love of a great man than all the world and the company of little men like you."

Sasha blushed an angry red and turned aside.

"Let's search him out," he said. "He's here somewhere."

As he spoke there came a deep roar of laughter from one of the barns.

"That's him. Drunk in the hay!"

The three sons strode across the yard to the hay barn. There, in a broad hollow in the haystack, they found their father, Amroth Jahan. Round him and over him there wriggled and squealed a litter of six-week-old piglets.

"Piggy, piggy, piggy!" he was crying, scrabbling with his great hands to take hold of one of the piglets.

His sons stared at him in shock. Their father, once so explosively powerful, had become an old man. His cheeks had sunk and his hair was gray. His laugh was the same as ever, but his eyes when he looked up and discovered them were cloudy and pale.

"Go away!" he shouted at them. "Don't need you any more. Got new sons—much pinker—much more wriggly!"

He managed now to grasp one of the piglets. He held it up and kissed its nose.

"You shall rule after me," he crooned. "Piggy Jahan!"

The piglet wriggled from his hands and burrowed into the hay. From somewhere out of sight came the deep grunts of the mother sow.

"Father," said Sasha. "You know why we're here."

"Piggy, piggy, piggy," said Amroth Jahan. "Where did you go?"

"Father! Listen to me!"

"Listen to you?" The Jahan goggled at Sasha as if this was an incomprehensible request. "Why should I listen to you? You're my son Sasha, the lump head. You've never said anything worth listening to in all your lump-headed life." His withered face cracked into a wide grin. "I'd rather listen to my piggies squealing. Piggy, piggy, piggy!"

He roared with laughter.

It was the laughter that snapped Sasha's self-control. He drew his blade and jabbed it in the air and burst into a stream of violent abuse.

"You're drunk!" he screamed. "You're a joke! Everyone laughs at you! I laugh at you! Ha-ha! The Great Jahan! Only you're not so great any more; you're sick and old and a joke! You shame the whole Orlan nation! You've bullied me all your life and now it's over, it's over, it's over! And I'm laughing, I'm happy, because I've always hated you, I've always wished you were dead, so hurry up and die, old man! Everyone wants you dead!"

Amroth Jahan was not laughing any more.

"You want me dead?"

Sasha struggled to regain his dignity.

"I want you to name me as the Jahan of Jahans."

"While I still live?"

"It's over, Father. We all know it. The Orlan nation must have a new leader."

Amroth Jahan heaved himself slowly to his feet and fumbled at his waistband for the silver-handled whip. His sons watched him, unsure what he meant to do. If he gave Sasha the whip, he would be handing over his title and his power. Instead he held it up before them.

"You want this," he growled, "you'll have to kill me for it."

"If I have to," said Sasha, raising his blade once more.

"Stop this!"

A commanding voice cried out from behind him. Amroth Jahan smiled.

"Meet Caressa, boys."

Caressa had a spike in one hand and a blade in the other and a look about her that said she was ready to use both.

"Back away!"

"Then you make him see sense," said Sasha. "It's over. He's a joke."

"What's the joke?" said Caressa, never dropping her guard. "Tell me, so that I can laugh, too."

All three of the Jahan's sons were struck by the fierce cutting edge to her voice, but it had not yet occurred to them to fear her.

"He's sick and old and sleeps with the pigs," said Sasha. "Look at him."

Caressa looked.

"I see the man who conquered the world," she said.

"Oh, beauty!" cried Amroth Jahan. "What a woman!"

"Have him!" said Sasha. "Keep him! But I must have the whip!"

He made a grab for the whip and caught the cord and wound it tight round his right arm. Amroth Jahan had a firm grip on the handle, but he was far weaker than he had once been and Sasha knew it. He pulled on the cord and dragged his father towards him.

Caressa's cool, clear voice sliced the air.

"Let go or die!"

The threat stopped Sasha only for a moment.

"I'm not afraid of a woman," he said.

"Mistake, son," said Amroth Jahan. "You're not half the man she is."

He roared with laughter.

"Don't laugh at me!" screamed Sasha. He pulled on

the whip's cord, yanking his father close, and in the same movement thrust into him with his sword. Caressa saw and struck.

The spike hissed through the air and buried itself deep between Sasha's shoulder blades. Sasha uttered a single grunt and dropped to his knees. Amroth Jahan stood motionless before him, his eyes on Caressa.

"Oh, you beauty!" he said.

Sasha's sword was protruding from his belly, where it had been plunged halfway to the hilt. The Jahan now grasped the sword with both hands and pulled it out. Blood gushed from the wound. Caressa ran to him and caught him as he fell.

"Help me here!" she shouted. Alva and Sabin, too shocked to know what else to do, came to her aid.

Together they laid the Jahan on the hay and bound his wound as tightly as they could, to staunch the flow of blood. They looked to Sasha too, but he was beyond help. That one awesome blow had killed him instantaneously.

The rest of the band of Orlan officers, having heard the fracas, came running to the barn and stared at the scene. Sasha Jahan dead. The Great Jahan dying before their eyes. Alva and Sabin white-faced by his side. And the beautiful dark-haired woman commanding them all.

The Orlans dropped to their knees in grief and respect. Amroth Jahan looked at them and nodded.

"Nearly over," he said. "Bring me Malook. Bring me my horse."

"You can't ride," said Caressa.

"Do as you're told, woman!"

The exclamation cost him more strength than he had. He closed his eyes and bowed his head.

"It's the Orlan way," said Alva. "Orlans die on horse-back."

So Malook was found and led into the barn. The Caspian bent his head low and snuffled at his master's face, and the touch gave the Jahan renewed strength.

"Here, beauty," he said to Caressa.

She knelt by his side. He took her hand and pressed it to Malook's brow.

"I give him to you. But Malook must carry me one last time."

Together they heaved the Jahan up onto Malook's back. The blood was streaming from his wound and down his thigh. Once mounted he pulled himself upright and looked down at the ring of faces round him. He raised his silver-handled whip, which had never left his grasp.

"I name my successor," he said. He reached the whip down. Alva stepped forward. "Not you, baboon," said his father. "Here is your leader." He handed the whip to Caressa. "I give you your new Jahan of Jahans. Obey her as you have obeyed me."

Caressa took the whip in her hand and heard the dying Jahan's words with perfect amazement. She had neither sought this honor nor expected it. She saw bitter fury on Alva's face, and sheer bewilderment on Sabin's, but neither spoke a word. Their father was not dead yet.

His strength was failing fast. He lowered his body so

that he was lying on Malook's back. Caressa kissed him for the last time. His ugly face, pale from loss of blood, cracked into a last grin.

"Always wanted to die young," he said.

He murmured softly to Malook and the Caspian moved away, stepping carefully across the farm to the open gates. From there he picked up speed until he was cantering steadily westward over the parched land. Caressa and the Orlans watched in silence, knowing this was his last ride. They saw the Great Jahan rise up from his slumped position and sit tall on Malook's back. They saw him reach out his arms on either side in the Orlan victory charge. They saw him hold this proud pose for a few moments in the sun, and at last they saw him fall.

They dug him a grave on the spot where he fell, according to the Orlan fashion. They dug a second grave by his side for his eldest son. While the men were engaged in the slow labor of digging the dry ground, Caressa sat by the dead man and stroked his hair and thought long and hard about his crazy final gift.

They lowered the Jahan of Jahans into the ground, and Sasha Jahan too, and covered them with earth, and left no marker where they lay. This too was the Orlan way.

"An Orlan lives on in his sons," they said. "He needs no headstone."

Alva Jahan never spoke. His eyes were on the silver-handled whip, which Caressa now wore in her belt.

They returned together to the abandoned farm, where there was brandy to drink to the memory of the dead men. Then after due honor had been done, Alva spoke at last—in a low bitter voice.

"My father was not in his right mind before he died," he said. "The words he spoke were madness."

"You think so?" said Caressa.

"What he said—it's impossible. You're a woman. You're not an Orlan. You could never be the Jahan."

"So who's to take your father's place?"

"I am," said Alva. "I'm his son."

"So am I," said Sabin.

"I'm the elder," retorted Alva.

"Why does that give you the better right?" said Sabin. "Younger sons have been chosen before."

"Our father is no longer here to choose." Alva was struggling to contain his fury. "It must be me."

"Where does it say that the older man is always the better? I know of no such law."

"Then," said Alva, his eyes flashing, "perhaps we had better decide this the Orlan way."

"I'm ready," said Sabin.

"You mean to fight each other?" asked Caressa.

Alva stared angrily round the watching Orlans.

"I'll fight any man who stands in my way!" he said.

"If it's the best fighter you want," said Caressa, "why not open the contest to all comers?" She too turned to the Orlan captains. "One of these may win."

"Let them try," growled Alva.

"We can't have everyone fighting everyone," exclaimed Sabin.

"How has this decision been made before?" said Caressa. "What's the Orlan way?"

"The Great Jahan always names his successor before he dies. That way the Orlan nation remains united."

Caressa pulled out the silver-handled whip and held it up before them.

"Then hear me now," she said. "Amroth Jahan did name his successor. He named a woman and a stranger. You can fight each other and go on fighting until the biggest brute among you is left standing on the corpses of your own people. Or you can say, better a woman if she has true claim. Better a stranger if she unites the Orlan nation."

A silence followed this speech. Alva looked round and saw that his brother and his fellow Orlans were looking at one another, each waiting for the first to give a lead.

"What!" he cried, his voice charged with contempt. "You'd grovel to a girl?" He drew his sword. "Not I!"

Caressa held up the silver-handled whip. She took two steps forward to stand before Alva, whip outreached. Alva stared, and then he smiled, believing that she offered him his rightful inheritance in fear of his rage. He sheathed his sword and raised his right hand to take the whip. As he did so, Caressa's left hand flashed and her blade sliced down and across in a long shallow cut, leaving a stripe of blood across Alva's chest.

He cried out in pain and bent over, clutching at his wound.

"I am the Jahan of Jahans!" Caressa cried. "I will be obeyed!"

Sabin was the first to kneel. Then one by one the others followed. Alva, wounded more in pride than in body, saw their homage, and spat out at Sabin.

"You shame our father!"

"I honor his last wish," said Sabin.

"You always were a weakling!"

With that, Alva turned and stalked proudly away.

"Rise, my friends," said Caressa. "The Orlan nation is on the march again."

Sabin rose.

"We have no army any more," he said. "What are we now but bands of robbers on horseback?"

"Robbers on horseback who once were warriors," said Caressa. "Let the Jahan of Jahans ride out to the sound of trumpets and drums, and they'll know they're Orlans again!"

They all felt it then, as they heard her fierce and passionate words: somehow, inexplicably, this stranger, this woman, was a true leader. More extraordinary still, she was their leader.

"I didn't ask to be the Jahan," she said. "But give me brave hearts and fast horses, and I'll give you the world!"

⚔ 5 ⚔

There Has to Be More

THE TOLL-KEEPER WAS SITTING ON A CHAIR RAISED HIGH
above the road. He wore a broad-brimmed straw hat to
shade his eyes from the sun. Beneath him stood the heavy
timber barrier he had erected, with its single narrow gate;
and on the other side of the barrier, visible through the
cracks between the timbers, prowled his pack of attack
dogs. The toll he charged was entirely for his own bene-
fit and, strictly speaking, was a form of banditry; but he
had been controlling this remote hill pass for so long now
that he had come to think of himself as officially appointed
and of the money as his fairly earned wage.

He saw the young traveller making his way up the road
to the pass and noted that he was moving fast, but he
thought nothing of it. Then, when he was closer, he began
to pay him more attention. There were other travellers on
the road, carrying packs on their backs or driving laden

bullocks before them—the usual trickle of traders willing to pay his price for the direct road over the pass. But this young one was different. He was lean and hard, his face burned by the sun and scoured by the wind. He went barefoot and wore simple gray clothing, like a beggar priest; but he had the far stare of a hunter.

Seeker came striding at speed up the stony track, overtaking other travellers without a word or a glance. He saw the toll-keeper draw a loop of rope tight in his hands. He heard the creak of the bolt in the dog-cage door as the rope tightened. He heard the whining and yelping of the dogs as they broke into flurries of fighting among themselves.

The toll-keeper called out to him as he approached the gate.

"You pass, you pay."

Seeker did not pause, and he did not pay.

"Stop right there," cried the toll-keeper, "or I loose the dogs!"

Seeker looked up and raised one hand. The toll-keeper gasped and sagged in his chair. His broad-brimmed hat fell first; and after it, his body tipped and toppled to the ground. Seeker then made a single impatient sweep of his arms and the high barrier burst before him, as if hit by a hurricane. The flying fragments of timber fell on the cages, smashing the frames, and the dogs broke free. Crazed with terror, trained to attack and kill, the howling pack flew at Seeker. He raised one hand and fixed them with his hard clear gaze, and they fell before him, one after another, as if he had punched them.

The toll-keeper, limping to his feet, looked round at his smashed barrier and his writhing dogs.

"Who are you?" he said.

But Seeker did not stop. He strode on to the nearby summit of the pass. There he stood still for a few moments, gazing intently at the long road that wound down on the far side into the sunbaked plain. Far away a horse-drawn wagon was moving fast over the dusty road towards the distant forest. In the open wagon, just visible from the pass, lay two white-canopied litters.

Now the other travellers on the road were coming up to the pass. The nearest of them had witnessed the stranger's astonishing power, and they hurried after him, reaching out to him, trying to touch him.

"Let us come with you," they called to him. "Protect us. Save us."

They saw the attack dogs crawling to him on their bellies, whining. Some travellers in their excitement and awe fell to their knees.

"Who are you?" they cried. "You must be a god!"

He turned when he heard that, and his brown eyes were filled with sadness.

"I'm not a god," he said. "My name is Seeker. And I can't help you."

With that, he continued on his way. As they watched him go they saw him break into a long loping run that covered the ground at great speed. In a short time he was beyond reach of their cries, descending the hill road to the plains.

Those who had heard him speak passed on to the others what they had learned.

"His name's Seeker. He's not a god. He can't help us."

"Then he must be an evil spirit."

The toll-keeper picked up his hat and rammed it back onto his head and said, "He's worse than an evil spirit. He's a monster. He's come to destroy us all."

"A destroyer!" They looked at one another with wide eyes. "He must be the Assassin!"

High in the branches of a beech tree, deep in the forest, Echo Kittle sat in a swing seat twisting this way and that in the dappled light, listening to Orvin Chipe propose marriage.

"I don't believe there's anyone else you like better than me," Orvin said. His voice sounded squeaky and hurt, which made her feel annoyed. "And we've known each other all our lives. And you're the only one for me. So there it is."

For some reason all she could think about was how long his neck was and how his throat wobbled when he talked.

"I'm not the only one, Orvin," she said.

"Yes, you are. I don't want anyone but you."

"That's just stupid. If I died you'd marry someone else."

"I'd marry them, maybe," said Orvin doggedly, "but I wouldn't want them. And anyway, you're not dead."

"Well, I can't marry you."

She knew she should say that she was sorry, and say nice things about him to soften the rejection, but she just couldn't. She didn't see that it was such a compliment to ask someone to marry you who didn't want to be asked. It just showed how stupid he was.

"I think I have a right to know your reasons."

"Why?" Now she was angry. Her voice rose. "What gives you the right? Saying you want to marry me doesn't give you any rights over me."

"I'm not just saying it," said poor Orvin, bowing his head. "I'm feeling it. I can't help it. You're so beautiful."

"That's not my fault."

"But listen, Echo." He looked up at her, so lost, so puzzled. "You have to marry someone."

"I don't have to."

"Then how will you go on?"

"I'll just go on being me."

At this there came a crashing among the nearby branches and Echo's mother appeared out of the leaves, pink in the face, her mouth agape with horror.

"Echo Kittle! What are you saying?"

"Mother! Have you been spying on me?"

"Certainly not! Watching over you, yes, and why not? Am I to stand by and see my only daughter disgrace us all? Of course you should marry Orvin Chipe! Who else are you to marry? It's been understood between the Kittles and the Chipes for years. And as for not marrying anyone, well, that's just a jar of moonbeams. You want a family, don't you? You want a home. Then, you must have a husband."

Echo stopped swinging to and fro in her seat. She was trembling very slightly and didn't want her mother to see it. She glanced at Orvin and saw that he was nodding in agreement with her mother.

"Look at me, Echo!" said her mother sharply. "Tell me this is all no more than a fit of nonsense."

"I don't know what it is, Mother."

"Then let's have no more of this *can't* and *don't-have-to*. What's Orvin to make of all that? He doesn't want a *don't-have-to* wife. Nor does any other self-respecting young man."

"No, I expect they don't."

"Which means you'll end up with nobody."

"Yes, I expect I will."

"Echo!" Her mother was now bewildered as well as angry. "Do you want to throw away your whole life?"

Echo gave no answer. How could she tell her mother that to her, marriage to Orvin Chipe would be throwing away her whole life? Her mother would never understand. The great forest called the Glimmen was her mother's whole world, and the Glimmeners the only people in her world. But Echo had travelled far from the Glimmen and had met many different kinds of people, and down on the ground between the trees grazed her beloved Caspian, Kell, ready to carry her far away once more, if only she knew where.

There has to be more.

"Echo!" Her mother stamped her foot, making the supporting branches shake. "Orvin is waiting for your answer."

"I've given Orvin my answer," said Echo quietly.

Before Mrs. Kittle could speak again there came the sound of running feet from the ground below, and they saw a strange little procession hurry down one of the forest paths. Two men were running along bearing a litter between them. The litter was covered by a white canopy and was the kind used to transport the dead. Behind the men and the litter came another two men, also running, carrying a second litter.

The Glimmeners had fallen silent at the first sound, trained from earliest childhood to go still when groundlings passed through the forest. They waited until the footfalls faded into the distance. Echo's mother was just drawing breath to deliver another angry speech to her daughter when they heard a distant cry.

"Echo Kittle! Help me!"

Echo knew that voice.

Seeker stood staring at the horses and wagon abandoned in the forest road. The canopied litters were gone. He had no idea which way the ones he was hunting had taken, except that they had disappeared into the Glimmen. He called again.

"Echo Kittle!"

Getting no answer, he took the nearest path and raced off in pursuit. He came soon to a fork in the path, and another, and another. All round him rose tall trees, their heavy foliage cutting out the sunlight and shutting off his view ahead. Whichever way he turned, he saw only the great gray tree trunks and the tangle of wiry undergrowth, with here and there a patch of bright sunlight or the passing flash of a bird. Every path looked the same, and the deeper into the forest he ran, the narrower the paths became. He forced himself onwards, driven by the conviction that at last he was close to the quarry he had hunted for so long. Somewhere in the shadows of the trees, they were fleeing from him, on foot now, slower than him. He could run them down, if only he knew which way to run.

He searched the trees for clues, but they all looked the same to him, and they all stood in his way. He came to yet another fork in the path and stopped, panting softly. He no longer knew north from south, left from right. Maddeningly, enragingly, he was lost. To come so close and to let them go again! He let out a cry of fury. The trees were in his way, the trees fenced him in, the trees suffocated him. He raised both his arms and, in his frustration, released a blast of power, together with a howling cry.

All round him the trees fell. Some snapped where they stood, some tore their roots from the ground, some were crushed beneath the fall of bigger trees. Within moments the deep shade was rent apart to reveal the dazzle of the summer sky.

Seeker stood motionless in the sudden sunlight, shocked at what he had done. Then out of a tree that was still standing dropped the lithe form of Echo Kittle.

"Seeker!" she cried. "No more! Please!"

He stared at her like a fool.

"Don't hurt the trees!"

He blinked and passed one hand across his brow. The sunlit air was still heavy with dust from the fall of the trees, and the smaller branches could be heard crackling under the weight of the toppled trunks as they settled.

"No more," said Echo with tears in her eyes.

He didn't know what to say.

"They were in my way. I had to find—I have to find—they were getting away."

"The men carrying the litters?"

"Yes! Have you seen them?"

"They were heading north. To the coast."

"How can I find them?"

"I can track them for you," said Echo.

"Then, guide me!" cried Seeker. "Quickly!"

Echo gave a long high whistle, and Kell came trotting through the trees. She swung herself up onto his back and rode to Seeker's side. She made her decision without a moment's hesitation. Seeker had fascinated her ever since their first meeting, when he had refused to help her, saying, "You have your duty and I have mine."

She held out one hand.

"Ride with me."

Cheerful Giver came to a stop at the northern end of the forest road and pointed triumphantly through the trees ahead.

"There it is! The Haven!"

The forest ended where the heavy soil gave way to the sand dunes of the coast. The road continued a little way farther to its most northerly point, a spit of land from which a long timber causeway reached out to a small island. This island was surrounded by a high rampart, and its only entrance, the causeway gate, was guarded by armed men. In these troubled times it had become necessary for the richer citizens of the old empire to find places of refuge where they and their families could live in safety; and nowhere was as safe as the island called the Haven.

Cheerful Giver, his wife, Blessing, and his two sons had been travelling on foot for two days to get here. Now that the island was at last in sight they paused for a much-needed rest. Cheerful Giver mopped the sweat from his scarlet face and spread his long winter coat wide to let the coastal breeze cool his body.

"Our troubles are over," he said to his wife. "A new life in a new home."

Blessing sighed. She had announced after the disaster had struck Radiance that she would never be happy again. Her one remaining satisfaction lay in each new proof that she was right.

"It's horrible," said their eldest son, scowling at the bleak coast. "All sand."

"We're not there yet, son," said Cheerful Giver, keeping his tone light even though he felt like smacking the boy's ears. "Can't say that yet."

"Can," said the boy. "Have."

"Well, yes, you have said it. But you don't actually know what it'll be like till you see it."

"Yes, I do," said the boy. "It'll be horrible."

Two men came pounding down the road out of the forest, carrying a litter. Their coats flapped as they passed, and the white cloth covering the litter flapped. Behind them came another two men with another litter, its cover flapping in its turn. They passed, onto the causeway, and boomed over the planks to the closed gate in the island's protective wall. The guards opened the gate for them, and so they disappeared into the Haven.

"Dead people," said Blessing, giving vent to a shrill little laugh. "I suppose it's to be expected. We're to live on an island of dead people."

"I should think not!" cried Cheerful Giver, mopping the sweat from his cheeks. "Dead people don't pay these kinds of prices."

The Haven was indeed the most expensive refuge of its kind, a fact that Cheerful Giver found reassuring. His former life was in ruins, his house overrun by thieves, his oil presses smashed, his sunflower fields gone to weed. But his chest of gold shillings had never been found, and the coins were even now hanging heavy in the lining of his winter coat. He had worn the coat throughout the blazing summer days of their journey. The heat had been unbearable, and the weight insupportable; but he had struggled on for the sake of his family. He had reflected from time to time with bitterness on how little gratitude they showed, no gratitude at all, to be exact; but in time he had found he experienced a curious satisfaction in suffering so much for so little return. The startling unfairness of his lot had become for him a badge of merit, and he found in his bitterness an edge of sweetness.

"Come along," he said, resuming their journey. "Almost there."

———

Echo and Seeker rode out of the trees, following the forest track, onto the coast road. There ahead lay the undu-
lating sand dunes leading to the seashore. The salt smell of
the sea hung in the hot summer air, and they could hear
the ripple and hiss of the waves.

Echo studied the marks in the sandy track with care.
Then she pointed down the road to the causeway at the
far end and to the fortified island to which it led.

"They went there."

"You're certain?" said Seeker, staring at the distant
island.

"I'm certain."

Seeker slipped down from Kell's back and began to
walk down the road, scanning the details of the island's
wall and gate.

"Nowhere left for them to run," he said.

Echo followed on Kell, marvelling at him. She felt his
utter concentration and his urgency. He was like an arrow
in flight. Nothing deflected him from his goal.

"Who are they?" she asked.

"An old woman. An old man."

"Old people? What do you want with them?"

"To finish what I've begun."

He never looked at Echo once. He had no interest in
her. She had briefly been a means to his end, no more.
Echo found this indifference refreshing. His drive and
certainty infected her, whether he meant it to or not. He
seemed to her to be launched on a mission that was greater
than himself; and she wanted that, too.

There has to be more.

"Don't follow me," he said. "You could get hurt."

With that, he set off down the road to the island.

Just ahead there was a roadside barn, a long building with low-hanging eaves. Here Echo dismounted and found shade. She watched, her eyes straining against the bright light, as the distant figure approached the causeway. Sounds came from the other side of the barn wall, soft whimpering sounds, followed by low sobbing.

"Who's there?" she called.

⊰ 6 ⊱

Welcome to the Haven

CHEERFUL GIVER AND HIS FAMILY PASSED THROUGH THE second set of security gates and were greeted by a square-shaped man with a flat head and tiny but piercing eyes.

"Company manager," he said. "Name's Pelican. Welcome to the Haven."

Before them lay a wide-open space in which teams of laborers were hard at work in the noonday heat. On all sides were houses in various stages of being built, and between the building sites snaked long lines of men and women silently performing repetitive tasks. Some were hauling stones, some were carrying timbers. Most were passing baskets of soil from hand to hand in one direction, and buckets of mortar back in the other.

"What you see before you," said Pelican, "is Phase Two of the Haven. By next spring the work will be complete. The grass will be seeded. This will be a charming neighborhood. Children will play on spreading lawns. Their parents will sit in the shade of a cool terrace, served their drinks by well-trained servants, looking forward to an excellent dinner prepared by the best chefs. And all walled, gated, and guarded. Security guaranteed."

"Dusty," complained Cheerful Giver's youngest son.

"Horrible," said his brother.

"I can't imagine where they find the servants," said Blessing.

"No need to worry about that," said Pelican. "All company staff are polite, obedient, and clean. Perhaps you've already noticed that even our building workers are clean."

"They are clean," admitted Blessing.

"When they come to us, they're little better than animals. Filthy, starving, in rags. The company gives them new clothes, new purpose, new pride."

As they watched, one of the workers stumbled under his load of earth and spilled it. A supervisor pulled him to his feet.

"Pick it up! Keep the line moving!"

"How much are they paid?" asked Cheerful Giver.

"The company gives them life," said Pelican. "Who can put a price on life?"

"So, no actual cash money?"

"What use is money to them? Prices rise. Shops are burned. Bandits steal. No, sir, the company repays its workers by giving them what is far more precious—self-respect."

"Please don't think I'm criticizing," said Cheerful Giver. "I've been an employer myself, on a large scale, too. I've always suspected that forced labor is the answer."

"Not forced labor, sir." Pelican looked pained. "Structured labor."

He led them through the building site to the inner part of the island. Here the work had been completed, and a number of large handsome houses stood on a grid of neatly raked gravel paths. Beyond them, on the island's far shore, rose a squat windowless tower built of dark stone blocks.

"And here we have Phase One," said Pelican.

This inner region presented a charming scene to the weary visitors. All was calm and still but for the coming and going of a number of small children carrying watering cans or rakes.

"You see, my dear," said Cheerful Giver approvingly, "here are the happy children at play."

Pelican coughed, then addressed Blessing.

"You raised the question of servants, madam. The company has found its own original solution to the problem. We recruit and employ children between the ages of six and twelve. The company has found that children are better adapted to domestic tasks than their parents. And of course their parents are more naturally suited to the heavier building work."

Cheerful Giver's boys were intrigued.

"Look!" they cried. "They've got dog collars!"

"For training purposes," said Pelican.

He beckoned to a boy who was at work raking a gravel path. The boy dropped his rake and came at once. Pelican fingered the leather collar buckled round the boy's neck.

"You see here, at the back, an iron ring. During training, the junior help are kept on leads. You'll often hear people say that spiker children can't be taught. Not so. Keep them on a lead. Give clear, simple instructions. Beat them if they disobey. It really is as simple as that. A few weeks, and they can come off the lead. Eh, young fellow?"

He patted the boy on the head.

"Yes, sir," said the boy.

"Back to work, then."

The boy ran back to his rake.

"Dad!" cried Cheerful Giver's older son. "Can I have a spiker boy on a lead?"

Cheerful Giver was pleased. It was the first sign of enthusiasm his son had shown since they had left Radiance.

"I don't see why not," he said.

"And can I beat him?"

"If he's naughty."

"I want one, too!" cried his brother.

The two boys ran off to inspect the child with the rake. Cheerful Giver turned complacently to his wife.

"Well, my dear. I think you'll allow that life here could be bearable."

"Life must be borne, I suppose," said Blessing.

"The tower over there," said Cheerful Giver to Pelican, "what is its purpose?"

"Security within security," said Pelican. "The last redoubt. In event of emergency."

"Yeow!" shrieked one of the boys. "He hit me! Beat him! Put him on a lead! He hit me with his rake!"

"You poked him," said his brother.

"He hit me with his rake!"

The spiker child fell to his knees, sobbing and shaking. Pelican strode over to him and grabbed him by the shoulder.

"Please, sir, he poked my eye. I had to, sir. He was jabbing my eye."

Blessing clasped her son in her arms.

"Has he hurt you, darling? Show me where it hurts."

"I want to beat him! I want to see him cry!"

"He's crying already," said his brother.

"That's just snivelling. I want proper crying."

Cheerful Giver didn't want his son's newfound enthusiasm to fade.

"I know we've not yet made our payment," he said to Pelican, speaking low, "but I am in a position to proceed. Would my lad be allowed to beat the spiker boy on account, as you might say?"

Pelican tipped his head on one side to consider the proposition.

"On payment of the deposit," he said. "I don't mean to be difficult, but we do get people looking round the Haven, and when it comes to the point"—he smiled and opened an empty palm, to indicate the absence of money.

"Understood."

Cheerful Giver extracted some gold shillings from his heavy coat and pressed them into Pelican's hand.

"All I want is for my boy to be happy."

Pelican attached a lead to the spiker child's collar and handed the lead to Cheerful Giver.

"Give it to me!" cried Cheerful Giver's son. "I'm the one he hit, not you."

"Here you are, son," said Cheerful Giver hastily. "I was giving him to you."

"Get me a stick!"

Pelican volunteered his own staff.

"I'm going to drag him about a bit first. Then I'm going to beat him."

The spiker child shivered and whined.

"Please, sir. Won't do it again."

"Too bad! You hit me. Now you get a beating."

He gave a sharp jerk on the lead and the spiker child trotted, sobbing, after him.

A sharp cry sounded from the ramparts. A bell began to clang. Pelican looked round, suddenly alert.

"Intruder alarm," he said.

"Intruders!" cried Blessing.

"Nothing to fear. Walled, gated, and guarded. Security guaranteed."

"Can I go on with the beating?"

A creaking sound filled the air.

"The bolts! Look at the bolts!"

The bolts that secured the gates were bending. Some massive force was pushing at the gates from the far side.

"What—!"

The bolts snapped. The gates burst apart, slamming against the walls, kicking up a cloud of dust. Out of the dust stepped a lone unarmed man with staring eyes.

"Seize him!" cried Pelican.

The guards all broke into a run at the same time, converging on the lone figure.

He looked through them as they came, searching the

area beyond them. They launched themselves at him as he strode forward, but somehow they missed him and found themselves striking at empty air. On he came, untouchable, unstoppable.

Pelican gaped in amazement. The building workers laid down their loads. Cheerful Giver's son let go of the spiker boy and began to howl.

"Make him stop! I don't like him!"

Seeker's sweeping gaze identified Pelican. He came to a stop before him and fixed him with his staring eyes.

"Where are they?" he said.

Pelican meant to resist but found he could not.

"In the tower," he said.

Seeker knew now that his long hunt was over. The last two savanters had nowhere left to run. Mere stone walls could not stand in his way.

He drew one long deep breath that made all his body vibrate. Then he raised both his hands and pointed his fingers at the tower. The air before him turned dark. A stream of pure force flowed from the tips of his fingers.

The stone wall of the tower shuddered and cracked open. A cloud of dust belched out of the gaping hole. The cracking and tumbling of falling masonry filled the air. Then out of the dust came the figure of a woman in black.

She came slowly, walking with great difficulty, a stick in each hand: a stooping, frail old lady.

Seeker began to move once more, slowly now, his eyes locked on to her aged eyes. She came to a stop and waited for him.

Cheerful Giver and his family looked on with jaws agape, as did Pelican and all the others in the Haven. This was not their battle. There were powers at large here that were beyond their understanding.

When he was close, the old lady spoke to Seeker, her voice as thin and frail as her body.

"You don't know what you do," she said.

"I do what I must," said Seeker.

It had already begun, the conflict of wills. Neither struck a blow. They held each other's eyes and fought for domination, mind over mind.

"You have strength, boy," said the old lady, "but no love."

Seeker said nothing. Little by little he was overwhelming the savanter. The proud spirit within that aged body was bending before him. He was the hunter. With each day that had passed since he had begun his hunt he had grown stronger. Now nothing and no one could resist his power.

Seeker felt no joy, no pride. This was what he had been empowered to do. He was a destroyer. Now he would destroy.

The old lady uttered a small cry and tottered on her sticks. A look of terror distorted her deeply wrinkled face. Seeker did not relent. Slowly, helplessly, she slid to the ground, and lay there curled up on one side. For a few moments more she could be heard whimpering softly. Then she fell silent.

Seeker knelt down by her side to satisfy himself that all was truly over. He rolled her onto her back. Her eyes opened.

"No love," she hissed.

With that, her withered arms shot up and seized his head. She pressed her face to his lips and kissed his mouth. She held him with ferocious strength, and her kiss sucked at his face, and he could not shake her off. He struggled to break her grip, but even as he did so he could feel her face softening against his, losing its outline, melting into his. He thought her intention was to suffocate him, to fill his mouth and nostrils with her decomposing flesh, so that he would die, too. But then he felt her breath in his mouth and knew that it was more dangerous by far. She meant to live on within him.

He choked as he fought, and twisted his head from side to side, but she held fast. Now her face and his were fusing into one. If he were to tear her from him he would rip his own flesh from his skull. She was dying, he could feel the power draining out of her, but in the last moments of her dying she was binding herself to him forever.

He heard sounds ahead. Someone else was moving in the shattered tower. The last savanter. The final kill. Seeker knew then that he had very little time and only one way to release himself.

Let her in. Let her death feed on my life.

He released his grasping hands. He let go his resisting mind. He let her fall into him through the kiss, like one who loses their last prop. She had not expected it. She fell fast, and in falling, she loosed her grip on him. In this way she fell deep into him even as her withered body dropped away from him; and he found himself free once more, looking down at a lifeless, faceless corpse.

There came the grinding rumble of timber on stone, the snap of a boat's sail in the wind. Seeker jumped up and raced to the tower. He vaulted over the rubble of the breach he had himself made, then bounded through the ruins of an inner hall to a doorway beyond. Here the doors were open wide, giving onto a stone launch ramp that sloped steeply down to the sea. A small sailing boat was slicing into the water, the wind driving it rapidly from the shore. Beneath its sail Seeker saw a single litter, shrouded in a white canopy.

The last savanter.

In a rage of despair he poured his power into the water and caused the sea to seethe and boil. But all his anger served only to drive the boat farther out to sea; and great though his power was, the ocean was greater. His little storm was soon dispersed into that boundless immensity.

He watched the craft sail away out of his reach towards the far horizon, towards other lands, and a terrible desolation possessed him. His power had been given him for a single purpose, and he had failed.

Leave one alive and it will all begin again.

⊰ 7 ⊱

Share the Joy

THE DAY WAS ENDING AS MORNING STAR AND HER LITTLE band of spiker children took the hill road out of the village.

"Where are we going now?" said Burny.

"To find the happy people."

"I never seen any happy people," said Libbet.

Morning Star was puzzled and concerned for her parents. Her father never strayed far from his flock. But she had found the sheep on the hillside without a shepherd.

She had no way of knowing where they had gone, and so she was taking the road that led along the ridge of hills to the lowlands. She followed the long slanting track that climbed the flank of the last hill, panting now. Hem strode stolidly beside her, just half a pace ahead to show he was the leader, but glancing back from time to time to make sure he was leading in the right direction. Burny held tight to one of her hands, and little black-eyed Deedy held tight to the other.

Hem crested the brow first and came to a stop, staring down into the plains below. Morning Star joined him, with the rest of the children. They all looked in silent surprise at the scene now laid out before them in the light of the setting sun.

An immense crowd of people was gathering in the river valley. From all directions more groups of people could be seen making their way to join this crowd, so that it was growing all the time. These were not soldiers, or bandits. Even from this distance it was clear that the crowd was made up of women and children as much as men. From the crowd rose up the sound of singing and laughter.

"What's them all doing?" said Burny, tugging at Morning Star's hand.

"Don't know," said Morning Star. She was trying to read the aura of the great crowd. It was hard, because as the sun set, it sent streams of red light over the plains; but as far as she could make out, the crowd's color was rose pink, the color of happiness.

"Only one way to find out," she said. "Who's coming with me?"

"Me," said Burny.

"Me," said Deedy.

Hem, the leader, was already on the way down. So they all descended the steeply sloping hillside together.

The sun had set by the time they reached the fringe of the crowd, and fires were burning brightly. As they approached, they were spotted by a stout middle-aged woman who had unpinned her long hair to let it fly wildly about her head. She hurried to meet them, arms spread wide, a great beam of welcome on her face.

"Joy!" she cried. "Joy to young and old! Share our joy!"

She embraced Morning Star as if they were long-lost friends.

"Thank you," said Morning Star, backing out of the embrace.

She gestured to the milling crowd.

"What is all this?"

"This! Don't you know?" The beaming lady gave a happy laugh and spun round and round, arms waving and hair flying. "This is the Joyous!"

"The Joyous?"

"The gift of the Beloved to all people! To you, and you, and you!"

She patted Libbet and Burny and Hem. Hem jerked back from her touch.

"Oh, you young separator!" cried the happy lady, wagging one finger at Hem. "I was just the same as you once. But the Beloved has shown us that separation is pain. Let go of your pain! Come to the Joyous!"

"Who is the Beloved?" said Morning Star.

"The Beloved?" The happy lady rolled her eyes upwards and clasped her hands to her chest, momentarily unable to put into words the intensity of her feelings. "The Beloved is our teacher and our guide. You must go to him—yes, and you, and all of you! Look on his dear beautiful face just once and you'll follow him for the rest of your life."

"Does he have a name?"

"A name? He is the Beloved. He is the Joy Boy."

With that, she ran dancing and skipping back to her own group, to be received with hugs and laughter.

"Funny in the head," said Libbet.

"Maybe," said Morning Star. "But she's not the only one."

They made their way deeper into the crowd, and on every side, clusters of people were holding hands and laughing. Many were dancing, linked in small rings of five or six, spinning round and round, their heads thrown back, kept from tumbling to the ground only by their clasped hands.

"Drunk," said Hem.

A sharp yap drew Morning Star's attention. She caught a flash of white between the legs of the crowd.

"Lamb!"

The dog came bounding towards her, wagging the whole back half of his body in his excitement at finding her. He sprang up, his front paws on her thighs, and made small squealing sounds of delight.

"Oh, Lamb! Are you drunk, too?" She rubbed his head and face with her hands and pressed her cheek to his wet nose. "Where are they? Where's Mama and Papa?"

Lamb understood her well. He scampered back through the crowd, and Morning Star followed, and after her trailed her train of small children. The dog led her to a circle of dancing people and came to a stop. Morning Star looked at the dancers as they whirled round and round.

One of them had something of the look of her father, Arkaty. She knew it could not be Arkaty because he was grinning like a lunatic and swinging his head from side to side as he danced in a way that her shy, grave father would never have done. But there in the middle of the circle was Amik, her father's sheepdog, her head on one side, looking disapproving. And the woman who had just danced by laughing so merrily looked very like her mother, Mercy. How could it be? What had happened to her gentle sadness?

Morning Star felt her face flush red with embarrassment. The spectacle was so undignified. She wanted to call out to them to stop. She wanted to shut her eyes and pretend she hadn't seen them.

Burny and Deedy, still holding her hands, were excited by the dance and started trying to mimic it. Morning Star refused to be spun round and round.

"But them's doing it," said Burny.

"I don't know what they're doing," said Morning Star.

"The joy dance," said a man standing nearby. "We all do it. You should try it."

"No, thank you," said Morning Star. "We're new here."

"You'll be meeting the Joy Boy soon, then. Once you've met the Joy Boy it'll all make sense to you."

The dance came to an end in a laughing tumble, with all the dancers hugging each other on the ground, Amik and Lamb running round them in circles, barking. Morning Star waited for her parents to emerge from the heap.

"Papa," she said reproachfully. "Mama."

They were astonished to see her, and unself-consciously delighted. They leaped to their feet and embraced her.

"Star!" they cried. "Share the joy!"

They seemed to feel no shame that she had watched their dance.

"What's happened to you, Mama?"

"We've found the Joyous! Oh, my darling, I'm so happy. And now you've found the Joyous, too!"

"You're drunk," said Hem.

"Yes, my friend," said Mercy with a ringing laugh. "Drunk on joy!"

Arkaty took his daughter's hand in his and held it, his eyes shining as he spoke.

"Your mother's sadness," he said. "All gone."

"Oh, my sadness!" Mercy laughed again. "The Joy Boy saw that for what it was as soon as he set eyes on me. Separation, of course. All gone now."

Morning Star wished she could be happy in this transformation, but the truth was it frightened her. She felt as if her real father and mother had been stolen away and replaced by these two laughing impostors.

"Papa," she said, "you've abandoned your flock. What are you doing here?"

"The old life is over," he said. "All gone now."

"But what will you do?"

"The same as everyone else." He swept his arms over the crowd. "We're all getting ready for the Great Embrace."

"What great embrace?"

"It's why the Joy Boy has come. Ask him and he'll make you understand."

"I want you to make me understand, Papa."

"It's the end of separation forever," said Mercy.

Arkaty took Morning Star's hands in his.

"You remember the nights we spent on the hillside, you and I?"

"Of course I do, Papa."

"You remember how we sat there holding hands under the rug, not talking, watching the dawn?"

"Yes, Papa."

She couldn't help it. Tears rose to her eyes as she remembered. They had been some of the happiest moments in her life.

"When the Great Embrace comes, it'll be like that for everyone, forever."

She shook her head. Those had been special times, just for the two of them.

"I don't want that," she said.

"You just don't feel it yet." He put his arms round her and held her close. "I didn't feel it at first. The Joy Boy will make you feel it."

Morning Star was quite sure this Joy Boy was a trickster and a fraud, and the more she was told how much she would love him, the more she hated him. But Burny was pulling at her tunic and complaining that he was hungry, and Deedy had started to cry.

"The poor darlings," said Mercy. "Take them to the long tables. Let them eat."

"I've no money," said Morning Star.

"Money!" Mercy laughed happily. "No money in the Joyous. Everything is given freely, out of love."

"Let's grab it quick, then," said Libbet, "before the others get it."

Mercy smiled at this and shook her head.

"No need to grab," she said. "Share the joy."

Libbet had already run off towards the trestle tables set up at the heart of the great crowd. The other children went chasing after her, so Morning Star followed.

"I'll find you again soon, Mama."

"Find the Joy Boy first, darling."

The long tables were set in rectangles, four tables to each side, with supply wagons at either end. Cooks were hard at work on the inside, boiling up great vats of rice and beans and spiced vegetables. People crowded round holding out mugs or bowls, and the cooks dolloped the food into them until they were brimming over. There was no pushing or jostling, because there seemed to be a limitless amount of food in the vats.

Morning Star's band of hungry children wriggled their way to the table side and, having no bowls, were served in their outstretched hands. Morning Star looked on the laden supply wagons and the bubbling vats with amazement and some suspicion.

"What do you put in it?" she asked one of the cooks.

"Rice, beans, onions, tomatoes," said the cook.

"Nothing else?"

The cook laughed. "Joy," he said.

Morning Star couldn't stop the hungry children from eating, but she took nothing for herself.

"How does the Joyous pay for so much food?" she asked.

"Oh, there's always plenty of money," said the cook. "We don't use money here, so anything we have when we join goes to the Joyous. And every day more and more people join us."

"Look, lady!" cried Burny.

He had both hands piled high with rice and beans. He held them up before Morning Star, gazing at her, his eyes bright with happiness. Then he plunged his face into the sticky heap, rubbing rice and beans all over his cheeks and chin and brow, eating whatever came within reach of his mouth. The other children all started to copy Burny, squealing with delight. Some of the food stuck to their faces, and some of it fell to the ground.

"Don't do that," said Morning Star. "You're wasting it."

"Let them be," said the cook. "It takes us all that way at first. It's hunger makes folk greedy, same as being poor makes folk steal."

Hem nodded vigorously at this. He couldn't speak because he was eating as fast as he could, afraid that at any moment the food would be taken from him.

The smaller children, their bellies full, announced that they were sleepy. Morning Star led them to the nearest fire, and the people round it made spaces for them as if they were their own children.

"Come along, little ones. Curl up here. My, that's a big yawn!"

"They're orphans," said Morning Star, feeling she should make it clear she was not their mother.

"Not any more, they aren't," came the friendly answer. "They're children of the Joyous now."

Morning Star had no way of knowing that the children who had attached themselves to her would be safe in the care of these strangers; but they were already asleep, exhausted by the day's long tramp. And who was she herself, she reflected, but just another stranger? So she left them by the fire and went off alone into the crowd. It was time to meet the source of this phenomenon: the one they called the Joy Boy.

Everywhere her eyes fell she saw happy people. If this was a drug, it was a highly effective one. She studied the colors of the people she passed and saw that the joy was genuine. It was impossible to fake the colors. And yet she could not rid herself of the conviction that something here was terribly, dangerously wrong. It was just all too easy. Joy was not to be had for the asking.

Her eyes fell on a random stranger, and the stranger gave her such a warm smile in the firelight that she felt ashamed of her suspicions. Maybe life was easy, and she alone made it hard. Maybe—

Her train of thought was broken by a comical sight ahead. A group of young people were standing round a crate of large overripe tomatoes, picking them out and tossing them high into the night air. They were pushing and jostling each other as they did so, to stand under the falling tomato, faces upturned, eyes screwed shut, competing to be the one on whom the tomato landed. The sight of a tomato exploding over a face was irresistibly funny. A single tomato made a surprising amount of mess. The pulp and juice went everywhere, leaving the drenched victim to wipe the skin from his eyes and shake the pips from his collar.

"Me, me, me," they chorused as another plump red globe arced up into the air.

The one last hit was bent laughing over a water vat,

sluicing his head with splashes of water from a tin mug. When he rose up he caught sight of Morning Star and gave her a friendly smile. He was a chubby youth of perhaps fifteen, with smooth, short black hair and strong black eyebrows and full pink lips. There was nothing about him to mark him out from his fellows but for one detail that only Morning Star could have spotted: he had no aura.

Clearly something about her drew his attention. Waving a cheerful good-bye to his companions and drying his hands on his sleeves, he came towards Morning Star without taking his eyes off her for a second.

"You're new, aren't you?" he said. "You're welcome."

"I've not come to join," said Morning Star. "I was looking for my parents."

"Have you found them?"

"Yes, I have."

She became aware that the people round them were paying closer attention to her than before. In fact, she and the chubby youth seemed to be the focus of general interest.

"I hope you found them well."

"Oh, yes," said Morning Star. "They were dancing."

The youth smiled. "You disapprove."

"No, I don't disapprove. But it's not like them."

"You don't dance, I take it?"

"Not really. I'm not much good at dancing."

"Does that matter?"

"I'm sorry?"

"Suppose you were to dance and not be much good at it, would that matter?"

He went on smiling at her in the friendliest way. All the people gathered round were also smiling. Morning Star began to go red.

"No one likes to look foolish," she said.

"Indeed not," said the youth. "But when everyone is dancing, no one is looking."

A soft patter of applause greeted this statement. One young woman had a notebook in one hand and hurriedly began to scribble in it with a pencil.

This must be the one they call the Joy Boy, thought Morning Star in surprise.

"Are you—" she began, but found she could not utter the ridiculous words. "Are you—the leader?"

"The leader?" He put his head on one side, weighing the word. "No, I'm not the leader. What am I? What shall I tell our new friend?"

He looked round the crowd and gave a sweet noiseless laugh.

"I'm the disease."

The people gathered round clapped their hands in admiration.

"A harmless disease, I hope. I infect all who come near me. It's quite involuntary on my part, I assure you."

"Oh, I see," said Morning Star, not so easily impressed. "You infect people with joy, I suppose."

He nodded, not offended by her sardonic tone of voice.

"I am called the Joy Boy."

"So all this"—she glanced round to take in the great crowd—"is because of you."

"Not because of me," he said, gently correcting her. "Because of joy."

Morning Star found herself looking for a way to wipe the smile off that chubby face.

"You've got tomato in your hair," she said.

"Have I?" He brushed his hair absently with one hand. "I'll swim in the river tomorrow."

Then he held out his hand to her. It seemed needlessly rude to ignore it, so she held out her hand and he clasped it in his. His hand was dry and firm and pleasing to the touch. She understood at once that he was holding her hand in order to know her better.

"Ah." He raised his black eyebrows. "You're a rare person. May I ask your name?"

"Morning Star."

"Morning Star. You are a Noble Warrior."

"Not really," she said. "I was trained by the Nom, but I left before the training was complete."

"How is that possible?"

"That's a long story."

"But your power remains strong. No"—he furrowed his smooth high brow, searching for the right word— "there's more than power in you. You possess an immense gift. You feel what others feel."

Morning Star was surprised.

"How can you know that?"

"I too have a gift," he said. "My gift is that I am nothing. So I see you as you are."

"You are—nothing?"

She stared at him. He had no aura. How could a person be nothing? She didn't even know what it meant. But nothing about the Joy Boy was as she had expected. Even his fat pink cheeks and plump pink lips were taking on a different appearance. The very smoothness of his face now spoke to her of innocence.

"I know it's hard to understand," he was saying to her. "But it's not hard to feel, is it?"

She could feel him: like an empty space before her, drawing her in.

"It's your own choice, Morning Star. You can go on being unhappy if you wish."

She looked down and spoke low, suddenly afraid.

"Don't talk to me like this."

All this time he had been holding her hand. Now he let it go.

"So much darkness. So much fear. But what is there to fear? Joy is as simple as daylight. Step out of the shadows into the sun."

He made her a slight bow and turned back to his companions. They linked arms with him and strolled away together through the crowd.

Morning Star found she was trembling. While they had been talking she had stiffened all the muscles of her body as if to repel an attack that had not come. She only became aware of this extreme physical tension when the Joy Boy left her and she started to shake.

So much darkness.

She made her way back to the food tables and accepted

a bowl of rice. Here her mother found her, and they sat down together by one of the fires.

"You've met him, haven't you?" said Mercy, watching her daughter closely.

Morning Star nodded.

"Everyone changes after they meet him. You've changed."

"What is he, Mama? Who is he?"

"I don't know, darling. All I know is that he has led me out of the darkness."

"He told me he was nothing."

"Maybe he is. Nothing or everything, like a god."

"Do you think he's a god, Mama?"

"No, not yet. But soon. That's what we're all waiting for. Your father told you."

"He called it the Great Embrace."

"That's when we become god."

Morning Star searched her mother's face in the firelight.

"Can you truly believe that?"

"Now that you've met him," said Mercy, "can't you believe it, too?"

"No. I doubt everything."

"Even your own doubt?"

"Yes. Yes! Most of all my own doubt. Oh, Mama, I don't know what to think any more."

"Then, no more thinking," said Mercy, taking her in her arms and hugging her like a little child. "You're tired. Sleep now, and see what tomorrow brings."

⊁ 8 ⊁

A Blue Flower

THE BARN DOORS WERE BOLTED ON THE INSIDE. THE bolts shattered at Seeker's first blow. As Echo looked on, he kicked the high doors open and the bright sunlight streamed into the space within. There, blinking in the light, eyes wide with fear, lay hundreds of small children, tethered in open stalls like dogs.

Seeker stared at the scene in silence, and the anger in him turned hard and sharp. He strode towards the stalls and the children shrank back in terror, covering their heads with their arms.

"Don't beat me!" they cried. "I'll be good!"

"There'll be no more beating," said Seeker.

The children had collars fastened round their necks. A short chain linked each collar to an iron staple in the wall. Seeker felt the collar of one child with careful fingers, but it was too tight round his neck to remove without hurting him. He took hold of the chain and snapped it with his bare hands. This simple violent action gave him some relief. He moved on to the next child and the next, breaking their chains one by one.

Echo followed Seeker into the barn. As the children found themselves able to move out of their stalls, they came to her and clustered round her, seeing her as the latest of the many adults who had come to give them orders. It never occurred to them to run away.

"At your service, lady," they piped, bobbing their heads and jingling the trailing ends of their chains. "What's your pleasure, lady?"

"You're free," said Echo. "You can go."

They gazed at her with their wide uncomprehending eyes, some of them as young as four years old, waiting to be given the orders they had been trained to obey.

"But we must serve you, lady."

"No, no. Not any more. The bad people who tied you up can't hurt you any more. You don't have to serve anybody. You're only children."

"Children do what they're told, lady. Or they get beaten."

All the little heads nodded at that, and their chains clinked.

"That's all over now," said Echo, pointing behind her through the open doors and down the road to the Haven. "Look."

A great exodus was under way. The workers were flooding across the timber causeway to the mainland.

"The men who beat you have run away. You've got no masters now."

"No masters!" The children's faces fell. "Who's going to feed us?"

Some began to whimper and then to howl.

Seeker had now snapped the last of the chains and rejoined Echo. The barn had filled with the sound of lamentation.

"We can't just leave them here," said Echo. "Who's to look after them?"

Seeker saw the miserable faces of the crying children, and the anger in him turned to bitterness. However he used his power, no good came of it. All he wanted now was to be far away and on his own.

The workers from the Haven reached the barn. It was at once clear that they were the parents of the chained children. Voices cried out on all sides, as fathers and mothers found their children and clasped them in their arms, sobbing and weeping with joy. Even now the children clung to their training.

"At your service, ma'am. What's your pleasure?"

"No, no, you don't have to serve me. I'm your mother."

"Please don't beat me."

Echo watched the pitiful reunions with tears in her eyes. When she turned to Seeker, he was gone.

He was outside in the sun, surrounded by a small crowd. In the forefront of the crowd a red-faced man wearing a heavy coat was shouting and waving his fist at Seeker.

"Go on!" he cried. "Smash me! Smash my wife! Smash

my sons! You've smashed everything else I have. Why stop there? Why not just kill us all and put us out of our misery?"

Others were calling out to Seeker too, but theirs were cries of admiration and reverence.

"Tell us what to do! Lead us and we'll follow you!"

Seeker put his hands to his ears and shook his head and tried to move past them.

"I don't know what to tell you," he said.

But they followed after him, tugging at his clothing and pleading with him. The mothers and fathers with their newfound children came out of the barn and joined in the procession.

"He's the one with the power," they told each other. "He'll make our lives good again."

Seeker began to walk faster.

"Don't follow me," he said. "I've got nothing for you."

But still they jostled to be close to him; so he broke into a run. His long loping strides carried him at a speed none of them could match. The shouts of the crowd now turned to grumbles of discontent.

"What does he expect us to do now?"

"That's nice, isn't it? Off he goes without a word."

"All that power and he keeps it for himself."

Echo watched Seeker out of sight. Then she called to Kell, and the Caspian trotted to her side.

"We'll go after him, won't we, Kell?" she said, rubbing his neck. "He has to stop to rest sometime."

Kell pushed gently at her shoulder with his soft nose. She whispered to him.

"He's our future, Kell. No going back now."

Then she swung herself up onto the Caspian's back and set off down the road south after Seeker.

The bucket boomed as he lowered it down the well, bouncing from side to side against the walls of the old shaft. He let it fall all the way to the end of the rope, but it did not hit water.

Slowly, wearily, Seeker drew the rope up again and looped it by the well's side. The sun was hot and the air was dry and he was tormented by thirst. His lips were so dry they were cracking.

Why not? Nothing to be gained by dying of thirst.

He gathered his lir and sent it streaming down the well shaft. There came a series of small explosions from far below, then a rising hiss, then a deep gurgle. Shortly water came brimming up to the lip of the well.

Seeker stooped and drank from his cupped hands, gulping and gulping till he could drink no more. He splashed cool water over his face and neck. Then he shook himself all over and drew a long deep breath.

All that power and all I can do is get myself a drink of water.

He longed to be a novice once more, standing in line with the others, learning the skills of the Nomana; or even a schoolboy, sitting alone in the classroom, hearing the cries of his fellows as they played in the yard. Then he wished Morning Star were with him again, so that he could tell her of his unhappiness and know that she understood. Then he wished for the Wildman, with his bold cry and his beauty. The three of them had been happy together, it seemed to him, not so long ago.

Now what?

Follow the road. Find the ruined wall. Go back through the door. Lie in the dirt before the Garden and confess his failure to the All and Only. Pray for guidance.

He felt a sudden giddiness in his head and heard a sound, a thin, high distant scream, that seemed to come from behind him. He turned round, but there was no one.

It's because I'm hungry, he thought. I must find food.

He looked down the empty road south. On either side lay neglected farmland, a featureless region of spiky grasses bleached gray by the sun. A shimmer of hot air hung over the land, melting the horizon.

Water was still gushing out of the well. It was finding its way down ditches into dry streambeds, away towards some distant unseen river, and so to the sea. He thought then of the ocean and the fishing boats he had watched from the overlook on Anacrea. He thought of the quiet evenings he had spent with his brother Blaze, skimming stones over the waves.

The old life was gone and would never return.

Then through the heat-haze he saw a figure walking, far down the road. He rubbed at his eyes and squinted. The figure was distorted by the shimmering horizon, where the land itself seemed to ripple, but he could see that it was a man and that he was walking away. Something in his outline, a hint of head-covering, a glimmer of a stick, made him think it was the strange old man called Jango.

He set off at once, striding down the road. He moved

much faster than the hazy figure ahead and was confident he would soon catch him up; but after a little time, he found he had not got nearer. He broke into a run.

As far as he could tell, the figure ahead was not hurrying, but still he could not catch him up. If anything, the gap between them was widening. He heard the far-off scream again, and the giddiness returned. The ripple of the land ahead was like the waves on the sea. He shut his eyes, thinking he might be affected by the glare, and at once felt a lurch of vertigo that forced him to slow to a stop. He opened his eyes again.

The distant figure was gone.

He stood still, one hand to his mouth, and slowly the sickness passed. Before him he saw a fork in the road he had not registered before. He had kept his eyes fixed on the lone walker, but he had no idea which road he had taken. To the left and to the right the horizon was the same. Worse still, he had no idea which fork led to the ruined wall.

A second wave of nausea swept through him. Afraid he would fall, he sat himself down on the ground and rested his head on his knees.

"I must be ill," he said.

But it didn't feel like an illness. It felt like an intense inner disgust. He wanted to be sick, but not from his stomach. He wanted to be sick from his mind.

Then he remembered. He was not sick. He was possessed.

"Don't fight me," he said, speaking to the alien life within him. "I'm stronger than you can ever be."

He heard the thin faraway cry once more. Now it sounded from deep within his mind.

"You'll live with me," he said, "and you'll die with me."

Slowly the nausea passed.

The sun burned down from a cloudless sky. He couldn't stay here by the fork, where there was neither food nor shelter. So he rose to his feet and set off once more, taking the way to the left for no good reason, and walked on down the road. Now as he covered the ground, he found the open scrub and weed on either side giving way to stubby sun-dried grasses that stood up stiffly in clumps. A little farther and the grasses grew closer and taller, until he was passing down a road between high and shivering walls. The dry summer grass clicked and rustled in the breeze. This must have been the cause of the rippling of the land he had seen ahead of him earlier. He had entered a land sea and was sailing in billows of amber grass that reached as high as his shoulders.

The road narrowed steadily until it was little more than a path running on straight before him, his only guide in this shivering world. All he could think to do was keep walking, knowing that in time he must come to a river or a coast. Then, over the fringes of the grass, not far to one side, he saw the shingled roof of a house. He parted the stalks before him and looked. He saw white clapboard walls, a blue door. His hunger returned with full force. Where there was a house there must be people. Where there were people there was food.

He left the path and pushed through the tall grass directly towards the house. It was not far, and he expected to shortly emerge from the golden sea into a clearing. But there was no clearing. He stamped and beat his way to the very doorstep of the house, to its soft lavender-blue door. The house was one story only, and small, its board walls painted a chalky white, its roof bleached gray by the sun. The grasses grew right up against its window, the higher fronds touching the eaves. No path to the door, no tracks of wagon wheels. No one had been this way for many years. And yet the door looked as if it had been painted not so long ago. Its color charmed him. He touched the paintwork, finding in it the promise of a kindly welcome.

The door handle turned. The door opened. He stepped directly into the principal room of the house, which was lit by two windows, one on either side. The tall grass pressing against the windows acted as natural blinds, softening the glare of the sun. The wooden interior walls were whitewashed the same chalky white as outside. The floor was plain worn boards, on which lay a rug woven in stripes of faded colors. There was a table, two chairs, an iron stove, a set of shelves on which stood dishes and kitchen implements. And on the table, in a water glass, there was a single long-stemmed blue cornflower.

Seeker stared at this flower. He had seen it before. Jango had stood in a doorway with his wife by his side, and behind them there had been this whitewashed room, this table, this glass, this blue flower. Was this therefore Jango's house? But that house had been entered through a door in a ruined wall. This house stood in a sea of grass.

He moved round the room, looking and touching, and as he did so he found a new mood was taking possession of his troubled spirit. The house was peaceful. In its simple way it was beautiful. He didn't understand many things: how it could have been unoccupied so long that grasses grew up to the door and yet have on its table a flower that had not withered; how there could be no dust on the white plates ranged along its shelves. But the calm space resisted questions.

Why should I understand everything?

Two further doors opened off the main room. One led to a small washroom, where clothes hung from an overhead rack to drip into a brick trough below. There were two white undershirts, both stiff and dry. The other door opened into a bedroom barely big enough to contain a high box bed. The bed was made up, ready for use, with a plump white quilt, lying in hummocks over a sailcloth mattress, and two sturdy white pillows.

He returned to the main room and looked in the cupboard by the stove. There he found a jar of pickled eggs and a jar of honey. He ate three of the pickled eggs, and then opened the honey and put in his finger, dipping and licking it again and again. His hunger satisfied, he remained sitting on the wooden chair by the stove, gazing at the blue cornflower and the plain white walls and the flicker of sunlight coming through the windows.

Whoever lives here, he thought to himself, has a good life.

Sunlight on the blue petals of the cornflower, on the crushed, crumpled burst of pure color that sprang like a new day from the stiff green stem. He looked more closely, and as he looked he saw that the blue of the bunched petals was not uniform after all, there were flashes of a darker purple, where shadows fell, and the palest blue, almost white, in the direct light of the sun. How had such a joyful extravagance of summer sky exploded from the green stalk? He drew the glass nearer, and with his face now at the level of the flower, he searched for the join, for the point at which green turned to blue, as if somewhere within the stem he would find blue veins that ran down in the growing flower to the source of the blueness, some hidden shaft of sapphire buried deep in the ground. But there was no join. The petals grew from the stem as the narrow green leaves grew from the stem, sharing the same substance and yet transformed. He felt that he had never properly looked at a flower, had never before appreciated the miracle of the colored world. This plain white sun-dappled room made him this gift. In the midst of simplicity, a thing of wonder.

Why does this place make me feel so happy?

He heard the echo of a laugh. The savanter within him was mocking his pleasure. The laugh brought in its wake a taste of bitterness; and after the bitterness, anger.

Am I poisoned? Am I never to be happy again?

He no longer wanted to stay. He rose and replaced the two jars in the cupboard and moved the chair back into the position in which he had found it. Then he left the little house and drew the blue door shut behind him.

Once back in the tall grass, he pushed his way towards the road, knowing it was no great distance away; but the road did not appear. He realized he must have mistaken the direction. He tried again, tramping on through the grass for a longer time, but had no better luck.

He decided he had better return to the house with the blue door, but looking round in all directions, he could see no sign of it. The little house had disappeared. So, it seemed, had the road.

He was lost in the sea of grass.

THE SECOND STAGE
OF THE
EXPERIMENT

HYPOTHESIS

In the heart of the violence and superstition
of the world, I will place a new breed of men and women.
They will seek no riches, no dominion, no glory. They will
be warriors but not conquerors. They will have power but
they will never rule. By the example of their lives they
will lead others to act justly and to love peace.

Can such noble warriors endure through the years?
Can they remain strong but uncorrupted? Can they renew
themselves generation after generation? Can they fall sick
and heal themselves? Can they die and be reborn?

If all this can be done, then I will know
there is more good than evil in men's hearts,
and I will go to my rest content.

⇥ 9 ⇤

Yes, Beloved

MORNING STAR WAS WOKEN BY HEM. HE HELD OUT A tin plate on which there was a piece of bread smeared with honey.

"Breakfast," he said.

"Oh, Hem. You are sweet."

"Share the joy," he said.

"Hem! Have you joined them?"

"Why not?" said Hem. "There's food. There's fun. Who wants to go back to being hungry and sad? Not me."

"Nor me."

Hem squatted down beside her as she ate her bread and honey.

"How old are you?" he said.

"I'm seventeen."

"I don't know how old I am. How old would you say I am? Fifteen?"

"Maybe a bit less than that."

"If you'll wait for me, I'll get older quite soon."

"Wait for you, Hem?"

"Then you can marry me."

"Oh, I see."

"Unless there's someone else you want to marry more." He avoided her eyes. "Which I expect there is."

"No," said Morning Star. "There's no one else at present. But even so, I think it's too soon, don't you?"

"I knew you'd say that. That's why I said to wait. I hate being young. It's not fair."

He got up and stomped crossly away.

Morning Star found this little exchange put her in a good mood. She took her tin plate back to the food tables, where everything was in the process of being packed away into the wagons. The Joyous was preparing to move on.

"Where are you going?" she asked the ox handlers.

"Just moving on," they said.

"But there must be somewhere you're going, or why move at all?"

"So people can find us."

This was the way the Joyous grew in numbers. For days now, the followers of the Joy Boy had been slowly crossing the land, drawing in their wake the people of villages and towns. This was a time of uncertainty, following the collapse of the old ruling power of Radiance. The army of the Orlans had broken up into rival bands, and no village was safe from their horse-borne raids. The roads were full of refugees driven from their homes by feuding bandits. At such a time, the vast throng that was the Joyous proved an irresistible draw to the rootless frightened people of the hills and the plains; and so it grew larger with every passing day.

Morning Star now found herself unsure what to do. She had left Spikertown thinking she could return home, but home for her meant her father and mother. Did she therefore propose to stay with them here in the Joyous?

At this point, she was approached by a smiling young woman who bowed politely to her and said, "The Beloved would like to see you."

Morning Star realized at once that she wanted this very much. She followed the young woman through the crowd, past people putting out fires and packing up belongings into kit bags, to the circle of favored devotees that had formed round the Joy Boy. He was kneeling on the ground, his head bent, while an older man poured water over him from a bucket.

Morning Star waited and watched. She supposed the water was to wash him clean, but the manner in which he knelt there, so humble and unresisting, made it look like a ritual of greater significance. As before, Morning Star felt both irritated and impressed.

He looked up now, face dripping, and smiled to see her before him.

"You came. I'm so glad."

The washerman stepped forward with a cloth and patted the Joy Boy's face dry as if he were helpless. Then, when the ablutions were all done, the Joy Boy rose and came to Morning Star. Once more she saw that he had no aura. This frightened her and excited her.

He looked at her with his smiling eyes but didn't speak. The silence was only awkward for a moment. Then she found herself held by those eyes. They seemed to draw her in and calm her thoughts. Then, still without speaking, something passed from him into her that caused a sweet melting sensation all through her body. Startled by it, she looked away and found that everything round the Joy Boy, the other people, the distant hills, the small clouds in the blue sky, had all become more intense, their colors more vivid.

"You see so much," he said. "Too much."

"Yes."

"I've been thinking about you, and why you've come to me now."

"I told you. I was looking for my parents."

"So you did." He smiled gently like a father who knows his child is lying, but sees no need to challenge the lie. "I've been thinking about your gift of feeling. I have a question to ask. Do you have the power to make one person feel what another person feels?"

"Yes," said Morning Star slowly. "I have done that."

"Can you do it with many people?"

"Yes."

"It's as I thought. You have a wide embrace. You're a unifier. That is the greatest gift there is."

Morning Star saw the brightness of the colors all round her and felt that something strange was happening to her. This plump-faced youth made the world fresh and new.

"You've done this before, I think," he said.

"Yes. With the spikers. I joined them into an army."

"An army? You used your gift to bring men together to kill?"

He spoke without sneering. He was puzzled.

"Yes," she said. She felt ashamed.

"You can do better than that."

"Tell me what I can do."

She had no intention of becoming the Joy Boy's disciple, and she thought as she spoke that she would listen but not necessarily obey. However, the melting sweetness within and the vivid brightness round her made her less resistant. She wanted to please him now.

"You can use your gift to share the joy," he said.

This time the phrase that had so annoyed her sounded different. She heard it from his lips as a simple innocent statement of the obvious. Why would she not want to share the joy? What was to be gained by keeping herself apart and in pain?

"I know you're afraid," he went on in his gentle voice. "You have so little protection against the darkness. You're made of smoke and moonlight. You don't know where you end and others begin. But what you think of as your weakness is your strength."

Morning Star had never had anyone speak to her in this way. It seemed to her he read her innermost heart.

"I fear more than you know," she said.

"You fear the loss of yourself. It's what everyone fears. But you stand closer to the edge than others."

"I'm weaker than you know."

As she spoke, she thought to herself, Why am I telling

this boy what I've told no one else? And she answered herself: because no one has ever known me as he knows me. Not even Seeker.

"So weak," he said, "that you have loved where you have not been loved in return."

So he knew that, too. She bowed her head.

"And so weak that you can never be a true Noble Warrior."

"Yes."

"What's the use of you, Morning Star?"

It was like her own voice, speaking outside her.

"Nothing."

"You've already failed. And yet your gift remains. How can that be?"

She looked up. She saw so much love and understanding in those dark eyes that in spite of herself she began to feel happy. What did any of it matter after all?

"I don't know," she said.

"Maybe whether you succeed or fail doesn't matter. Maybe whether you're strong or weak doesn't matter. Maybe you don't matter. Maybe all that matters is your gift."

"Yes," she said.

"Your gift and how you use it."

"Yes."

"You can remain alone, or you can share the joy."

"I want to share the joy."

It was so simple after all.

"I told you before that I'm nothing. Like you, I have a gift. I come to make men into gods."

The claim was outrageous, but Morning Star heard it without surprise. She had recited the words of the Catechism often enough in her time in the Nom.

Why did the All and Only bring us into being?

To become gods.

"This will happen," said the Joy Boy, "when we overcome the separation that keeps us apart. We will become god."

"What am I to do?"

"Reach out to those who are the farthest away from joy. Use your gift to make them feel what they fear to feel. Bring them to join us."

"Am I to travel to other lands?"

"Not to other lands. To other minds. To those who have kept themselves so far apart that they have lost sight of others and become trapped in themselves."

"Who are they?"

"The Noble Warriors."

Morning Star shivered as she heard the words. It was a shiver of recognition. So her time in the Nom had been for a purpose after all.

"You are a bridge, Morning Star. Lay yourself down across the chasm that separates us, and let your brothers and sisters cross to joy."

"How am I to find them? The Noble Warriors are dispersed."

"There is one with greater power than the rest."

"Seeker!"

"Find him. The others will follow."

"Find Seeker!"

All her memories of her friend came flooding back. Of course she must find Seeker. There was nothing she wanted more. The Joy Boy knew her heart of hearts. He assigned her the task that was most special to her in every way.

"I know him well," she said.

"Bring him to us. Let him share the joy."

"Yes, Beloved," said Morning Star.

⊰ 10 ⊱

The Old Man in the Mirror

SEEKER CROUCHED LOW AND CLOSED HIS EYES. THE giddiness had returned. He shivered and felt the sweat on his face. Then once again came the rising surge at the base of his throat and he thought he was about to be sick. He wanted to be sick. He wanted to vomit up the poison in him. But nothing came.

"Stay, then," he said. "You can't hurt me."

He rose to his feet once more and looked round him. The sea of grass extended on all sides as far as he could see. No roads, no tracks—not even the track he had made in coming here. The grasses had erased all signs of his passing.

"Very well, then," he said to himself. "Since I don't know which way to go, I'll go nowhere."

He closed his eyes and set off walking blind. He pushed his way through the long grass, not caring where he went, hunter turned wanderer.

Meet your plan like a stranger, so they taught in the Nom.

At first he moved hesitantly, fearing that he might stumble and lose his footing. But finding the ground remained firm beneath his feet, he gained confidence and strode along at a brisk pace. By shutting his eyes and therefore refusing to seek a single destination, he made all destinations available to him. He might end up anywhere in the world. If he could only keep his eyes shut long enough, he was bound at the very least to go somewhere new.

After some time, he felt that the grass was changing round him. He heard the croaking call of rooks. Where there were rooks there were trees. He stopped and opened his eyes. He saw the trees not so far ahead of him, and between the trees a building. It was not the house with the blue door; this was something far grander. The waving grasses now ceased altogether, and he found himself walking over what had once been lawn and was now an expanse of sun-parched weeds. Before him stood a veritable mansion. Colonnaded single-story wings reached out like embracing arms on either side of a two-story central block. He was approaching what must be the back of the mansion, a wide stone terrace onto which opened a line of five tall windows. In one of these windows, standing gazing out towards him, was an old man, thin and stooping, holding a long slender stick.

Seeker hurried forward, his hopes rising. The old man, he was sure, was waiting for him. He found the steps that gave access to the terrace. He saw now that all the glass in the windows was gone. Fragments of glass lay among the terrace weeds. The wooden frames of one pair of windows stood open, but the figure he had seen waiting there was gone. As he hesitated, unsure whether or not to enter, he heard an inner door open and close. A sensation of extreme urgency possessed him. He must find the old man.

The room he entered through the open casement was long and high, its five tall windows matched by windows on its facing wall. Between each pair of windows hung tall mirrors, many of them cracked, adding to the dazzle of daylight. The room was empty but for a single wing-backed armchair, set in the middle, and an empty wineglass on the polished floor at its feet. At the far end were double doors. One of these doors was slowly swinging shut.

Seeker strode down the room, catching glimpses of his own shivered reflection as he went, and opened the swinging door. Beyond, there was a smaller hallway, out of which rose a handsome staircase. At the foot of the stairs stood three large leather trunks, all open, all spilling out a jumble of clothing. Farther up the stairs lay evidence of looters long departed: a broken picture frame, a lady's shoe, a small blue-glass perfume bottle lying uncorked on its side.

Footsteps passed overhead.

Seeker bounded up the stairs and saw before him a long central passage with doors on either side, all closed. He tried one of the doors. It was unlocked. The room within had been a bedroom, but the looters had stripped it of all linen, leaving only the heavy bed-frame and the remains of a mattress. A mouse, startled by Seeker's entry, scuttled out of the slashed mattress and disappeared into the skirting board. The window was open, its latch broken.

Seeker made his way on down the passage to the far end, where a second staircase descended to the ground floor. Here he came to a stop and listened for the sounds of the man he had seen. He heard the buzz of flies and the cries of the rooks in the trees outside. He heard his own breaths. Nothing else.

Then from below there came a faint clink. At once into his mind there flashed the image of that solitary wineglass on the floor by the armchair. He ran down the stairs and back into the long mirrored hall. It was empty, as before. But the wineglass lay on its side, rolling slowly round in an arc.

Seeker stood still, looking round, trying to work out what was happening. The mirrors on the facing walls reflected him into infinity. He stared at his overlapping image, then spoke aloud.

"Here I am," he said.

No response.

Then his roving gaze caught something new reflected in the mirrors: the armchair, with its high back to him. On its arm, an old man's hand.

Seeker spun round to the armchair itself, took the few paces necessary to face it front on. It was empty.

He turned his back on the chair and looked into the mirror. There he saw himself, standing with the chair beside him. And in the chair sat a very old man.

It was not Jango. This old man was far, far older. His face seemed to be dried and shrunken with age, and he had no hair at all. The bones of his head, his brow and nose and cheeks, all jutted out like a grotesque mask. His neck was so thin you could see his windpipe and the two tendons on either side, all sharply distinct. But these signs of extreme age counted for nothing, because his eyes glowed with life.

Seeker could not look away. He met the old man's eyes in the mirror and he saw there an intent probing intelligence, and a compassionate understanding, and an immense reservoir of latent power. The body might be crumbling, but the eyes showed that the force within was as vigorous as in youth. Seeker gazed into those eyes and felt that he was falling into them and that there was no end to his falling.

He jerked his head away from the mirror to look directly at the armchair. It was empty.

Stupidly, wanting to believe his eyes deceived him, he felt the armchair with his hands. Nothing. He looked back into the mirror. Nothing. He sat himself down in the armchair, assuming the position taken by the old man, one hand on the chair's left arm, the other hand on—what had the right hand been holding? He recalled the image. A stick. No, a sword. The right hand had held a long slender blade. Why had he not paid attention to that before?

He arranged his own right hand as if he too held a sword, then looked up again at the mirror. There, gazing back at him from the armchair, sword in hand, was the old man.

This time Seeker did not turn away.

"Here I am," he said.

The old man nodded in acknowledgment. Seeker saw now that over his shoulders he wore a badan, faded almost to white, and frayed down the sides, but for all that, a badan.

"You're a Noble Warrior," Seeker said.

Again the old man nodded.

"And you are Seeker after Truth," he said.

His voice was like his eyes: deep and clear and filled with power. It made Seeker shiver to hear him. He looked into his eyes as he listened, and he felt as if he were falling again, and his hands grasped the arms of the chair.

"You've done well," said the old man.

"No," replied Seeker. He had nothing to hide. Those eyes held him and penetrated him. "I've failed to do what I was sent to do."

"There's little to fear in failure," said the old man. A sudden smile made sharp wrinkles in the dry skin round his mouth. "Failure is the end of one road and the beginning of the next. You've come a long way. You have farther to go."

The more Seeker looked into the old man's eyes, the more he liked him. He felt the old man's gaze on him as a child feels his father's loving scrutiny. He sensed that he was known, approved, and loved.

"Who are you?" he asked.

"I am Noman," came the reply.

Seeker now looked on that shrivelled face with awe. This was the only living being ever to have entered the Garden and come face-to-face with the All and Only. This was the man who had founded the Noble Warriors and written their Rule. This was the warlord who had surrendered all his power to live simply and in the truth, to possess nothing and to build no lasting home. Here at last he would find the answers he sought.

"Tell me what to do," he said. "Tell me how to use the powers given to me. Tell me where to go. I can't go on like this, lost and alone."

"Lost and alone?" The old man's eyes reproved him. "Am I not with you? Have I not always been with you?"

"I didn't know it."

"But now you know. And you know you have always known it."

"Yes." So it was. The certainty that now came to him somehow included the past, as well as the future.

"You have so much more knowledge than you know. It waits for you."

"Tell me now. Make me understand now." Seeker heard his own voice rise in agitation even as he saw the old man slowly shake his head. "Why must I be kept in darkness?"

"I can't live your life for you," said Noman. "This is your journey, not mine."

"What journey?"

"You must find your own way."

"How? Why?" As Seeker understood that he was not to be given the commands he longed for, he gave way to a rush of disappointment. "How can I know where I'm to go? You say you've always been with me. Then, guide me. Instruct me. Order me. I'm ready to do all I can. I'm ready to obey, but how can I obey if I don't know what it is I'm to do?"

He was close to tears and ashamed of his own weakness, but he couldn't help himself. He bit his lip to stop

himself from crying, then fixed the old man with his pleading eyes.

"Seeker," said Noman, "I don't want your obedience.
I have known what it is to command men. Those who
carry out my orders are no wiser than my own hands."

He spread his frail bony hands before him.

"My hands know nothing. My hands will die with me
when I die."

He looked up, and the brilliance of his eyes shocked
Seeker once again.

"You must live your own life and die your own death.
Your life is an experiment in search of the truth."

"What if the experiment fails?" said Seeker. "What if
I'm not strong enough?"

"You may fail. It has happened before. If you fail, I will
know I have been wrong."

"I have failed. I was sent to kill seven savanters. Five are
dead. One I carry within me. But the seventh got away."

"Then you will continue to search for him."

"He got away on a boat. I saw the litter carried away.
I saw the boat sail out to sea."

"That litter was empty. It had been empty all along.
The last savanter is here, now, in the old kingdom."

Seeker heard this with amazement. So the hunt was
not over yet.

"Where?"

"He's at the center of a great gathering of people. He's
getting ready to harvest their lives." Noman's voice took
on a bitter edge. "His name is Manlir. You think you are

the only one to have failed? Manlir was my first and great-est failure."

"Manlir?"

Seeker recalled the savanter in the land cloud, who had spoken of one of his fellows as Manny.

"Manlir was the best of us," said Noman. "He chose the path of knowledge. I chose the path of faith. Both are necessary. It was he who discovered the force in us, the force in all living things, that he called lir. But as Manlir grew old and saw his own death approaching, he became angry and afraid. He dreaded death. He used the power of his knowledge to find a way to prolong his life. To be young again."

"He takes the lir from others," said Seeker. "I've seen it."

"He believes that if he can take enough lir into him-self, he will become immortal."

"Is he right?"

"Possibly. No one knows."

"And the people whose lir he takes?"

"You say you've seen that for yourself. There's no life without lir."

"And I am to stop him!" This was a clear goal. This was a purpose for his power. "And if I do, I'll have done what I was sent to do."

The old man's eyes flashed with anger, and his voice cut like a knife.

"You child!" he cried. "Can you only act when others give you orders? When will you be a man? When will you come out of the shadow and walk in your own light?"

"If I'm a child," said Seeker, angered in his turn, "then let me alone! Let me grow up in my own time."

Noman's ancient face stared back at him out of the mirror. Slowly, he nodded his head.

"You're right. Old men lose the luxury of patience. I want to see the proof before I die. I have failed once. I want to see the experiment succeed."

"And if I kill the seventh savanter, will you have your proof?"

"The experiment is far bigger than that."

"Bigger than that?"

It struck Seeker now that he had paid too little attention to this so-called experiment. He had supposed it to be the test of strength in which he was enlisted: the battle between the Noble Warriors and the savanters.

"What is this experiment?"

Noman closed his eyes. Seeker remained silent, sensing that Noman was debating within himself how much to reveal. After a few moments, without opening his eyes, Noman began to speak.

"Imagine," he said, "that a farmer sets out to grow a field of corn. He knows that so long as he protects the seedlings from frost, and clears the weeds from the young shoots, and waters the plants in the dry months, his corn will come to harvest and feed his family. But he also knows that he can't be in his cornfield all day. He has other concerns. He may fall ill. He may die. One day he must die. So he says to himself: How can I plant my seed so that it will grow and survive without me? Then my family will be fed after I'm gone. He knows the many dangers of this cruel land. He fences his field, and he irrigates it, and he picks only the hardiest seeds. Then he watches and sees the corn grow to ripeness all by itself. The autumn winds blow. The seeds scatter. Winter comes, and the land freezes. The frosts pass, and the land wakes into spring. The farmer could return to the field and plant new corn, but he chooses not to. He watches the scattered seeds take root but does nothing to protect them. Many die. He does not intervene. Why not? Because if the seeds he planted so long ago show that they can renew themselves without him, the farmer will know that he has planted living corn. He may die, but the corn will return each spring. Living corn will feed his children, and his children's children, forever."

With that he opened his eyes, but even as he looked on him, Seeker felt his withdrawal.

"Don't leave me," Seeker said, suddenly afraid.

Noman raised his long sword over his head, as if the slender weapon in his frail hand had the power to protect them both.

"I am always with you."

The blade flashed, reflecting the light from the tall window, making Seeker blink. When he looked again into the mirror, the old man was gone. There was the reflection of the armchair. And in the armchair, his right hand upraised, the reflection of himself.

Slowly he rose from the chair, and slowly he made his way down the long mirrored room. His reflections, repeated forever, walked with him.

He left the room by the end doors. Here was an entrance hall. The outer door stood open. A flight of steps led down to an overgrown driveway flanked by tall trees. At the far end of the driveway ran the high road. He was lost no more.

As he stood looking out of the mansion, a horse and rider came down the road and stopped to gaze on the great house. Seeker recognized the rider. He descended the steps and walked down the drive to her side.

"We meet again," said Echo Kittle. "Is this your house?"

"No."

"So where are you going?"

"Wherever the road leads," said Seeker.

"Would you like company on your way there?"

"I may be poor company."

"Any company's better than none," said Echo.

So they set off down the road together, Echo riding Kell, and Seeker striding by her side. From time to time Echo glanced down at Seeker, and when he caught her look, she smiled.

"Since we're travelling together," she said, "let's at least be friends."

⊰ 11 ⊱

The Wildman Dances

THE CASPIANS WERE GRAZING ALONG THE BANKS OF
the river. There were a hundred and more of the beautiful beasts, running wild now that the Orlan army had dis-
integrated. The grass was short and dry, and they had to
keep moving to find enough to eat. Where the bank was
shallow, they picked their way carefully to the river's edge
and drank the yellow water. The day was hot and the air
round the Caspians was swarming with flies. From time to
time one of them looked up, attentive to the smallest
sounds; then a shake of the long golden mane, to disperse
the flies, and the head dropped down again to resume
grazing.

A splash from upriver, and into view shot a long canoe
paddled by four men. The Caspians sprang back from the
river's edge. A second canoe followed, and a third. The
men in the canoes began shouting at the herd and hurling

small stones. The Caspians wheeled about and trotted away from the riverbank, putting distance between themselves and the river men.

But ahead of them, over the brow of the slope, there appeared a line of spikers holding a long net. The net hung from their raised hands and dragged over the stiff grass. The Caspians wheeled again, to run south, only to find a second line of men approaching from that direction, too. Sensing that a trap was closing in round them, they came to a stop, huddled close together, nostrils flaring with fear, and looked about them to see where the danger was greatest.

When the ring round the herd was complete, the spikers with the nets stopped advancing and stood still in the bright sun. Over the brow of the hill, stepping slowly, came a horse and rider. The ring parted to let them through, then closed behind them. It was the Wildman, riding the Caspian called Sky.

He rode with an easy grace, his long golden hair floating as he came, like the Caspian's golden mane. He wore scarlet and amber and brilliant green, and all down his bronzed arms, his silver bracelets flashed. He rode the Orlan way, without saddle or harness, and Sky responded to his slightest pressure.

He came close to the frightened herd of Caspians and spoke to them quietly, then let them smell both him and Sky and know that they meant no harm.

"Heya, my beauties. Quiet now, my beauties."

The men in the canoes, drifting downriver in the slow current, set about paddling to stay by the herd. The swish

of the paddles spooked the edgy Caspians, and one of them
made a break for a gap in the ring of men. The gap closed
at once, but now half the herd was on the move, and the
line of spikers on the northern rim faced a panicky charge.

"Let them come!" cried the Wildman. "Let the net
have them!"

The spikers in the line of charge held the long net before them, only releasing it and throwing themselves clear
as the Caspians struck it. The net was swept forward, dragging with it long lines of spikers, to right and left, but it
did not break. The Caspians found themselves packed together into a thrashing bunch and tried to turn about to
escape and so became even more entangled.

"Stand steady!" called the Wildman. "Hold them there!
Be strong! Be still!"

He himself proceeded on Sky at a walking pace to the
terrified herd, now bundled on all sides within the net. He
slipped off his mount, leaving Sky free, and vaulted over
the net into the heaving, shivering mass of horses.

The surrounding spikers watched with smiles on their
faces as the Wildman pushed his way among the captive
beasts. He moved from Caspian to Caspian, embracing
them one by one, pressing his face to their heads, speaking to them, letting them feel the nearness and the harm-
lessness of his body.

"Heya, my beauties. Nothing to mind; no one to hurt
you. There, beauties, friends now. Friends and comrades."

He touched them as a victorious commander touches
his weary men after a battle, transmitting to them his
power and his glory. Slowly the Caspians calmed down and

allowed him to climb on their backs. There, lithe and barefoot, standing tall, he stepped with expert balance from back to back, his jingling arms outstretched and shining in the sun, and cried out to his admiring followers.

"Heya, bravas! Do you lo-o-ove me?"

Back came the eager cry.

"Wildman! Wildman! Wildman!"

The Caspians were accustomed to the leadership of men, and once they had accepted the Wildman's authority, there was no more need for restraint. The nets were unwound, and the Wildman, mounted on Sky once more, led the herd back to the spiker army camp.

As the men and horses made their way along the high ridge path, they heard the distant sound of singing and laughter. Shortly there came into view below them a great crowd of people, too far off to make out in any detail, advancing slowly across the plain, singing and dancing as they came.

The Wildman called a stop to look.

"What is that?"

No one knew.

"There must be thousands of them."

Shab stepped forward.

"I've heard the Orlans are reforming," he said.

"Those aren't Orlans. There's women there, and children. Listen."

The singing voices drifting up towards them on the warm breeze were both light and deep, and here and there they caught the shrill laughter of children.

"Let me go and find out," said Shab.

"Alone?"

"Better for one man to go. That way I'm just another spiker on the road."

The Wildman thought for a moment, then nodded his approval.

"Do that, Shab. Come back and tell me."

The Wildman rode on towards Spikertown, leading the riderless Caspians after him, and his men strode with him on either side.

As they reached the outskirts of the great camp, the cheering began. The Wildman rode down the broad central street, at the head of the captured herd, and the people roared their approval.

At the heart of the camp, beneath the long canopies, he dismounted and gave orders for the Caspians to be fed and watered. Then he went to his own tent. Pico, his bodyguard, was squatting outside.

"Let no one past, Pico," he said.

Pico had been with him from the start and could read his moods. He was a big man, with long black hair and a thick black beard, a strong man not much given to speaking. He nodded and held the tent flap open and drew it shut once more, after the Wildman had passed through.

When he was alone at last, out of sight of his men, the Wildman's smile faded. He stood for a few moments in utter stillness. Then, with slow movements, he drew off his brightly colored shirt and lay down on the floor, arms outreached, face to the ground. As he lay, he groaned and beat his brow softly on the rough weave of the rug.

Here he lay, neither eating nor drinking, till nightfall.

At last he rose and drank a cup of water and ate a cut of bread; just enough for the basics of life. Then he called Pico to join him in the tent, and he handed the big man his whip.

"Do it, Pico," he said.

"Don't like this, chief."

"Do it for me, Pico."

He knelt before him, and the whip rose and fell, lashing down on the Wildman's bare brown back. A tracery of red weals from earlier whippings striped the skin. The Wildman received the lashes in silence.

When he was finished, Pico handed back the whip, shaking his head.

"What's done is done and won't be undone."

"Same time tomorrow, Pico."

The big man believed the whipping to be an act of atonement for the death of Snakey; but the Wildman sought the punishing sting of pain for so much more than that. He had fallen into a dark place where he felt nothing and no longer loved his life. Surrounded as he was by a vast army, he felt entirely alone. Able to command whatever he desired, he desired nothing. The beautiful youth who had danced on the Caspians' backs, crying out, "Do you love me?" had been playing a part, acting the carefree bandit leader that his followers knew and revered. In himself, when alone, the Wildman felt empty, as if he had been hollowed out. The only true and certain joy left to him was the one he had felt as he had squeezed the life out of Snakey: the wild joy of the kill. It frightened him that this was all he craved. Better to feel nothing than to come alive only through such acts of violence. He was frightened too by his own temper. It exploded suddenly, unpredictably, beyond his control, and was dangerous in its intensity. So for this too, to atone for his minor cruelties, he knelt and was silent beneath the lash.

In the command tent, where he joined his men at last, the talk was all of the Orlan resurgence.

"They have a new Jahan, who they say is even greater than the old one."

"The old one wasn't so great. I saw him on his knees."

This angered the Wildman.

"Who says the Jahan wasn't great? He was a warlord!"

"I saw him begging on his knees."

"So did I," growled the Wildman. "Every one of us would be on his knees before that one."

They all knew who he meant by "that one," but the name was never spoken aloud. He had been the Wildman's friend. Now he could no longer bear to hear his name.

The Wildman sat with the others for the night meal, but he ate nothing. In the course of the meal, Shab returned. He was tired and dusty, but a beaming smile creased his lean features. In place of his petulant whine, he greeted them all with a ringing laugh.

"Friends!" he cried. "Share the joy!"

They stared at him.

"Have you been at the brandy?"

Shab went to the Wildman and threw his arms round him.

"Chief! Be happy!"

"Get off me!" The Wildman gave Shab a sharp push to get him away. "Don't tell me how I'm to be."

Shab smiled all the more cheerfully. He seemed to have lost all fear of the Wildman's anger.

"Those people we saw, they call themselves the Joyous. They're not soldiers or bandits, they're the followers of the Joy Boy. They're preparing to be gods."

"So they're a flock of fools," growled the Wildman. "I don't need to know any more."

"But chief! The Joy Boy! You must meet him! He made me see things I've never seen before." He turned on the gathered spiker chiefs sitting round the table and extended his arms. "Look! None of you are happy. Don't you want to share the joy?"

At that, the Wildman shot out one arm and seized Shab by the throat and shook him.

"No!" he shouted. "We don't want your fool joy!"

Shab was beyond fear.

"Meet him," he croaked, grinning even as he choked in the Wildman's grip. "Meet the Joy Boy. Find out for yourself."

"The Joy Boy!" The Wildman hurled Shab to the ground in disgust. "You're a bad joke, Shab. You always were."

Shab picked himself up and brushed the dirt off his clothing.

"Maybe I'm a joke," he said. "But I'm the only one here who's laughing."

———

The next day, the Wildman called up fifty of his men to act as his escort, and mounted on Sky, he rode out to see the Joyous for himself. Shab led the way.

As they came close, the Wildman saw the heavily laden supply wagons.

"Bandits," he said. "Just another gang of thieves."

"No," said Shab. "It's all freely given."

"Why would anyone give for nothing?"

"Because they've no need of personal possessions where they're going."

"Where's that?"

"They call it the Great Embrace."

They went on and so entered the outer fringes of the crowd. The Wildman looked with irritable gaze on the singing, dancing groups.

"Cracked," he said. "Funny in the head."

"Happy," said Shab.

Smiling faces called out to them, "Share the joy!"

"So where is he?" the Wildman grumbled. "Where's the chief fool?"

"He'll be in the crowd somewhere."

"In the crowd! There's thousands here. We'll never find him."

"He'll find us."

There was nothing to mark him out, no retinue of servants, no crown or throne, but the Wildman knew it was him at first sight. The Joy Boy was sitting on the ground, leaning back, supported on his elbows, talking and laughing with a crowd of children. When the Wildman rode to a stop before him, he looked up, shading his eyes with one hand, and nodded a friendly greeting as if he had been expecting him.

The Wildman addressed him sharply.

"You're in my territory," he said. "Everyone who crosses my land pays a levy."

"By all means." The youth waved one hand to either side. "Take whatever you want. We don't have much, but you're welcome to all you need."

"I don't take," said the Wildman. "You give."

He meant to establish a relationship of authority between himself as warlord and this plump-cheeked youth. Annoyingly, every time the Joy Boy spoke, all those round him nodded and smiled as if he had said something clever.

"I do give," said the Joy Boy, smiling. "I give the greatest gift that can be given. I give it to you. But do you receive?"

The people round him clapped softly. The Wildman looked away, not liking the sensation of meeting those big dark eyes. He gazed over the heads of the great throng and spoke with an air of indifference.

"I see that your people aren't armed. Move on today, out of my territory, and my men will see you safely on your way."

"And who will see you safely on your way?"

The Wildman chose not to answer this. He didn't like these soft questions, so barbed with presumptions about his needs. He wheeled his Caspian about and signed to his men to begin the journey back to camp.

The Joy Boy called after him.

"Go in peace," he said. "Seek your own peace."

The Wildman went on riding, and his men strode with him on either side, but these last words had done their work. They echoed and reechoed in his brain. Did the Joy Boy know that these same words had been spoken to him long ago? Did the Joy Boy know that it was just this very search for peace that had turned him from a carefree bandit into the lonely self-hating warlord of today?

The more he thought about this, the angrier he became. This pudgy Joy Boy was just another one of the tribe of dreamers who ruined lives with promises that could never be met. Peace! There was no peace in this life. And joy, this joy that he was told on all sides to share, it lasted a few moments, at the most, before turning to ashes.

Suddenly the rage came swelling up from the belly of his misery and burst forth in a howl of refusal.

"No!" he cried. "There is no peace! There is no joy! You're all fools!"

He swung Sky round and cantered back to the Joy Boy. He threw himself to the ground and seized the youth's fleshy neck in his powerful hands and squeezed it and shook.

"Don't tell me what to do!" he shouted. "Don't goop at me with your fish eyes! Don't preach at me! You've got nothing! Nothing!"

The Joy Boy offered no resistance. None of his followers sprang to his defense. After a few moments, the Wildman's anger cooled and he let him go. He wanted very badly to fight, but even he couldn't fight a limp sack like this.

"So don't go smirking about as if you've got the answers to everything," he said, aware that he was beginning to sound sulky. "You've got nothing."

The Joy Boy stood there, massaging his neck, with a puzzled look on his face. At least this was an improvement on the smile.

"You're quite right," he said. "I've got nothing."

"There!" The Wildman shouted out to all the crowd gathered round them. "You hear that? He admits it! He's deceived you. He's got nothing!"

The men and women smiled as he said this and nodded their heads, as if this was well known to them and, more, was exactly what they wanted.

"But I can dance," said the Joy Boy.

"Dance!" The Wildman's voice was heavy with contempt. "What's the good of dancing?"

At the Joy Boy's words, several men in the crowd drew forth musical instruments—flutes, hand drums, small pot-bellied guitars—and began to play. As the chirpy little melody filled the air, the Joy Boy began to dance.

His dance was like nothing the Wildman had ever seen before. Every part of his body moved as if he were made of rubber. His hips undulated from side to side, his head swooped forward and back like a chicken's, his arms drew spirals in the air, and his legs moved sometimes in a sinuous creeping motion, sometimes in sudden hops. The sight of all this wiggling at once was so absurd that the Wildman burst into laughter. The Joy Boy grinned back as he danced, in no way offended, and as the instruments hit a sustained musical climax, he began to spin.

He spun at an astonishing speed, all on one spot, with his hands on his hips and his elbows flapping like wings. Then the music slowed its pace and his spinning slowed its speed, and there he was, still once more, entirely unruffled, gazing at the Wildman with deep and quizzical eyes. Now, as the music stopped, the Wildman felt no inclination to laugh. He knew that what he had witnessed had been a remarkable display of controlled precision. What was more, he felt within himself an overwhelming urge to be in motion, to reach out his own arms—in short, to dance.

As if sensing this, the musicians started up again, this time with a simple tune that ran to a driving beat. The Joy Boy held out his hands, and people on either side of him clasped his hands and held out their other hand in turn, and very quickly a ring formed. The Wildman found his own hands taken and held, and without ever meaning to, he became part of the dancing ring.

Round they went to the right, stamping to the beat, and then round to the left; then twice round to the right, and twice round to the left, pounding the ground a little faster; then three times each way, faster still. As the tempo of the drums increased, so it seemed natural to stamp harder, and in doing this, the body crouched and leaped with ever more pronounced motions. It was hardly a dance, it was more like a charge, but the Wildman found this accelerating motion took over his body without any act of will. He heard grunts and cries accompanying the stamping beat and found to his surprise that he was uttering them himself, along with everyone else. When the dance reached the very limit of speed and urgency, he shouted aloud at the top of his voice along with all the other dancers, throwing his head back and yelling at the summer sky, the sweat streaming down his cheeks and neck.

A last crash of the drums and it was over. The dancers were swept on by their own momentum, but with the rhythm gone, they tumbled and crashed into each other and fell laughing into a heap of bodies.

The Wildman felt himself pulled to his feet by friendly hands. He stood there panting, glowing, grinning like a fool, and all round him he saw happy, answering smiles.

"Now you're thirsty," said the Joy Boy, smiling at him. "You would like a drink."

"You must be a mind reader." The Wildman meant to speak mockingly, but the dance had filled him with such simple good feeling that his words came out as a sweet tribute.

The Joy Boy led him to the food tables, and they drank juice crushed from oranges and lemons, and it was the most delicious drink the Wildman had tasted in years.

"This is excellent!" he said. "You must teach me how to make it."

"Certainly," said the Joy Boy. "All you need is oranges and lemons and an eagerness to drink."

"Preaching again, boy."

"You're right. It's my vice. The temptation is so strong."

He sighed and then smiled affectionately at the Wildman.

"You preach to me," he said. "I would far rather learn."

"Me preach? I've nothing to say."

"Nothing? Has your life so far taught you nothing?"

"It's taught me that friends betray. It's taught me that pleasures fade. It's taught me that the best days of my life are over."

"What then do you live for?"

"Habit. Fear of death."

"I see."

The Joy Boy reflected in silence for a few moments, furrowing his brow.

"It seems to me," he said, "that almost anything would be better than that."

"Anything real. Don't trick me with dreams."

"What if the dreams are real?"

"No, no. I must see it. I must touch it. I must feel it."

"Like this?"

He was looking directly into the Wildman's eyes. A sudden intense spasm of pleasure shot through the Wildman's body, making him gasp. It was over as soon as it had begun, but it left him trembling, in shock.

"You felt that?"

He nodded.

"That was joy."

The Wildman shook his head in amazement and spoke slowly.

"I've never, ever had a feeling like that before."

"And yet," said the Joy Boy, "it is what you were made for. That is your natural condition. You were born to be joyous. You have learned to be unhappy."

This time the Wildman did not urge him to stop. The aftereffects of the shock of joy were still shivering through his nerves.

"You have chosen to be unhappy," said the Joy Boy in his soft steady voice. "You can choose joy."

"How?"

"Join us. Shed your armor. Let your anger fade. Let the bitterness drop away, and the cynicism, and the suspicion, and the fear. When a stranger smiles at you, smile back. When he holds out his arms, embrace him. When the music plays, dance. Share the joy."

"And after the smiling and the dancing—what then?"

"You become god."

"Ah, preacher. More dreams."

"Why not? That's the biggest dream of all." He looked round the ring of smiling faces that surrounded them. "They all believe it. And the people beyond them. And all the people beyond them who make up this great gathering that we call the Joyous. But of course they're all fools, and you know better."

The words were teasingly spoken, even lovingly. The Wildman found himself in a dilemma. His pride demanded that he walk away from this soft-spoken youth and have no more to do with his seductive promises. But he no longer wanted to go. That one touch of joy held him; that, and the memory of the bitter loneliness to which he would return.

What if they're all fools? he thought to himself. I've been a fool myself before and I'll be a fool again. What would I rather be? A lonely wise man or a joyful fool?

The Joy Boy understood his hesitation.

"Go back to your men," he said. "Live as you have

lived. If your true place is with us, you'll know it and you'll return."

"If I do return," said the Wildman, "and if some of my men wish to come with me, will they be welcome?"

"They will be welcome. They are welcome. Every day they come from your camp and are welcomed into the Joyous."

"My men?"

"Of course." He looked round the crowd. "There. You see some of them."

The Wildman looked, and there indeed stood a band from his own spiker army, grinning foolishly, a little ashamed at being drawn to the attention of their former chief.

Shab then stepped forward.

"I want to stay, chief."

"You too, Shab?"

"I want to be here when it happens."

He looked at the Joy Boy, shy of claiming to understand the transformation they all anticipated. The Joy Boy supplied the words in his gentle voice.

"He wants to join in the Great Embrace. He wants to become god."

"What is this?" The Wildman asked because he wanted to know. Gone were his angry dismissive sneers. "When will it happen?"

"Very soon now, I think," replied the Joy Boy. "Every day more people join us. How can I turn any away? How can I deny to any who want it the chance to become god?

I long for the Great Embrace with all my heart. But I am like the captain of a ship at anchor in the harbor of a dying country. Soon I will raise anchor and set sail to a new world. But the people of the old world clamor to come aboard. How can I leave them to destruction and death? So each day I say, tomorrow we sail. And each day more people crowd aboard. As you see."

"And where will you take them when you sail? What is this new world?"

"A place where all men become one. And that one is god."

The Wildman shook his head.

"I can't understand that," he said.

"Of course not," murmured the Joy Boy. "To understand god you must be god. But all of us have felt, if only for a moment, what it's like to be god. We call it joy."

He smiled and bowed politely and left him to his own thoughts.

The Wildman called for his Caspian and swung himself up onto Sky's back. Silent and pensive, he rode back to the spiker camp, escorted by his men.

That evening he said to Pico, "There'll be no more lashes."

Pico nodded, to show he had heard, but did not speak.

"What would you do, Pico," said the Wildman, "if you had to choose between everything you've got and the one thing you want?"

"I'd watch my back," said Pico.

⚜ 12 ⚜

Fear Makes Us Cruel

CHEERFUL GIVER, HIS WIFE, BLESSING, AND THEIR TWO boys tramped dismally back down the road towards Radiance. Cheerful Giver was silent, as he had been for many miles. Each day, he grew more weary. He still wore his winter coat, weighed down with gold shillings, but the true burden that stooped his shoulders and silenced his tongue was his loss of hope. He could see no future for himself and his family in this lawless world. He was still rich. He was still, in his own mind, a person of distinction. How then had he come to this? He was wandering the land like a homeless vagabond. He had become—the thought struck him with peculiar horror—he had become a spiker.

Blessing made quiet noises of her own as she went along. She was singing the song of the temple choir from the old days at Radiance.

"O Radiance! O Radiance!
This life we humbly give!
Return to us! Return to us!
Through you alone we live!"

Then in a high piping treble she broke into her solo.

"Receive our tribu-u-ute!"

Her boys groaned aloud.

"You're doing it again, Mum."

"Am I?" said Blessing, startled.

"You're going funny in the head, Mum."

"Husband, husband!" wailed Blessing. "What's to become of us?"

Cheerful Giver made no reply. He was staring down the road ahead. A man had come into view, a very big heavily armed man. He had a short-handled axe in his belt and a chain wound round his waist.

"Axer!" he cried.

His spirits lifted. The axers had been the imperial enforcers in Radiance. In Cheerful Giver's eyes they were the guardians of order and authority. He hurried forward to greet him.

"I am Cheerful Giver," he said, "formerly the Handler of the Corona to his Imperial Radiance! Thank the great sun above that we've found you! Please lead us to your captain."

The axer stared at Cheerful Giver and his family.

"Handler of the Corona, were you?" he said. "Heavy, was it?"

"Not so very heavy," said Cheerful Giver. He didn't like the way the big man was looking at him.

"These your sons, are they?"

The axer reached out one brawny arm and seized the oldest boy. The boy shrieked. The axer threw him to the ground and put one foot on his midriff. The boy screamed and struggled. The axer pressed down. The screams subsided into gasps.

"What are you doing?" cried Cheerful Giver.

"Call it an experiment," said the axer. "See if the lad can take my full weight."

"Stop! You'll crush him!"

"True. I might. So what are you going to give me so I don't?"

"Give you? I don't understand."

Blessing, who had been briefly shocked into silence by the turn of events, now found her voice.

"Give him your coat, husband! Your coat!"

"Your coat, eh?" said the axer, looking with interest at Cheerful Giver's coat. "Let's have a closer look at your coat."

"No!" cried Cheerful Giver, pulling his coat tight round him. "You can't have it!"

The axer applied more of his weight to the squirming boy.

"Seems to me the boy's not got the solidity," he said.

Blessing screamed.

"Give him the coat!"

"No!" Cheerful Giver clung even tighter to his coat. It was all that remained of his former status.

"He'll kill our child!"

The axer trod down a little harder, peering down at the boy as he did so.

"All fat," he said. "No muscle. Fat offers no resistance at all."

"Husband!"

At just this point Morning Star came round the bend in the road, walking towards them. In desperation Blessing cried to her for help.

"He's killing my child! Give him the coat! Tell my husband!"

"That's right," said the axer, turning to the newcomer. "You tell him."

Morning Star raised one hand. The axer gasped and staggered as if he had been clubbed in the belly. Morning Star passed her hand from side to side in the air, and he toppled over backwards, releasing the boy on the ground. The boy scrambled away, whimpering with terror, to be clutched tight in his mother's arms.

"My baby! My little one! Are you hurt? Oh, the brute!"

She looked up to thank their saviour, and suddenly recognized her.

"You!" she cried.

Morning Star too had known her as soon as she had seen her. But now she wanted only to go on her way.

"Husband, look! It's the girl you brought us, who had the dreams! It's my own daughter!"

Morning Star shook her head.

"Not your daughter," she said.

"You're one of them," said Cheerful Giver, gazing at her clothing. "You're one of the smashers."

For a moment it seemed he would start shouting at her, but instead his voice cracked and began to tremble.

"Noble Warriors, that's what you are." His body began to shake. "You saved my son."

He looked from the stunned axer lying on the ground to his son sobbing in his wife's arms, and he dropped to his knees and began to weep.

"What am I to do?" he said. "Where are we to go? The world has gone mad. Save us all, Noble Warrior! Save us all!"

Morning Star heard the clinking sound of Cheerful Giver's coat as he fell to his knees, and she guessed at what it held.

"The axer tried to rob you of your coat?"

"My gold! All that I have left. All that I have."

"Not all. You have a wife and sons."

"My gold is to protect them."

"And yet it seems your gold makes you less safe, not more."

"How else are we to live?"

"Your sons are young and strong. Let them find a way for you all to live."

"My sons?"

Cheerful Giver stared at his boys. They looked back at him, and for the first time, the sullenness was gone.

"We can do that, Dad."

"Don't you worry, Dad. We'll get food and stuff."

Blessing hugged them both.

"There! Didn't I always say they were fine boys?"

"But," protested Cheerful Giver, "how—what?"

"Take off your coat," said Morning Star. "Hang it on a tree by the roadside. And follow your boys."

With that, she went on her way.

Blessing watched her out of sight.

"I know she was my daughter in another life," she said. "Whatever she says."

"Well, well," said Cheerful Giver, standing up and dabbing at his eyes. "Maybe she was."

Slowly he drew off his coat and hung it over the branch of a tree. He stood tall, no longer bowed down by the weight of the gold. He felt the cooling air on his skin. He looked down the road south. The land was in chaos. There was no order. But perhaps there was opportunity; if not for himself, then for his sons.

"Come along, my dears," he said. "We've nothing left to lose. Things can only get better. Lead on, boys."

They set off once more, stepping carefully round the insensible axer, and Cheerful Giver held his head high as he followed his sons.

Morning Star had already forgotten the encounter. She was moving fast, and she was moving in a state of fearful wonder. Ever since her meeting with the Joy Boy, the world had taken on an intensity of color she had never known before. The roadside trees trembled with blues and greens as if they strained upwards in prayer. Birds darted by, leaving orange trails in the air. Slow plodding oxen hauling heavy carts moved in dull yellow clouds, while beside them strode travellers wrapped in layers of maroon and turquoise. The very ground she trod on shimmered with a mist of shell pink, as if happy to bear her weight.

She was on her way to Seeker, even though she had no way of knowing where he was. Inspired by the Joy Boy, she now believed that this was her task and the purpose for which she had acquired her special gifts. She never doubted for one instant that she would find him. All she had to do was pass through this newborn world with her eyes wide open and she would reach him.

Towards the end of the day, she was overtaken on the road by a troop of Orlans on horseback. The men's auras were a harsh mustard yellow, the color of brutality, but the horses shone pale blue, innocent of their riders' coarser natures. They were a ragged band, their belts bristling with weapons in the manner of bandits, and they were in high spirits. They called to her as they rode by.

"Looking for company, sweetheart? It's a long lonely road. You can ride with us for a kiss."

Morning Star shook her head.

"Don't be shy, gorgeous." They surrounded her with their Caspians, jostling her with their legs. "You'll be proud enough to know us soon. We have a new Jahan! The Orlan nation rides again."

"A stranger too," cried another, "with eyes that all men obey."

Hearing this, Morning Star became interested.

"What stranger?"

"Who knows? We go to see for ourselves. But they say

the old Jahan's boy Alva tried to seize the whip, and the stranger felled him with a single blow."

"This stranger has unusual powers, then?"

"Looks that way. We're to gather at the old fort. Then we'll see for ourselves."

With that, they rode on their way. Morning Star knew of no old fort but presumed it was farther down the road. As for this stranger who had made himself the new Jahan of the Orlans, she could only guess that he was Seeker himself. It was Seeker who had smashed the Orlans in their pride. Who else had the power to command such an army?

She could see him now in her mind's eye, walking beside her as he had done long ago, on the road to Radiance. To others he might be the possessor of power beyond understanding. To her he was the best friend she had ever had. He was the only person before the Joy Boy who had known her well, even if he didn't know everything. When they had parted many months ago, he had said to her, "Don't say good-bye." It had been his way of saying they would meet again, and she had never doubted it. She had known from their first meeting when they had touched hands that he would always be there for her. She understood now, as she walked the twilight road, how important that certainty was for her. It made her feel that somewhere there was safety in a hard world, and love in a cruel world.

Is that what I feel? Love?

She had loved the Wildman. With Seeker it was different, not love at all, really, not that hurting, desperate need that had so shamed and excited her. When she thought of Seeker she just felt glad that he was there. She had no secrets from him. Even now in the midst of such dangerous times she looked forward to telling him about her foolish passion for the Wildman, and how it had ended as suddenly as it had begun. He would laugh at her and understand her and be her friend. She remembered lying on her back on the grass, beside just such a road as this, looking up at the stars, hearing Seeker speaking softly to the Wildman. He had talked about the hurting of the world, and how he wanted to make there be light, and how he wanted to come close to the light. "So close that I'm dazzled and flooded. So close that I'm not even me any more." Those were his words. The Joy Boy had said the same thing in different words. "When we overcome the separation that keeps us apart, we will become god." Seeker would understand.

Night was now falling, her first night in this new and more brilliant world. As the shadows deepened, the many colors faded, and the trees and the road and the sky above stilled themselves for sleep. So too must she.

On either side of the road the summer grasses grew high, as high as her waist. She went a little way into the grass and flattened a space big enough for her to lie down in. The trampled grass made a bed, and the standing grass made walls, so she had a little secret house for the night. She lay down in her clothes with her rolled-up badan beneath her head for a pillow.

Once she was lying down and twilight deepened into night, a great calm came over the world. Such breeze as had troubled the air in the day now died, and the tall grass stood motionless. High above, stars began to appear, glowing with faraway colors like jewels. She lay quiet and watched them steadily and felt as if she were sailing, as if she and the earth beneath her were sailing away beneath the sequinned sky.

Then she heard a soft clicking in the grass and caught a movement nearby. She watched and listened. She saw it now: a darker shape among the grasses, no longer moving, but the grass round about shivered. Someone was watching her.

She calmed her beating heart and gathered her lir, as she had been taught. Then slowly, calmly, she rose to her feet, her hands loose at her sides, her senses keen, ready to respond to any attack.

The shape in the grass did not move. It was too dark to read its aura. Whoever it was must be crouched or kneeling, to remain covered by the grass. For a long moment she waited, absolutely still. Then a hand reached up towards her, and Morning Star sprang. In midair, her senses working at high speed, she saw the crouching figure below her, saw his startled attempt to rise, aimed the heel of her left foot, and caught him on the side of his head as she landed. He fell sprawling to the ground. She dropped down onto the flattened grass beside him. He lay motionless, half stunned by the blow of her foot.

It was Hem.

"Oh, Hem! Oh, you stupid fool of a boy! Why didn't you tell me?"

She rolled him onto his back and patted his cheeks. Slowly he came out of his stunned state and blinked at her.

At first he didn't seem to believe what he was seeing. Then he began to cry.

"I'm sorry," said Morning Star. "I didn't know it was you. Does it hurt very much?"

He shook his head and went on crying.

"What are you doing here? Did you follow me?"

He nodded.

"Oh, Hem." She sighed. "What am I to do with you?"

She spoke tenderly, touched by the look of misery on his thin young face.

"Don't matter," he said. "So long as I'm with you."

"You can't be with me, Hem. You'll make it harder for me. I have to go alone."

"You go alone," he said. "I'll come behind. You don't need to talk to me, or bother with me. It'll be like I'm not there."

He pushed the tears from his eyes with his fists, leaving smears all down his dirt-encrusted cheeks.

There was no point in saying any more that night, so she let him stay with her till the morning. They settled down to sleep, Morning Star in one grass-walled room, and Hem in another close by. Silently Morning Star resolved that at first light she would creep away before he was up.

She woke to the lavender mist of a new day. Her first thought was: How beautiful! Her second thought was: He's awake.

As she stretched the sleep from her body, there he was, standing chest deep in grass, staring at her, with his dirty face and his hungry eyes.

"Please, Hem," she said. "I'm asking you. Don't follow me. Go back to the others. We'll meet again later."

He scowled and looked down.

"Not going to leave you now," he muttered. "Not going to leave you ever."

Morning Star knew then that she had no choice.

"Look at me, Hem," she said.

She held his eyes, and for a fraction of a second, she flooded him with the force of her lir. He jerked as if she had hit him, then crumpled to the ground. She knelt by his side and touched him gently on the brow as he lay in the long grass. He was breathing evenly. He would wake unharmed.

Once more she set off up the road. As she went, it seemed to her that the colored land was singing. Then she realized that she was accompanied on her way by a thread of tinkling sound that came from the roadside ditch. It was running with water. The flow was too shallow and muddy to drink, but the farther she walked, the deeper the water burbling in the ditch. Then ahead she saw an abandoned farm building with a well in its yard. The well was gushing out water.

She splashed over the puddled ground and plunged her hands into the cool depths. Gratefully she drank her fill. Then, when she could drink no more, she splashed water over her face and hair and clothes, soaking herself to the skin, knowing the hot sun would soon dry her out.

Preoccupied with washing herself, her ears ringing with cascading water, she never heard the riders approach the well. When at last she straightened up and tossed her wet hair back out of her eyes, she found they were all round her. From their clothing and their horses, she knew they were another band of Orlans. They pushed close and stared at her and grinned.

"Look what we've got here," said one of them. He was broad-chested and black-haired, and his face twitched as he spoke. His pulsing orange aura told her he was in a dangerous state of overexcitement. "We've got ourselves a girl hoodie."

"Let her alone, Alva," said one of the others.

So this was Alva Jahan, the one who had lost the leadership of the Orlans to the stranger.

"I let alone who I choose," he barked, "and I meddle with who I choose. It was the hoodies who broke my father."

"But she's only a girl."

"Quite a girl, too," said another. They all laughed. Alva too grinned as he looked down at Morning Star.

"Look at you," he said, "in your wet clothes."

He signed to his men to dismount. Morning Star stood very still, preparing to defend herself. She reckoned there were about fifteen of them. Her difficulty was that they were all round her. She could handle the ones within sight, but the ones behind could be tricky.

Alva walked towards her, rolling his hips and flexing his arms as he came. He was still grinning.

"Wet clothes," he said, and wagged one finger from side to side. "No, no! You could catch a cold."

The others laughed at that.

Suddenly strong arms seized Morning Star from behind and held her arms in a powerful grip. At the same time, a coat was thrown over her head and pulled tight. Through the thick material of the coat, she could hear the laughter of the Orlans and the voice of Alva Jahan.

"Off with her wet clothes!"

A high scream sounded from one side. Whatever it was caught the Orlans unawares. She felt their grip loosen, and she seized her opportunity. She pulled herself free, shaking off the stifling coat.

A small screaming, thrashing figure was attacking Alva Jahan, pummelling and biting and kicking. Alva caught him in his powerful grip and dragged him off.

It was Hem, shrieking like a wild animal.

"Hem!" cried Morning Star. "Get away!"

"You little spiker rat!" shouted Alva. Holding Hem gripped in his left hand, he jabbed his right fist up under his chin in a vicious blow. There came a crack, and Hem's head snapped backwards. His body went limp. Alva threw him to the ground. He felt his own face and found blood.

"Little spiker rat scratched me," he said.

He turned on Morning Star.

"This one I want alive. Just long enough to have some fun with her. Eh, hoodie girl?"

He grinned at her. Morning Star felt an uncontrollable passion rise within her. The colors of the world went dark.

Alva approached, confident he would meet no resistance now. He held out his arms in a mockery of an embrace.

"How about a kiss for the big man? You never know. You might like it."

The darkness swept over the world like night.

"You look good wet. You should do it more often."

He was close now, dark in the darkness.

"I'm going to enjoy this."

Morning Star struck, all the force in her boiling out in a rage-filled attack. Alva flew backwards with a shout of pain and surprise and went on rolling under the impact of the bolt of power, skidding over slick mud to slam to a stop against the barn wall. Morning Star swept round the other Orlans, howling like a wild animal, pouring out her force, sending them and their Caspians scattering. Only when all were broken or fled and there was no one left to strike did she come to a stop, and even then a scream was sounding in her open mouth.

She fell silent at last, drained and trembling, afraid of the darkened world, afraid of herself. She heard the trickle of the water from the overflowing well. Slowly the darkness left her and the sunlight returned, glinting on the puddled ground.

There before her lay Hem's motionless body. She went to him and knelt by him, her entire body shaking with exhaustion. She knew before she touched him that there was no hope. The dead have no colors.

"Oh, Hem," she whispered, tears rising to her eyes. "You should never have followed me. I told you to go back."

She wept for him and for herself, knowing she had been the cause of his death.

"You wanted so much to grow up. And you did grow up, Hem. You were a man at the end. A real man."

Alva had limped to his feet and was now climbing unsteadily back onto his horse. Several of the others were already riding away. Alva threw a look of hatred towards Morning Star, but seeing her look towards him, he turned away and urged his Caspian into motion.

Morning Star crawled over to the old barn and lay down in its shade.

How can men be so cruel? she thought. What makes them want to hurt and kill?

The answer was in herself even now. She could see Alva Jahan's leering face. She could taste the sour terror in her mouth. Yes, she would hurt him if she could. She would kill him if she could.

Fear makes us cruel.

⊰ 13 ⊱

At the Old Fort

THE OLD FORT STOOD HIGH ON THE SKYLINE, ITS WATCH-tower silhouetted against the evening glow. At such a time, when the light was gone, the fort returned to its former grandeur and seemed to be a massive edifice that dominated the land. But as Morning Star made her way up the road towards it, she saw the sad truth: the fort was an overgrown ruin. Large sections of its walls had fallen away, and weeds and brambles grew over what remained. Not a single roof was still intact against sun and rain. Even the great watchtower was a skeleton of its former self, one face invaded by elder, the other crumbled away to expose the beams of the shattered stairway.

Morning Star was very tired. She should have stayed longer by the well, she should have slept there till next morning to replenish her exhausted strength, but she had risen after two short hours and resumed her journey. She wanted to find Seeker before night fell.

More bands of Orlans had passed her on the road, without paying her any attention. And now here before her was their destination, the gathering of Orlans. A large fire had been lit in the ruined hall of the old fort, which stood open to the road. Round the fire milled hundreds of Orlans, greeting each other and embracing. Each new band of arrivals dismounted and left their Caspians to graze among the rubble, then went to swell the numbers in the roofless hall.

Morning Star did not follow them, made wary by her treatment at the hands of Alva Jahan and his men. Silent and unseen, she climbed a mound of fallen stones to a position from which she could look over the whole scene. Here she settled down and searched the firelit crowd. She was looking for the new Jahan.

Her vantage point was some way distant from the fort. The road lay between them. Night had now fallen, and she could not distinguish faces, but she could pick out the faint glow of the Orlans' colors. At the far end of the hall, men were fixing torches on either side of a raised stone platform, and by the light of the torches, she could make out drummers and pipers assembling nearby.

Her attention was distracted from this scene by the sound of hoofbeats on the road. She turned and saw a late-arriving band of mounted Orlans approaching; but unlike the others, they came silently in the darkness. Their leader called them to a halt, keeping his voice low.

It was Alva Jahan. Morning Star saw the sullen glow of his colors and knew that he had come in anger.

I should have killed him by the well.

The band he led had grown in size. There were a hundred and more mounted men lined up on the road behind him. They waited while he rode forward and gazed towards the gathering in the old fort. As he stared, the drums began to beat and the pipes to play. Morning Star too looked to the platform at the far end of the roofless hall. There, serenaded by music, veiled by the rising smoke of the fire, the new Jahan presented himself before his people. She caught the glint of flame reflected on a silver breastplate and heard the Orlans cheer. Was it Seeker they cheered?

Alva Jahan returned to his waiting men.

"Orlans," he said, keeping his voice low, "our moment has come. One charge will end the shame of our nation. Are you with me?"

"Aye," they answered softly in the night.

"We have only one enemy—this impostor, this thief of honor, this false Jahan! Follow me, for the pride of the Orlan nation! One death is all I ask!"

Morning Star heard every word. She saw Alva position himself at the head of his mounted band. She looked to the old fort where the mass of Orlans were gathered round the platform, their backs to their silent enemy, listening to the exhortations of their new leader. Morning Star knew Seeker's great power, but the speed and surprise of the charge might catch him off guard. She could call out and alert the men in the hall to the danger, but a battle would follow and men would die. There was another way.

She dropped silently from her vantage point and padded to the road.

Alva Jahan drew his sword. Morning Star, unseen in the night, touched the arm of a mounted Orlan. Startled, he turned to look down at her.

"Sleep," she whispered.

He slid from his horse to the ground and lay there in a deep sleep. Morning Star stroked the Caspian's brow and swung herself up onto his back. The Caspian shivered and adjusted to her weight.

"Go!" cried Alva, low but fierce.

He set off at their head, and the hundred Orlans followed in a compact mass. Morning Star had exhausted her strength, but she still had her gift. She must force her thoughts to stillness. Riding behind the warriors heading into battle, she filled her mind with a simple memory. In her mind she was sitting on the hillside next to her father, watching the dawn. She was filling herself with calm.

Alva increased his speed. The Orlans, and Morning Star with them, increased their speed. The firelit gathering ahead came closer. Cheers sounded from the old fort.

Morning Star urged her Caspian forward and caused him to brush against his neighbor. With this touch, she sent her own colors flowing out like a lick of blue flame, and the Orlan beside her was embraced by the calm spirit that now possessed her. At the same time, his horse jostled the next, and the colors jumped from rider to rider. Even as Alva Jahan was spurring his Caspian to greater speed, his followers were beginning to fall back. The front line slowed, forcing the lines behind to press against them. So Morning Star's embrace caught them, too.

Alva Jahan had eyes only for the hated enemy ahead. Now choosing his moment and not looking back, he raised his sword high and cried, "Charge!"

He charged, but all unaware, he charged alone. The rest of his Orlans had slowed to a trot and were now looking about them with puzzled expressions.

"What's he so worked up about?" they asked each other. "We're all friends here."

Alva's lone charge caught the gathering of Orlans from behind and by surprise, just as he had intended. They threw themselves out of his way as he thundered across the great hall, howling his war cry as he went. Morning Star rode forward at speed, eager to follow the outcome.

Only the Jahan saw him coming. Through the smoke of the fire, Morning Star saw the Jahan draw a slender spike and raise it high. Alva closed on the platform, roaring to his men, "Follow me!" The Jahan's right arm flicked, and a flash of bright metal flew through the air. Alva fell.

It all happened so quickly that the men in the hall barely knew there had been any danger before it was over. Now they pushed round the fallen man and saw who he was. Morning Star heard shouts of anger. The Jahan himself was obscured from her view by his men. She heard a voice of the Jahan issuing orders she could not make out. She saw men bend low over the body, while others surrounded the Caspian on which he had made his charge. She saw ropes tied round the Caspian's neck and haunches.

Then they stood back, and a whip cracked. The Caspian bucked in alarm. The whips cracked again, goading the horse into motion. After it a long rope unfurled. Tied by the ankles to the rope was the dead body of Alva Jahan.

Morning Star watched as the horse bolted, dragging the dead body, bouncing over rubble and dirt, behind it. For all her hatred of the dead man, she felt sickened by the sight. It dismayed her that Seeker could give such an order.

She moved forward into the heart of the hall. Behind her, the Orlans who had followed Alva Jahan were dismounting and mingling with their former comrades, saying nothing of their brief allegiance to the dead man.

The Jahan was still standing on the platform, now surrounded by Orlan captains, all talking in animated voices about Alva's strange and suicidal charge.

"How could he attack like that, all on his own?" Morning Star heard. "He must have lost his wits."

"One throw, one kill!" said another, speaking admiringly to the Jahan.

Morning Star pushed on through the throng of excited warriors, drawing surprised looks as she went, but no one stopped her. Only when she was close to the platform did one of the Orlans raise the alarm.

"Who's that? What's she doing here?"

The group on the platform now parted, and Morning Star saw the Jahan clearly for the first time. She gaped in astonishment. The leader now staring at her so imperiously was a woman.

"Who are you?" demanded the Jahan.

"My name is Morning Star."

The Jahan frowned and looked more closely.

"I know you," she said.

Morning Star knew her, too. Impossible though it seemed, the Jahan was the Wildman's bandit friend Caressa.

Signalling to her men, Caressa turned away, as if no longer interested.

"She's a spy. Lock her up. I'll deal with her later."

Morning Star offered no resistance. She let herself be pushed through a doorway, and the door was closed after her. She heard the bang of a beam dropping into place to lock it shut.

She found herself in a square stone-walled space. Unusual for this ruined fort, all four walls were solid. She looked up and realized that this was the base of the watchtower. The tower rose above her, stone walls supporting timber beams, until the ruins took over again and the broken masonry gaped open to the sky.

From the other side of the door came sounds of laughter and singing as the now united Orlans celebrated their new leader. The night was clear, and the moon was shining. Morning Star brushed clear a strip of ground to be a bed for the night.

She was about to lie down when she heard the sound of the beam being lifted from the door. The door opened, and in came Caressa. The door closed after her, and the beam was replaced.

For a few moments Caressa stood looking at Morning Star in silence. Morning Star could see from her colors that she was in no danger. The new Jahan of the Orlans had come alone, to talk.

"I remember you," she said at last. "You were with him."

"I don't know who you mean."

"Don't lie to me, girly. I'm talking about the Wildman."

"Yes. I was with the Wildman."

Morning Star remembered it well: how they had met in Spikertown and Caressa had struck her and she had hit back. Caressa had said to the Wildman then, "You're mine or you're nobody's."

Caressa was watching her closely.

"They say he has an army now."

"Yes, he has."

"You've seen him with his army?"

"Yes."

"How is he? Is he beautiful? Is he fine?"

"Yes."

Suddenly Caressa began to rage.

"Now I have an army too, and my army will destroy him! I'll hunt him down and have him dragged before me on his knees and he'll beg me for mercy! I'll make him wish he'd never turned his back on me! I'll make him sweat and piss and cry and kiss my feet and die for wanting me!"

Morning Star saw it all clearly in the racing reds of her aura, the hurt and the anger and the undying love.

"He's unhappy," she said.

"Unhappy! I'll teach him to be unhappy!" But the information pleased her. "How's he unhappy? Why's he unhappy?"

"He's alone."

"Whose fault is that? I'm glad he's unhappy. Let him suffer."

But with every word Caressa's fury was subsiding.

"Does he have a woman?"

"No."

"How about you?"

"No."

"No, he wouldn't want a shrimp like you."

This reminded Caressa that the Wildman had not wanted her either, and her rage returned.

"I'll smash his army and take him prisoner and lock him up till he loves me!"

"I don't think that's how it works," said Morning Star.

"What do you know?" retorted Caressa. "Men are all fools about love. Leave them free to choose for themselves and they never love anyone at all. Lock them up! Tell them they have no choice! Then they get on with it."

A new thought struck her.

"You want him for yourself? Sure you do. All the girls want the Wildman."

"I did once," said Morning Star. "Not any more."

"Gave up hoping, did you? That was smart. You'd never have a chance."

"Why is that?" said Morning Star softly. "Because I'm sweet and dull, like a bun?"

"You said it, girly."

Morning Star was tempted, very tempted. But she restrained herself.

"What do you mean to do with me?"

"You? Nothing. You don't matter."

"So you'll let me go?"

"Not yet. I'll not have you blabbing to the men about me and the Wildman. No, you stay where you are."

With that, she banged on the door and it was opened for her.

"Keep her here till we leave," she said to the men outside.

And so the door was locked after her.

Morning Star lay down to sleep at last. As she lay there in the moonlight, she found herself smiling at a picture in her mind. In this picture the Wildman was in prison, and Caressa, in her armor, was standing beyond the barred door saying, "Well? Do you love me yet?"

Who knows? thought Morning Star as she slipped into the sleep she so desperately needed. It might be as good a way as any other.

⊰ 14 ⊱

Floggers and Stabbers

SEEKER AND ECHO FOLLOWED THE HIGH ROAD UNTIL IT met the old wall. Passing through what had once been a fortified gateway, Seeker took a new road running east.

"You seem to know your way after all," said Echo.

"We're in the old kingdom now."

"What old kingdom?"

"The wall was built by Noman, a great king long ago. It was to protect his kingdom."

Echo looked at the mounds of tumbled stones on either side.

"Doesn't seem to have protected it very well."

"The kingdom's long gone. Noman lived over two hundred years ago."

"So what do you want in the old kingdom?" Echo asked.

"A gathering of people."

"Are you to be the new king?"

"No. I've no wish to be a king."

"Why not?" said Echo. "There must be kings. If not you, who?"

"I have other work to do."

In a little while they came to a roadside stall with a smoking brazier. The stallholder was dozing beneath a faded canopy. Hearing their approach, he woke up and prodded his brazier to a brighter heat and began to call out his wares.

"Pancakes! Sweet tea!"

Seeker came to a stop and bent his head into his hands.

"Are you all right?" said Echo.

"It'll pass in a moment."

"You need food and drink."

"I've no money."

"Leave this to me," said Echo.

She dismounted and went up to the stallholder, who was a sturdy young man with a heavy lower lip.

"Hallo again," she said. "Remember me?"

The stallholder gaped at her.

"I never forget a face," said Echo, "but remind me of your name."

"Coddy," said the stallholder.

"Coddy! Of course."

She looked at him expectantly. Coddy looked back, perplexed.

"You don't remember me, do you?" said Echo.

"No, I don't."

"I thought we were friends."

"Did you?"

The young man saw the reproach in her lovely eyes and felt that in some way he must be to blame.

"That's all right," said Echo, making her voice small and sad. "You must meet so many people. You can't remember them all."

"Not so many," said Coddy.

Now that he looked properly at her, it began to seem to him that there was something familiar about her.

"I was so happy when I saw your stall," said Echo. "I told my travelling companion, that's my friend Coddy's stall. He'll give us something to eat, even though we've no money. He's a good friend of mine."

"You told him that, did you?"

"I made a mistake, that's all. I thought you'd remember me, and you haven't." She reached out her hand and touched him lightly on the arm. "But I've not forgotten you."

She gave him a sweet, sad smile, and went to rejoin Seeker.

"What are you doing?" said Seeker.

"Getting us some supper." She was standing facing Seeker, with her back to Coddy's stall. "What's he doing now?"

"Looking towards us."

"Count to three."

"Why?"

"Just count."

"One," said Seeker. "Two. Three."

He broke into a soft laugh.

"He's coming, isn't he?" said Echo.

"Yes. He's coming."

Coddy came, and shuffled his feet, and looked at Echo with puzzled eyes, and finally delivered himself of a decisive nod.

"I remember now," he said.

So they were both treated to free pancakes, with free mugs of tea to wash them down.

"Seeing as we're old friends," said Coddy.

He showed an inclination to stay with them and share their company, so Echo had to tell him that they were tired after their journey and needed to sleep. She found a grassy bank by the side of the road, and there they lay down. Coddy returned to his stall. They could see him standing there, gazing wistfully towards them, silhouetted against the twilit sky.

"Have you met him before?" asked Seeker.

"Of course not."

"So you're making a fool of him."

"How was your pancake? Has it made you feel better?"

"Yes."

"Then be grateful."

She smoothed down the grass by his side.

"Just so you know," she said, "I don't usually behave like this."

"Only when you're hungry."

"Well, what would you have done? Used your power?"

"To steal a pancake? No, I don't think so."

"So you're nobler than I am. I know that, anyway." She felt the little finger of her left hand as she spoke. "I've known I'm no good for some time now. So there we are."

Seeker had nothing to say to this. She glanced at him. He was gazing up at the sky.

"I did it for you," she said after a silence. "After all, you did save me from the Orlans."

"You owe me nothing."

"I don't call it nothing. I call it everything. I wish I knew how to repay you."

"You don't have to repay me."

Echo pushed her long fair hair back from her cheek and gazed at Seeker with her big gray eyes.

"So why doesn't it work for you?" she said.

"Why doesn't what work?"

"Other men say I'm beautiful."

"You are beautiful, Echo."

"Well, then. All you have to do is ask."

"I can't."

"Why not?"

"I'm a Noble Warrior."

"What's that got to do with it?"

"We take a vow when we enter the Nom to live our lives simply and in the truth. And to love no one person above all others."

Echo heard this with astonishment.

"Does that mean you can't marry?"

"Yes."

"Why? That's stupid. Whose stupid idea is that?"

"It's part of our Rule. The Rule was written by Noman, our founder."

"But what's the point of such a stupid vow? It doesn't make any sense."

"It's so that we're free to serve everyone."

"Yes, but—" Echo was so shocked by this revelation that she could hardly find words to express her feelings. "What happens if you do love one person above all others?"

"Then you separate from that person."

"So it does happen? Noble Warriors do fall in love?"

"We have feelings, just like everyone else."

"And what do you do with your feelings?"

"Nothing."

"Doesn't that make you sad?"

"Yes," said Seeker. "Sometimes very sad indeed."

He spoke so gravely that Echo was at once convinced he spoke out of his own experience. Who did he love? Echo was not blinded by vanity, she saw her own faults clearly enough; but just as clearly she saw that most men found her beautiful, and most men fell in love with her. Why should Seeker be so very different?

"So suppose," she said, "you were to fall in love with someone. Suppose you loved them even more than you wanted to be a Noble Warrior. Would you break your vow?"

Seeker did not reply.

The sun was now low in the sky, and she couldn't make out the expression on his face, but she sensed a struggle was taking place within him.

"Would it be breaking your vow," she said, "to tell the person you loved that you loved them?"

Seeker gave a low groan. His suffering had returned, not hunger this time. Echo thought she understood the cause and longed to take him in her arms and comfort him.

Seeker gave a second groan and turned onto his side.

"What is it?" said Echo, now becoming alarmed. "Are you ill?"

"It's not an illness," said Seeker, grimacing as he spoke, his eyes tight shut. "It'll pass."

But it got worse. He started to shiver violently, and sweat streamed down his brow. Echo dried his face with his badan.

"You must have a fever."

"It'll pass," murmured Seeker again.

The dusk had deepened so far now that she couldn't see to soothe him. She heard his breathing become slower and calmer, and shortly it seemed to her that he had fallen asleep.

She lay down close to him and watched him and saw that he was shivering in his sleep. The evening was warm. How could he be so cold? She put her arms round him, to soothe him, and drew his body close against her own. Now she could feel the beating of his heart.

It seemed to Echo as she lay with him in her arms that it was his caged love for her that made his body tremble; love that longed to be allowed to live and breathe.

She put her face close to his sleeping face and felt his breath on her lips.

"You can love me if you want," she whispered to him. "It's not hard."

She touched her lips to his lips and felt them tremble. She kissed him, and he responded in his sleep. Gladdened, she wound her arms tight round him and kissed him long and deep.

Then she felt a shudder pass through his whole body and a strange lurch in his chest. The vibration passed to his face, and then she too shook as she kissed him. He gave a cry from his throat, a burst of breath entered her mouth, she fell back gasping, and her whole body flushed first burning hot, then icy cold. She felt sweat break from her skin.

Seeker sprang up, now fully awake.

"What is it?" he cried. "What happened?"

"I don't know," said Echo. She felt sick and so stayed on the ground.

"Is there someone else here?"

"No. Just us."

Seeker looked round, and his mind slowly cleared.

"Was I asleep?"

"Yes."

"Why was I sleeping? I'm not tired."

"You're sick. You were shivering."

"I'm not sick. I'm not shivering."

It was Echo who was shivering now. Seeker looked at her closely.

"What have you done?"

"Nothing," she said. "I'm cold."

Now she felt her strength returning. The shivering stopped. She got up and found she was wide awake and eager to be on the move.

"We could ride on if you want."

"Are you sure you're all right?"

"Yes. I'd rather travel by night."

She called Kell, and Seeker helped her to mount. She

waved good-bye to Coddy, his face glowing red in the light of his brazier, and they set off down the night road.

As Echo rode along, the last vestiges of her strange sickness dropped away, to be replaced by a restless, prickly sense of excitement. New and strange ideas were buzzing about in her head.

"Whatever I want I can have," she said. "If I want it hard enough."

She was shocked to hear herself.

"Don't listen to me," she told Seeker. "I'm in a strange mood."

Seeker glanced at her from time to time as they went, but he said nothing.

"Everyone loves me," she said. "But I love no one."

Seeker still made no response.

"I don't know what I'm saying," she said. "Something's happened to me. Why don't you speak?"

"Speak to who, Echo?"

"Me, of course."

"And who are you?"

"You think you know so much," she snapped back, "but I know so much more."

Where did that come from? she thought, blushing in the dark.

She was saved from further embarrassment by the flicker of torches ahead, and the sound of chanting. As they rounded a bend in the road, they saw before them a band they took to be pilgrims, though they were not dressed in white robes. They all carried flaming torches in one hand, while in the other hand some wielded whips with which they were lashing themselves, and others waved knives high above their heads, dropping them now and again to stab at their own flesh.

"We are weak, we are wicked, but we bleed!" they chanted as they came. "Let our blood wash us clean!"

They did indeed bleed. Their shirts were bloody and torn.

"Great god, pity us!" they cried. "Turn away your anger from our land!"

When they saw Echo and Seeker approaching, they called out to them.

"You too are weak!" they cried. "You too are wicked! Join us in penitence!"

"Who has told you to do this?" said Seeker.

"No one has told us. We bleed freely!"

"I know him!" cried one of the penitents. "I was there! I saw him on that terrible day! He's the one that made the earth shake!"

"He must be a god!"

At once they fell into a frenzy of whipping and stabbing, their eyes shining as they punished themselves, their voices proudly lamenting.

"See, Lord, the blood on my shirt! All fresh today!"

"Look here, Lord! The scars of the whip never heal!"

"Count the knife holes in my jacket, Lord! Every hole a wound!"

"Stop!" cried Seeker. "I'm not a god!"

"Not a god?"

They lowered their whips and their knives and stared at him.

"Then how are we to appease your anger with our suffering?"

"I'm not angry."

There was a moment of silence. The floggers looked at the stabbers and the stabbers looked at the floggers.

"Some god somewhere is angry."

"Not me," said Seeker. "So you don't need to go on hurting yourselves."

"Not hurt ourselves?" They laughed bitterly at that. "Use your eyes. The whole world is hurting."

One of them spoke for all.

"Some god somewhere must be angry. Don't ask us which god, we're not priests. But I'll tell you this for nothing. It doesn't surprise me. The people have fallen very low. Lower than dirt, most of them."

He gave himself a sharp flick with his whip.

"When we bleed, it makes up for the lowness."

The others nodded in agreement.

"Flogging is elevating."

"And stabbing," said a stabber.

"Come on, friends! On our way! He's not a real god. He's not even angry."

With that, the penitents resumed their flogging and stabbing and set up their chant as they went on down the road.

"We are weak and we are wicked, but we bleed! Great god, feel our pain! Turn away your anger from our land!"

Seeker and Echo continued into the night, which was now all the darker after the glare of the torches.

"You could have stopped them," said Echo.

"I can't give them what they need."

"You mean you won't."

"I have other work to do."

"Other work!" Suddenly her voice was sharp with scorn. "What is it that's more important than saving people from their misery? Why have so much power and not use it?"

She had no idea what she was saying until she said it. But Seeker answered without surprise.

"My power has been given me for one purpose only."

"Who told you so? This Noman, who told you not to love?"

"Yes."

"Why listen to a miserable old man?"

Secretly Echo was astonished at herself, that she dared to speak her mind so freely. But the new force within her was driving her on.

I have life, she thought. I must give him life.

Seeker said nothing, so she spoke again, even more insistently.

"They've turned you into a killer. You go to kill on the orders of an old man who longs to die. But you're not old, you're young—like me. Why aren't you hungry for life? Why aren't you hungry for love?"

Seeker raised his hands to his ears.

"Leave me to do what I must do," he said.

"You're afraid to listen. You're afraid I'm right."

Seeker strode on in silence. Echo rode beside him on Kell, not knowing what had changed in her but filled with a new certainty.

He loves me, she told herself. Only his vow forces his silence.

Then came a further conviction, which was stronger in her than all that had gone before.

I bring him life. I will teach him how to live forever.

They travelled on in silence through the cool night hours until the drooping of Kell's head told Echo that they must stop to sleep. Dimly in the starlight ahead they saw a grove of umbrella pines; and responding to the natural instinct of all creatures to find a burrow for a bed, they lay themselves down within the circle of trees.

Both were unable to sleep. In time the moon rose, and by its pale light Echo was able to see Seeker's face.

"Are you angry with me?"

"Not with you, no."

"I'm cold," she said. "Are you cold?"

"A little."

"I could warm you, if you like."

He made no objection, so she wriggled close to him and laid her head in the crook of his arm.

"Am I warming you?"

"Yes," he said.

"And you're warming me."

She smiled in the night, happier than she had been for a very long time; and so smiling, she surrendered herself to sleep.

⚔ 15 ⚔

The Waterfall

WHEN MORNING STAR WOKE, SHE HAD NO IDEA WHERE
she was. All round her was the darkness of night, but this
was not her own private darkness, which she so dreaded.
This was the world's night, which glowed with quiet colors. Above her reached broad bars of amber. Round her,
walls of dark blue. A door glowed with the blue-red tones
of a damson.

So she remembered. She had been imprisoned here by
Caressa. She lay still and listened. No sounds of any kind.
The Orlans were either asleep or gone.

No sounds of soldiers, but there were other sounds.
The colored night was singing, a faraway round like the
voices of children repeating the same lilting phrases, one
after the other, a weave of sweet high song. Morning Star
felt as if all her senses had been magnified, so that even
under the blanket of night she could see and hear for

miles. It seemed to her that no living thing could elude her notice; that she could hear the soft breathing of rabbits deep in their burrows, and see the turquoise sheen on the breast feathers of pigeons in the trees.

I could see him, too.

Seeker was out there somewhere in this glowing, humming night. She needed only to see far enough.

Climb the tower.

It came to her as an urge more than as a plan. The tower was ruined and dangerous, its flights of stairs only half supported by its fragmented walls, but this was the way to the top. So Morning Star began to climb.

The darkness made it easier, because it turned the drop below her into a pool of dark blue. The air on either side was deep green and cushiony. She climbed boldly, feeling her way with her hands, marvelling at this new world. Above in the square of sky shimmered the first faint gleams of the coming dawn.

She kept close to the walls and made her way safely from step to step, feeling the treads shift beneath her weight. After the third flight, she reached a point where one side of the tower had crumbled away. Here the stairway, making its circuit of the walls, reached out into open air, supported by nothing more than its own structure.

She felt the nearest exposed tread with one foot and judged that it would hold her. She pressed on it. It creaked but did not break. She stepped fully onto it, and from there to the next step. So up and out she climbed, into the open air. As she stepped on the last of the unsecured treads, she reached for the solid stonework ahead and misjudged the

distance. She stumbled and righted herself, kicking back
hard on the stair. It gave a sharp crack. She grabbed for the
branches of clinging elder and pulled herself onto the stone
supports. The stair sagged behind her, and for a moment
the entire timber structure hung in the still dawn air. Then
it leaned and broke and fell crashing to the ground.

No way down now. But Morning Star wanted only to
go up and to be at the top to greet the rising sun; so on
she went, no longer fumbling her way forward, stepping
lightly and rapidly from tread to tread. The stairway rocked
beneath her, but she passed too quickly for it to give way.

The sky lightened as she climbed. The sun had still not
shown itself above the eastern mountains as she pulled
herself at last onto the platform on the top of the tower.
She stood up, holding on to the topmost branches of the
climbing elder, and drew a deep calming breath and looked
round.

A long stripe of the palest primrose yellow was spreading across the horizon. Below lay the gleam of the great
lake and the silver thread of the river running to the sea.
To the west loomed the dark mass of the Glimmen. To
the south, the hills where she had been born and the plains
where the people of the Joyous would soon be waking.
And all round the humming song, growing ever louder,
filling the air.

She heard a bird call, and another, and knew then that
there were birds singing everywhere and that their song
was part of the waking world's song. She turned east again,
feeling a tingling on her cheeks, and as she did, the sun
rose. With the burning scarlet disc came an explosion of

colors. The sky turned crimson and gold, and the land was lit amber and purple, and all that had been submerged in the deep colors of night now began to glow with new life. She gazed in wonder at the beauty of the world and heard the triumphal song of the new day carolling in her ears.

Somewhere out there was Seeker. She scanned the land more slowly now, her gaze taking in villages and early travellers on the roads, looking for the color that only Seeker possessed. She let her eyes idle, and listened to the singing of the world, and wondered why she had never heard it before.

The Beloved has woken me to joy, she thought, then smiled with happiness. Seeker would hear the singing too, when she brought him to the Joyous. He too would share her happiness.

Then, through the leaves of the clinging elder, she caught the faraway flicker of gold she had been looking for. It came from the northwest, close to the walled road. She looked intently, memorizing the location so that she could find it again on the ground. There was the road, and near the road, a group of spindly trees, and between the trees, the sparkle of gold aura that could only be Seeker.

She parted the high branches of elder and leaned over the parapet of the tower, wanting to be closer to him. As she did so, she saw the distances shrink and the colors of the land race towards her. She pulled back, alarmed, and shut her eyes. When she opened her eyes again, she found something strange was happening to her. The colors were closing in. The experience wasn't unpleasant. In fact, it was beautiful; but it was also frightening because it took away all measures of space. She no longer felt as if she looked down on the land from a high tower. The land was right there, before her. If she reached out a hand, she could touch it. Only it was no longer solid. It was made of color.

Is this good or bad? she thought to herself. Am I seeing the world as it really is, or am I going mad?

She looked again for the golden gleam that was Seeker, and it was there before her, now even more abundant, a cascade of gold; more than a cascade, a waterfall. She gazed at it and saw that the gold was the reflection of sunlight on falling water, it was a million dancing, tumbling mirrors of the rising sun, and the waterfall was high and broad—a streaming curtain that filled half the horizon before her. For all its immense size, the waterfall held no fear for her. She put out her hand to let it be splashed by the golden stream, but the waterfall was farther from her than she had at first realized. Nor was it gold alone. All the colors she had ever seen were bursting from that great plunging torrent, it was ruby red and jade green, sapphire and topaz and carnelian, its spray was silver and diamonds. She reached further, wanting to cup her hands in the beauty, wanting to splash her face with the jewelled water. But still it was too far.

So I must fall into it, then.

It seemed obvious to her now that this was why she had climbed the tower. The notion of falling wasn't strange. It had been with her all her life. But always before it had been a terror. Now it was a joy.

You don't know where you end and others begin.

She laughed to think of it. No end, no beginning. Everything flowed into everything else. Why should she not flow into the colors of the waterfall?

But I'm in the waterfall already. I'm falling already. Everything's falling. That's what the waterfall is. Why was I ever afraid? The stream carries us all away.

She leaned out more, reaching her arms towards the waterfall, and still she couldn't quite touch it. So she reached further.

Now, slowly at first, she felt herself begin to fall.

"Here I go," she said to herself, as the colors embraced her. "One perfect dive."

The children found her.

"She's dead," said Burny.

"Nobody goes up a tree to die," said Libbet.

Morning Star was lying in a deep hole in the tree with her eyes closed and her arms open, supported by a hammock of tangled creepers.

"Wake up, lady," said Burny. "Don't be dead."

"Stupid boggy baby," said Libbet.

They climbed the branches and broke the creepers one by one, and so Morning Star slithered by her own weight out of the dense growth to the ground below. Here she lay, motionless. They fetched water from the ditch and splashed it over her. When this had no effect, Libbet took hold of her arm and pinched her.

"Wake up, lady," she said. "We come after you. Don't be dead."

The pinching did it. Morning Star stirred, then opened her eyes.

She took in the little band of grave-faced children and then looked round her at the walls of the old fort, and the fields beyond. Then she looked back at the children.

"What happened to you?" she said.

"Nothing happened to us," said Libbet. "You're the one that got happened. We found you in a tree."

"Where did it go?"

Her voice faded to silence.

"We come after you," said Burny. "First Hem. Then us."

"Hem's gone," said Libbet.

"You got to come back," said little Deedy.

Morning Star's eyes slowly filled with tears. She was remembering Hem; but there was something else, too. Something she had lost.

"She's hurt," said Burny. "She's crying."

"Not hurt," said Morning Star. "Only bruised. I fell from the tower."

They looked up and were awed.

"You fell from up there!"

"What did you go up there for?"

"To look out at the world," said Morning Star. Then she remembered the brilliant colors of the dawn land, and she knew why she had tears in her eyes.

She had lost her colors.

The children before her had no auras. The land beyond them was no longer bright. She was seeing now as all others saw, but to her it was as if a veil had been drawn over the world. The melting beauty of the waterfall had been her last glory. She had dived into the colors, and now they were gone.

She wept for her lost gift. All her life she had taken it for granted, even resented it; but now that it was gone, she felt stripped of meaning. The only secret that had ever given her value was gone. What use was she now?

"Don't cry, lady," said little Deedy, starting to cry herself.

So Morning Star dried her eyes and rose to her feet, feeling the aching all over her body from the violence of her fall.

"You children must go back," she said. "The roads are dangerous."

"Not to us," said Libbet, drawing her knife.

"We're coming with you," said Burny.

"Hem got lost," said Libbet. "He always makes a muck."

Morning Star looked about her and considered what best to do. She had set out to find Seeker, at the request of the Beloved. Now more than ever she longed to find him. She would tell him all that had happened, and he would understand. She remembered exactly where she had seen his colors and reckoned it was not so far from the old fort. Once she had found him, she would be heading back to the Joyous, which was where she meant the children to go.

"Come along, then," she said. "We're going to find a friend of mine."

———

They saw the Caspian first, near the grove of umbrella pines. The beautiful beast was grazing in the roadside ditches where the grass was sweetest. The children were wide-eyed with admiration.

"Can I touch it? Does it bite? Look at its long hair!"

Morning Star left them to crowd round Kell, who accepted their pokings and pettings with patience. She herself went on to the trees.

It was still early in the morning, and the sun threw her shadow far before her as she approached. The hollow between the pines was also in shadow, and at first she couldn't see if there was anyone there. Then she came closer and saw a hand on the ground, reaching out into the sunlight. She came forward quietly and saw an arm, and then a head resting on a rolled badan. It was Seeker, as she had known it would be. But he was not alone.

Morning Star stood absolutely still and gazed at them as they slept: Seeker and the pale lovely forest girl called Echo. He was lying on his back with his arms thrown out beyond his head and his face turned a little to one side. He looked young and kind and familiar. Echo lay with her head resting on his chest, one arm reached across his body. Her fair hair spilled over his tunic. Her face was even lovelier in sleep.

A silent sadness welled up in Morning Star as she looked. Her body, already bruised and hurting from her fall, now felt the weary drag of a new burden.

Must everything be taken from me?

After this thought came a stab of shame. Seeker was her friend, nothing more. Why should he not love someone else? She saw again the look on his face as he had listened to her besotted ramblings about the Wildman. Not once had he reproached her. And she—she had taken his loyalty for granted, because he had always been there for her.

Until now.

What's wrong with me? she said to herself. Do I only want what I can't have?

She saw it so clearly now that it was too late. Of course she loved Seeker. She had always loved him. He had always been there waiting for her.

There came a shout from the children. Burny had tried to climb on Kell's back and had fallen off. Morning Star looked round and saw him clamber back to his feet unharmed.

The cry woke Echo. Her eyes opened. She saw Morning Star, saw that Seeker slept on, and made a sign, one finger to her lips, to let him sleep. Quietly she rose, and the two of them moved away so that they could talk without disturbing him.

"He sleeps poorly," said Echo. "Let him sleep while he can."

She sounded agitated. She kept looking from Morning Star to Seeker.

"Why have you come?"

"I've been looking for him. He has to come back with me."

"Why? What for? Why should he go with you?"

Echo spoke jerkily, and her face kept twisting.

"Maybe he won't," said Morning Star. "That's up to him."

"He's mine," said Echo, suddenly fierce. "He kissed me. He loves me."

Morning Star looked away, not trusting herself to speak. She had seen them as they lay together in sleep. Of course Seeker loved this beautiful girl.

"He's going to stay with me forever." Echo came very close and repeated the words in a whisper. "Forever and ever!"

The children, tiring of Kell, now came to them. They stared at Echo.

"Who are you?" said Libbet.

"You're pretty," said Burny.

Echo still had her intense gaze fixed on Morning Star.

"You hear me?"

"Yes, I hear you."

Echo then returned to Seeker. Kneeling down by him, she stroked his cheek.

"Seeker. Time to get up."

He woke and opened his eyes and, for a moment, was still half in dreams. Then he saw Morning Star.

"Star?"

"Hello, Seeker."

"Is it really you?"

"Yes, it's me."

He looked happy to see her. He rose and unrolled his badan and threw it over his shoulders.

"Where have you come from?"

"I've been in Spikertown," she said.

"Spikertown. Of course." She saw his expression alter

as he remembered. "How's the Wildman? Is he still beautiful? Does he still do that cry of his?"

Morning Star understood him well enough. He believed she was still in love with the Wildman. She wanted to tell him it wasn't so, that it was all over, that it had never begun; but pride kept her silent. He loved Echo now. Morning Star would not let it appear that she had come begging for love he no longer had to give her.

"Yes," she said. "He still does his cry. He's still beautiful."

"And always will be."

Seeker had an odd look on his face as he said this, which Morning Star didn't understand. Always before she had been able to read people's colors; but now her gift was gone. She felt clumsy and stupid.

"And you, Star? Where are you going?"

"I've come to find you."

"Me! Why?"

"I'm only a messenger. There's someone special who wants you. He's sent me to find you and bring you to him."

"So what?" said Echo sharply. "Why should he go just because he's sent for?"

"Who is he, Star?"

"He's a kind of a leader. You don't know him."

"A kind of a leader?" Seeker took in the children clustered round her. "They came with you?"

"Yes."

"This leader. He has followers?"

"He has thousands of followers."

"Thousands! So who is he? What does he do?"

"He calls himself the Joy Boy."

Morning Star then did her best to pass on all that the Joy Boy had told her, though she knew that the one thing she could not pass on was the gaze of those dark liquid eyes and the sound of that soft penetrating voice.

"He told you he's come to make men into gods?"

"Yes."

"How will he do that?"

"He calls it the Great Embrace. When it happens, there'll be no more separation. We'll all be one in joy."

Seeker was listening now with concentrated attention.

"It will be a large gathering?"

"Immense."

"When is this Great Embrace to happen?"

"Very soon, I think."

Seeker thought for a moment more. Then, "Take me to it," he said. "You're right, Star. This is what I've been sent to do."

"Let's go!" said Burny, tugging at Morning Star's hem. "I'm hungry."

"Can I ride the animal?" said Libbet.

"I want to hold the pretty lady's hand," said Deedy.

"Where is this gathering?" Seeker asked Morning Star.

"Follow the road south. You can't miss it."

"Come, then," said Seeker. "I don't want to arrive too late. Not a second time."

He strode away towards the road. Echo mounted Kell. Morning Star followed with the children. She was surprised by Seeker's sudden urgency, and puzzled by what he meant when he said, "This is what I've been sent to do."

She held the little ones' hands and Libbet walked stoutly by her side, but in a little while Seeker and Echo were out of sight. Morning Star walked on steadily and held her head high, not wanting the children to know how close she was to tears. He had left without a word of farewell, without a backward glance, as if she were nothing to him.

And I am nothing, she thought.

Then she remembered the waterfall.

The stream carries us all away.

THE THIRD STAGE
OF THE
EXPERIMENT

TRIAL

This is not a trial of god. This is a trial of
man's faith in god and of my faith in man.

I watch from the next room, through a doorway
that is always left open. I can pass through that doorway,
but beyond the threshold I am a child again. I go in ignorance.
All that I once knew is to be learned again.

I can give my noble warriors no help or guidance.
This is their trial. I have planted the seed. Now let it grow
as it will, and we shall see what we shall see.

I have given them secret friends. I have given
them secret enemies. There will be failures. There will
be suffering. But if one man among them dares to seek the
truth to the end, in all its terror and wonder, I will
know that my experiment outlives me.

That is all the immortality I ask for.

❧ 16 ❧

Lullaby

THE WILDMAN WAS UNABLE TO SLEEP ALL THROUGH the night after his meeting with the Joy Boy. The rhythm of the stamping dance still surged in his blood, he could still taste the oranges and lemons in his mouth, and most of all, he shivered to remember the spasm of joy.

All of us have felt what it's like to be god, the Joy Boy had said. We call it joy.

When morning came, he knew that he would go back; and the decision made, he slept at last. He woke late and found he had a keen appetite. He ate an immense breakfast of pancakes and bacon and stewed apple, and then called a meeting of the spiker chiefs.

"Bravas," he said to them. "All my life I've been told I'll come to a bad end. So all my life I've done what I pleased. Now, today, it pleases me to leave you and go my own way. I've decided to join the crazy people. I've laughed at them. Now you can laugh at me."

None of his men laughed.

"Could be that the crazy people are all being fooled," he said, "and I'll be fooled along with them. But could be they all end up as gods. I say that's a risk worth taking. And no one gets hurt but me."

It was as simple as that. When he'd spoken, he strode out of the big tent and mounted Sky and set off down the main street of the big spiker camp. As he went, riding slowly, men came out of their tents and followed him in a raggle-taggle procession. More and more spikers joined the march as they passed through the camp, and they drew in their wake a train of women and children and baggage wagons. When the Wildman reached the limits of the camp, he turned round on Sky to bid farewell and found that almost his entire army had come with him.

A slow grin spread across his golden face.

"Heya!" He raised both hands high above his head and sang out, "Do you lo-o-ove me?"

"Wildman!" they cried back. "Wildman! Wildman!"

So it was at the head of a great spiker army that the Wildman rode into the Joyous. When the Joy Boy came out to meet him, the Wildman said with a grin, "I'm back, and I've brought a few friends."

"The more people, the more joy," said the Joy Boy. "You're all welcome."

But a little later, to the Wildman alone, he said, "You bring new danger."

"What danger?"

"Travellers joining us bring news every day. The news is that the Orlans are on the march. Their new Jahan has sworn to seek out the spiker army and destroy it."

His plump face still smiled as he spoke, but his voice was grave. The Wildman rose to the challenge at once.

"Let them try!" he cried.

"Softly, my friend, softly," said the Joy Boy. "This is a beautiful opportunity. We must use it."

"I'm not afraid of Orlans!"

"Nor should you be. I will arm you with a weapon against which they will be helpless."

"What weapon?"

"What else but joy?"

"Joy? I'm to fight them with joy?"

"It will be the first battle in which the enemy will be defeated by joy. And then they will be the enemy no more. They will join us. They too will share the joy."

The Wildman gazed at the Joy Boy in disbelief.

"Is it possible?"

"Of course. If you have chosen joy, why should not they?"

"But how?"

"I will tell you."

Caressa rode at the head of the Orlan army, her luxuriant black hair streaming behind her, her breastplate glowing in the sun. Beside her rode Sabin Jahan, in whom she had full trust, together with her captains, seasoned veterans of many a campaign. Behind them, formed up once more in their old companies, rode more than a thousand warriors, the finest fighting men in the world. The Orlan army that had swept out of the north under Amroth Jahan had been ten times bigger, but Caressa Jahan's followers still made a formidable force. And who was there to stand against them? Here and there some pockets of axers, but they had no organization. The Nomana were scattered and showed no signs of using their powers to bring order to the land. So that left the spiker army. Caressa knew that if she could draw the spikers into a decisive battle, she could break their power for good.

Then the Wildman, their leader, would be defeated. He would be led before her, his hands tied, a helpless prisoner. She would have him at her mercy. What would she do with him? She thought she might cut off his long golden hair. Then she thought it would be enough to have him kneel and kiss her hand. Then she thought how fine it would be to show him mercy and set him free.

No, she told herself, her mouth curling into a smile of anticipation. I'll not set him free. I'll keep him for myself. I'll have him follow behind me on a chain, like a pet dog.

Ahead she saw her scouts riding back from a forward reconnaissance. From the eager speed with which they rode, she knew they had news.

The lead scout pulled up with a dramatic flourish and trotted by her side.

"Enemy sighted, Excellency."

"How far?"

"Less than an hour's ride."

"Do they know we're coming?"

"Yes, Excellency. They're drawn up in battle formation, Excellency. Many thousands, Excellency."

"So big!"

"But not fighters only, Excellency. Women. Children. Cattle. Chickens."

"Chickens!"

"And their weapons, Excellency. We saw none."

"They conceal them?"

"No doubt, Excellency."

Caressa rode on in silence, pondering this strange information. Some trick was being prepared, but what? She could only guess that the spiker women and children had joined the army because the Wildman hoped to inspire pity. Not many warriors would charge unarmed women and children. If so, was it a cover from behind which the fighters would draw their swords and launch a surprise attack? Or had the Wildman already conceded defeat?

"You saw their leader?" she asked the scout. "The one they call the Wildman?"

"Yes, Excellency."

"How did he seem?"

"Happy, Excellency. Laughing."

"Laughing, was he? We'll see if he's still laughing when I've finished with him."

But inside herself Caressa felt a secret glow of pride that the Wildman was happy and laughing. That was how she remembered him, always fearless, always beautiful. She spurred her Caspian to a canter, suddenly impatient to have the Wildman there before her. She longed to see the look on his face when he recognized her. He would be shocked. He would be proud before her and pretend he cared nothing for her new rank and her fearsome army. But he would respect her.

The Orlan warriors broke into a canter behind her; and so the great mounted army rode up the last hill.

The spikers were waiting for them. When the Orlans appeared over the ridge, the Wildman was more than ready. His army, if such a ragtag assembly could be called an army, had their orders. Soon now they would learn if their unorthodox battle plan would prove successful.

The Orlans approached in company order. The Wildman was impressed. The new Jahan, he saw, had restored discipline. There were large numbers of them—a further tribute to the authority of the new leader. It was not hard to pick out the Jahan, riding in the front rank, flanked by senior captains; but at this distance he could make out no details. He presumed the new warlord was one of the sons of the old Jahan.

When the enemy was within shouting reach, the Wildman raised his arms high above his head, and the entire great mass of spikers began to sing. Not a battle chant, not even a roaring drinking song. They sang a lullaby.

> "Little baby, don't cry
> Now the shadows are creeping
> See the stars in the sky
> Now it's time to be sleeping . . ."

A sweet song carried on the breeze in waves of gentle melody across the dry land to the Orlan army.

The advancing warriors heard the lullaby and looked round at each other uncertainly. The line wavered. The Wildman signalled his people again. Still singing, the spikers began to move forward, their arms now raised above their heads and swaying from side to side.

> *"Ferry softly cross the water*
> *Where the moonlight is gleaming*
> *Float away down the river*
> *To the ocean of dreaming . . .*
> *Sail to sleep, little baby,*
> *Little baby, sail to sleep . . ."*

The Orlans had now come to a complete stop. The spikers continued to advance as the lullaby drew to a close. The Wildman then stepped out in front of the line and spread his arms wide and called to his people.

"Do you lo-o-ove me?"

They shouted back, all waving their arms together.

"Wildman! Wildman! Wildman!"

He shook back his golden hair and laughed in the sunlight. Then he turned to the Orlans and cried out loud.

"We lo-o-ove you all!"

The spikers took up the cry.

"We love you!"

The Orlans stared back across the space that separated the two armies, waiting to be told what to do.

The Wildman now strode forward alone to meet the

new Jahan. He came with his arms extended as if to offer an embrace. Halfway across the space between the two armies, he recognized Caressa beneath her Orlan battle dress.

"Princess!" he cried with a joyful smile.

He ran to her and swung her down off her horse and seized her in his arms.

"Heya! What a beauty!" he exclaimed, gazing at her with open admiration. Then he kissed her. Then he looked at her again, his golden face bright with happiness.

"I love you, Princess!" he said.

Caressa had lost all control of the situation. From the moment the spikers had begun to sing, she hadn't known what to do. Now, in the Wildman's arms, all she could think was how she wanted him to kiss her again.

"Still crazy, Wildman," she said.

"Crazier than ever, Princess!"

He waved to his people and they streamed forward and clustered round the Orlan warriors, reaching up friendly hands, calling on them to dismount.

"We love you!" they said. "Share the joy!"

Caressa saw her army disintegrate into a laughing, hugging melee, and she no longer cared.

"I'm going to nail your ears to a door," she said to the Wildman. Then she kissed him long and hard on the lips.

Night had fallen by the time Seeker and Echo reached the summit of the last hill. Now below them Seeker saw the great gathering that was his destination. Fires and torches lit up the wide valley from side to side. The jangle of music and the shouting of thousands of voices echoed in the night air.

"He's down there somewhere," said Seeker.

"What will you do?"

"Find him. Finish it."

Echo leaned forward and stared intently down into the valley, as if she could see the one man they sought in all that distant crowd.

"So many people," she said. "He must be strong now. Stronger even than you."

"We'll see."

"And if you do kill him, what then?" She turned on him, her eyes glittering. "Will you kill me?"

Seeker said nothing. He kept his eyes on the gathering in the valley. From the sound of the music and the waving lines of torches, it seemed the people had started a mass dance.

"You know, don't you?" said Echo.

"Yes. I know."

Her face changed. Hard lines furrowed her cheeks, and her voice turned husky.

"I can't let you do that," she said. Then her voice rose to a shrill scream. "Assassin! Destroyer! I won't let you kill me! I won't let the knowledge die!"

She swung Kell round and rode off at great speed. Seeker let her go. He had work to do here.

When Morning Star and the children reached the hilltop, they found Seeker alone, kneeling on the ground. His head was bowed and his eyes were closed. The valley below echoed with music and the stamp of dancing feet.

"Whoa!" said Burny. "Big dance!"

Morning Star touched Seeker, thinking he must be asleep.

"We're here," she said. "Let me take you to meet the Beloved."

Seeker was not asleep. He spoke without opening his eyes.

"Soon," he said. "When I'm ready."

"Ready?"

Then Morning Star understood what he was doing. He was gathering his lir for combat.

"This isn't a battle, Seeker! You don't have to fight anyone!"

"I'm sorry, Star," he replied. "This is what I have to do."

"Why? Why do you think the Beloved is your enemy?"

"He's deceived you," said Seeker. "His name is Manlir. He's a savanter."

"No! No, Seeker, you're wrong! He's young, younger even than us! He's good, and kind. Meet him for yourself. You'll see."

"I will meet him," said Seeker. "When I'm ready."

The children were eager to be going on down the hill, to rejoin the Joyous.

"Come on, lady. I'm hungry."

"There's dancing. I like dancing."

"I'll tell him," said Morning Star to Seeker. "Then he'll know what to say to you."

She thought Seeker would try to stop her. She thought he wouldn't let her go ahead without him. But he seemed not to hear her.

"Seeker? I'm going to the Beloved now."

"Go," he said, his voice very low.

He had gone into the stillness. There was nothing more she could do.

"Come on," she said to the children. "Let's go and join the dance."

⊰ 17 ⊱

Love Him Enough
to Save Him

AT THE VERY CENTER OF THE JOYOUS, AT THE STILL point of the dancing throng, the Joy Boy sat on the ground, cross-legged and smiling, sipping a mug of juice. Round him swept a ring of linked dancers, capering first this way and then that, to the squeal of pipes and the hammer of drums. Beyond this inner ring danced a second, bigger ring, and beyond that, a third; and so on, out farther and farther, until the outermost ring numbered many hundreds of dancers.

Caressa Jahan was holding tight to the Wildman's hand and swinging round and round to the beat, her luxuriant hair flying, her eyes shining. Orlans and spikers were inter-mingled in the dancing circles, men and women, boys and girls. They had been on their feet for so long now that they had passed beyond tiredness into a pulsing trance that none of them wanted ever to end.

Morning Star and the children reached the Joyous while this mass dance was still in progress. The children ran off to the food wagons. Morning Star went in search of the Joy Boy at the heart of the dance. She ducked between the rings of dancers, envying them their ecstatic smiles and their abandoned movements. No one paid her any attention. She wondered if they even saw her as she slipped beneath clasped hands, passing from ring to ring. The music made her long to dance too, but first she had a message to deliver. So she stopped her ears and passed on to the center.

When she was on the outside of the innermost ring, she saw the Wildman dance by, and she stopped in astonishment. She followed him round with her eyes and saw how all the sadness had fallen away from him, and she marvelled. He looked more beautiful than ever, and more carefree.

Yet why should I be surprised? she thought to herself. He's been touched by joy, as I have been.

Then she recognized Caressa by his side, and she almost laughed aloud. So Caressa too had found the Joyous. Caressa who had boasted about the Wildman, "I'll lock him up till he loves me." Now here she was, dancing by his side, just another one of the thousands who had been transformed by the Beloved.

And this was the man Seeker meant to kill.

She could see him now, sitting very still in the center of the circling dance. And he could see her.

He beckoned to her to come to him. Morning Star ducked between the dancers and knelt on the ground by the Joy Boy's side. He looked on her with his gentle melting eyes and smiled.

"You have found your friend, I see," he said. "But you have bad news."

"Yes, Beloved. I have bad news."

The Joy Boy lifted one hand and the music ceased. The dancers danced on for a little longer, then they began to drop to the ground in exhaustion. The Wildman saw Morning Star and gave a whoop of delight.

"Star! I love you!"

He threw himself on her and wrapped her in his arms.

"You've come back! Will it be like the old days again? Where's Seeker? I want him to share the joy!"

"Careful, Wildman." Caressa peeled his arms off Morning Star, giving her a quick warning look as she did so. "Don't want to squeeze her to death."

Morning Star drew back, content to leave the Wildman with Caressa.

"Seeker's on his way," she said.

"Seeker coming! Heya! We stand together to the end of the world!"

"It's not like that any more." She turned back to the Joy Boy. "Seeker believes you're his enemy."

The Joy Boy raised his black eyebrows.

"Does he, now?"

"He thinks you're a savanter. He means to kill you."

The Wildman heard Morning Star's warning without understanding.

"Seeker wants to kill the Beloved? No, no! That makes no sense."

"He thinks I'm a savanter," said the Joy Boy.

"What's a savanter?" said Caressa. "What are you all talking about?"

"The enemies of the Noble Warriors," said Morning Star. "Seeker was given his power to kill them."

"Why should he believe the Beloved is an enemy of the Noble Warriors?"

"Because I am," said the Joy Boy, speaking slowly and softly.

The others stared at him.

"Consider." The Joy Boy spread his plump hands. "What is it that marks out the Noble Warriors from all others? Why are they held in such high esteem? They are champions of justice in a cruel world. For the Noble Warriors to have a purpose, there must be injustice and cruelty. There must be all the bitter fruits of separation. But after the Great Embrace there will be no more separation. The god of the Noble Warriors will be irrelevant. The mission of the Noble Warriors will be at an end. Of course the Noble Warriors see me as their enemy and seek to destroy me."

"But they're wrong!" cried Morning Star. "Beloved, you must make him see he's wrong! Talk to him. Let him feel the joy."

"I fear his heart has been hardened against me."

"But you must try!"

"And if I fail?" He smiled for her with a sweet sadness that almost broke her heart. "Your friend possesses more power than I. For myself I care nothing. But here are thousands upon thousands of good people to whom I have made a promise. Am I to let them down now?"

All those round him within hearing gazed at him, shocked by his words.

"Is the Great Embrace not to happen after all?" they said.

"Can't we do it now, Beloved? Before this killer comes."

The Joy Boy shook his head.

"The Great Embrace needs time," he said. "I fear that our angry friend will come soon."

"I'll meet him," said the Wildman. "I'll stop him."

"He's too strong for you now, Wildman," said Morning Star.

"Maybe so, but he's my friend. He'll listen to me. I'll make him understand. And if I don't, at least I'll slow him down."

All eyes now turned back to the Joy Boy.

"It's good that he should be greeted by a friend," said the Joy Boy after a moment's thought. "Meet him with love. But your love may not be strong enough to hold him."

"I'll not go alone," said the Wildman, "and if I have to, I'll hold him in my arms. What's he going to do? Kill me?" He laughed his ringing laugh. "You leave Seeker to me."

The Joy Boy bowed his head in respect.

"You have a great heart," he said.

Then he looked up and spoke for all to hear.

"The Great Embrace will proceed at once. Let the people take their places."

The word passed down the rings of the Joyous, and a ripple of excited chatter spread out through the crowd.

The Joy Boy touched the Wildman lightly on one arm.

"He will hate you," he said. "He will fight you. Is your love strong enough for this?"

"Try me!" cried the Wildman.

"Then, go with joy," said the Joy Boy. "Love him enough to save him."

The Wildman set off at once for the river bridge. Pico picked up a burning torch and followed behind.

Caressa said, "If there's a next time, that'll do for me, too."

She went after the Wildman, and a band of Orlans went with her.

Morning Star hesitated, but not for long.

"I can't go without my friends," she said.

She followed also, her heart heavy, dreading what was to come.

The Joy Boy then gave his instructions, and the people of the Joyous began to form themselves into lines. The lines began before him, and were arranged in a precise pattern. The first line was of two people only. Behind these two stood four more, close enough to touch the two in front with their outstretched hands. Behind them were eight, and then sixteen, and so on. As the lines grew longer they curved into arcs, so that all the people behind could reach one shoulder of one who stood in front. As the lines grew longer still the arcs extended into circles; and beyond the circles, more circles, into the darkness.

The people called out to each other as they took their places, filled with excited anticipation of the moment they'd all been waiting for.

"Share the joy!" they cried.

"Soon we'll be gods!"

The lines and circles overflowed wagons and tents and campfires all the way to the banks of the river. Those who failed to find a place in a line squeezed between the lines, attaching themselves like satellites to whomever they could reach. All the torches were thrown down now, to burn in the fires; both hands were to be free for the Great Embrace.

The Joy Boy stood silent and patient at the very front of the vast formation, facing the first line of two. He waited until the surging of the crowd settled at last into a bristling silence. Word then came up the lines that all were as ready as they ever would be.

The Joy Boy bowed and turned round, so that his back was to the two behind him. He fell to his knees on the ground.

"Kneel," he said to the man behind on his left. "Lay both hands on my left shoulder." To the woman on his right he said, "Kneel and lay both hands on my right shoulder."

They did so.

"Lower your face to your arms and close your eyes. Now let those behind you do the same."

So it was done, line after line, circle after circle, rippling across the valley, until every man, woman, and child was kneeling, linked in an unbroken chain of touch from the very outermost ring all the way to the Joy Boy at the center.

"Keep the contact," said the Joy Boy. "Once the Great Embrace begins, you must keep touching. If you break the contact you will be left behind."

This instruction too was passed down the lines.

"Now listen to the sound I make," he said. "Make the same sound yourself. And open your hearts to joy."

He closed his eyes and began to hum. The humming was soft and deep and musical. Those behind him picked up the note as best they could, and so the humming spread until the sound filled the valley like a coming storm. Here and there where the fires burned, the people could be seen beginning to sway from side to side, all instinctively adopting the same rhythm. Without any further instruction, the humming took on shape and melody, and wave after wave of wordless song swept over the swaying mass. Faint flecks of white foam appeared on the lips of those nearest to the front. And the Joy Boy himself, kneeling, his eyes closed, humming sweet and slow, smiled a beatific smile.

Seeker heard the wave of sound. He rose to his feet and looked down into the valley below. He saw the swaying mass of people and knew at once that the Great Embrace had begun.

He set off down the hillside. Ahead lay the dark river; and crossing the river bridge, striding towards him, lit by torches, was a line of distant figures.

His time of preparation had done its work. He felt sure and strong. Everything was simple now. No power on Earth could stand in his way.

The people ahead saw Seeker descending the hill and came to a stop, barring his way onto the bridge. One of them now stepped forward, his arms spread wide. Amazed, Seeker recognized the Wildman.

"Heya, Seeker!"

"Wildman! What are you doing here?"

"Come to meet you, my friend."

He stood there just like in the old days, smiling and beautiful in the flickering torchlight. Behind him, still on the bridge, was Morning Star.

"I can't stop, Wildman," said Seeker. "Give way."

"Can't do that, brava," said the Wildman. "Can't let you go. Not now I've found you again."

"This one you call the Beloved is fooling you, Wildman. He's a savanter. He means to destroy us all."

"I don't see the need for any destroying," said the Wildman. "We're friends, you and I. Remember? We stand together against the world."

"He's lied to you! He's lied to everyone!"

"You're wrong, my friend. All he wants is to share the joy."

"Listen to him, Seeker," said Morning Star. "It's not the way you think. The Beloved brings only peace and joy."

So Morning Star stands by the Wildman, thought Seeker. She takes his side, shares his destiny. So be it.

All the time, the sound of the wordless singing filled the night air. Seeker knew he was running out of time.

"Let me past," he said.

"Can't do that, brava."

Seeker took a step forward. The Wildman too advanced until they were face-to-face. The Wildman then reached out his arms and embraced Seeker.

Seeker drew a long breath.

"Let me go, friend."

From across the river the swelling song of the Great Embrace was rising now. The Wildman gripped Seeker tight. Seeker spoke more forcefully.

"Let me go!"

As he spoke he hurled the Wildman from him. But the Wildman was agile, and he recovered rapidly. He placed himself before Seeker, adopting the combat stance.

"You want to pass, you have to fight."

"I don't want to fight you, Wildman."

"So you know what to do."

"You can't win against me."

"I've never lost before."

"That was then. Tell him, Star."

"Stand your ground, Wildman," said Morning Star.

Seeker flashed her a bitter look.

"If you love him, tell him not to do this."

"You're the only true friend I ever had, Seeker," said the Wildman. "But I'll fight you to the end if that's what I have to do."

"Why? For a savanter who wants to destroy all Noble Warriors?"

"Seems to me you're the one wants to do the destroying."

"Listen to him, Seeker," said Morning Star. "You come to kill. The Beloved comes to bring joy. Why are you on the side of death?"

"I'll do what I've been sent to do," said Seeker. "Now clear my way!"

He struck at the Wildman, but the Wildman blocked the blow and struck back, making Seeker stagger.

"Don't make me do this," Seeker growled as he struck again. "I don't want to hurt you." He struck a third time. The Wildman reeled and was forced back.

"I love you, Seeker," he said. As he spoke he released a stinging blow that caught Seeker unawares and hurled him to the ground.

"Hold him down!" cried Caressa.

At her command a dozen Orlans piled onto Seeker, pinning his limbs to the ground. Seeker groaned and uttered a low howl of rage. His body shook. He began to rise up. As he rose he carried the men with him as if they were no heavier than fallen leaves, and like fallen leaves, were shaken from his back.

"What must I do," he growled, "to make you understand?"

"Share the joy," said the Wildman.

Seeker struck once, and again, and again. The Wildman broke under the power of the blows and sank to his knees.

"Now clear my way!"

Seeker strode forward. The Wildman threw his arms round him as he passed, binding him tight. His grip was powerful, and try as he might, Seeker could not shake him off. So he seized the Wildman by the neck and choked and shook him till his arms fell free and he folded to the ground. There, his hands flailing, he grabbed for Seeker's ankles and clung to them. Seeker kicked him away.

"It's over!" he shouted. "Do I have to kill you?"

"Yes," said the Wildman, rising unsteadily to his feet, smiling through his pain. "You have to kill me."

Morning Star saw the look on Seeker's face and saw how the Wildman could barely control his own limbs.

"No, Wildman!" she cried out. "No more!"

Seeker heard that cry, so charged with love and grief, and tried to stop himself, tried to turn away from the horror into which he had fallen, but the Wildman stumbled after him once more, embraced him once more, called to him once more—

"Heya!"—the voice a faint echo of past glory—"Do you love me?"

Trapped by memories, trapped by the net of lost love, Seeker knew only that he must free himself. Enough now! No more failure, no more hesitation. Strike and let it be over. Strike and be free.

His last and greatest blow exploded the Wildman up into the air, arms spread wide, body arching, golden hair flying, high up and over and down again, to land with a crunching crack on the hard ground. There he lay, unmoving, eyes gazing up, unseeing, into the darkness.

"No-o-o!" cried Morning Star, throwing herself onto his inert body.

"Die! Die!" shrieked Caressa, lashing at Seeker with her silver-handled whip.

Seeker seemed not even to feel the blows. No one now stood between him and the bridge. In the valley beyond, kneeling in a night mist that covered the ground, the people of the Joyous swayed and hummed in the Great Embrace.

"He's dead!" cried Morning Star, sobbing with grief and anger. "You killed him! He loved you, and you killed him!"

⚜ 18 ⚜

The Great Embrace

SEEKER MADE HIS WAY AS FAST AS HE COULD THROUGH the lines of people, stepping over outstretched arms, heading for the heart of the gathering. The humming had swelled to a full openmouthed keening cry, but the people still had their heads on their arms and their eyes closed. Then in the flickering light of the dying fires Seeker saw that from their mouths dribbled the white creamy ooze he had seen before in the land cloud. As it stained the night-cool ground it turned to vapor, forming the ghostly mist on which the ring upon ring of kneeling swaying bodies now floated.

The nearer he got to the center, the more possessed were the people. The life force that flowed down the chains gathered strength like a river into which flows many streams; but the people themselves did not grow stronger. If anything, they seemed to become more lifeless, and from their mouths dribbled ever more white ooze. The ground mist grew deeper, rising now to waist height. The lines were shorter, the spaces between the kneeling people wider. Then at last there were four, then two. And then there was one.

The Joy Boy knelt in the mist with his head bowed, his companions' hands vibrating on his shoulders. Seeker came round to stand before him, and as he did so, the Joy Boy raised his head and opened his eyes and smiled. He looked so young and innocent that for a moment Seeker hesitated.

"Join us," said the Joy Boy. "Live forever."

He reached out his hands. Seeker jerked back.

"Don't touch me!"

"What are you so afraid of, my friend?"

"Let these people go," said Seeker. "This is between you and me."

"Too late," said the Joy Boy. "They and I are one now."

Seeker said no more. He stilled his mind and gathered his power.

"So much pain," murmured the Joy Boy.

Seeker struck. He felt the pulse of force leave him. He sensed it rippling like a shock wave over the Joy Boy. But it had no effect.

"We're strong now," said the Joy Boy. "You come too late."

Seeker struck a second time, with all the power he could command. This time he felt the Joy Boy give a slight shudder. That was all.

"You can't kill me," said the Joy Boy. "So join me."

He held out his hands once more.

Everything in Seeker shrank from that offered touch; but as he looked on the Joy Boy's smiling face, he knew that this was the only way. He dropped to his knees in the mist. There, surrounded by the heartbreaking song of thousands of people giving up their life force in a cause they did not understand, Seeker bowed to the Joy Boy and let him lay his hands on his shoulders.

"Let me share your joy," he said.

He felt the surge of power flowing into him. He did nothing to resist it. One by one he threw open the gates with which he defended his own lir until he was at the mercy of the Joy Boy's torrent of force.

Funny thing, strength. You can drink it in.

His gaze remained fixed on the Joy Boy's plump smiling face.

"There now," said the Joy Boy, "that's better, isn't it?"

As the Joy Boy spoke, he gave a small tug, not with his hands but with his mind. Seeker felt himself tip and pour like a jug. He let the lir stream out of him until he was so light and empty that he barely existed any more.

"There now," murmured the Joy Boy. "No more separation."

Seeker could feel the flow of strength entering the Joy Boy from the Great Embrace. Now it was entering him, too.

"I am you," he said.

"Ah," said the Joy Boy. "You begin to understand."

"No separation," said Seeker. "No escape."

It was so easy after all. This was the limitless power he had been given: the power to absorb the strength of others. All that the Joy Boy had gained for himself, drained from the thousands upon thousands ranged round him in the rising mist, now belonged to Seeker.

Gently, almost tenderly, he drew the lir back towards himself. The Joy Boy felt the reverse of the flow, and shocked, stiffening, he tried to close down the channels between them. But he could not do so. He tried to raise his hands from Seeker's shoulders. But they were fixed there fast. He tried to look away but could neither turn his head nor close his eyes.

"I've come so close!" he cried. "Why stop me now?"

As the lir flowed out of him, the Joy Boy was changing. His plump young cheeks grew sallow and began to form wrinkles. His smooth black hair faded and became thin. His sweet voice turned husky.

"Let me live," he cried. "For the love of Noman."

"Noman has no love for savanters."

At that, the Joy Boy's fast-withering face twisted into a bitter smile.

"How little you know," he said. "Everything we have done has been done in accordance with Noman's will."

"You may deceive others," said Seeker, never relenting for a second, sucking the lir from the dwindling figure before him. "But I know who you are."

"And who am I?" said the Joy Boy.

"You are Manlir."

Kneeling before him now, helpless in his power, was an old man. With each passing second, he grew older still.

"He told you that?"

"You chose the path of knowledge," he said. "He chose the path of faith."

"And did he tell you why I chose the path of knowledge?"

"To live forever. To be forever young."

"But before that? No, he never told you how it began, did he? Listen to me before it's too late. Don't you feel how close we are to you? We are Noble Warriors—like you. Noman himself created the order of the savanters, to protect the All and Only from the greatest enemy of all."

"You lie," said Seeker.

"And you are charged with the same duty. You've been called by the All and Only. You have heard the voice."

Surely you know it's you who will save me.

Manlir caught the moment of hesitation.

"The Assassin is coming," he said. "The Noble Warriors must defend the Lost Child. The savanters are part of that defense."

"You are our enemy."

"We are the necessary enemy. We were created to make you strong. Did Noman not tell you? He is my brother."

"You lie!"

"And you—you begin to doubt."

By now Manlir was shrunken to the form of a living corpse. Only the sharp eyes had energy in that skull of a face. Seeker tried to block the doubts, but once begun they multiplied within him. The powers of the savanters were similar to the powers of the Nomana, it was true. In his battles with them, just as in his battle with Manlir now, he found himself attacked by his own secret skills. Perhaps it was true that savanters were Nomana gone bad. All the more reason to destroy them, as Noman commanded.

"Why has my brother let us live?" said Manlir. "Ask yourself that."

"The powers of the Noble Warriors have limits."

"But you have been given power without limits. Why you? Why now?"

"The savanters have grown too strong."

"The savanters were made to be strong. My brother said to me, 'Pursue knowledge without limits. Make yourselves lords of wisdom.' Why did he do that, Seeker? Why?"

The voice was faint and dry with extreme old age now, and the shrill tones bored into Seeker's brain. He realized with horror that he was losing his certainty, and that with it his strength was weakening. Manlir knew it, too. Like a fisherman drawing in his net, he began now to haul back the power that Seeker had taken.

"We are all Noman's legacy, Seeker. We are all necessary for the protection of the All and Only."

"No! I won't believe it!"

"If you destroy the last of the savanters, you leave the All and Only to the mercy of the Assassin."

"Noman has given me the power. I do as he commands."

"You think your power comes from Noman? Think again, Seeker. Noman is mortal, just as I am mortal. The power you have been given has no limits."

It was true. Seeker saw again the bright light shining from within the Garden and knew that this was the power that had existed before the world came into being. He heard again the voice in the Garden crying to him. *Save me!*

The humming song of the Great Embrace had never ceased. Now he found himself too making small sounds, the beginning of the same song. He licked his lips and felt how dry they were. Manlir knelt before him, gazing at him, and little by little he was growing young again.

"We need each other, Seeker. We each have our parts to play."

Seeker found he no longer possessed the clear killing rage that had driven him across the land in pursuit of his prey. And if he was not to kill the savanter before him, what was he to do with him?

End this charade. Put a stop to the Great Embrace.

He looked into the night, his eyes scanning the nearer men and women among the kneeling masses. Their heads lay on their arms, making it hard to see their faces; but he caught glimpses of the white cream that trickled from their mouths, and he knew what it meant.

"Let these people go," he said to Manlir, "and I'll let you go."

"Too late," said Manlir. "Their lir is in me now. Their time is over."

"Give it back to them!"

"That would kill me. And I mean to live. I mean to live forever."

"I'll make you do it!"

"Your moment has passed, Seeker."

Manlir sounded like the Joy Boy again. His flesh was filling out. He had regained the Joy Boy's full-lipped smile.

"I fear now," he said, "that you are the one who must leave us."

Seeker felt the lurch within him of Manlir's renewed power. He struggled to resist it, but to his dismay he found he was helpless. The tide of lir had flowed once more to Manlir and was flowing ever more strongly all the time. Seeker tried to rise from where he knelt, but his muscles wouldn't obey his commands. He tried to do as he had done before and drink in Manlir's strength and make it his own, but the savanter was ready for him this time and was too strong for him.

"You grow in knowledge, Seeker," he said. "To know is to doubt. To doubt is to fail."

Seeker broke away from that penetrating gaze and hunted through the rings of people in the mist, looking in his desperation for any source of help.

Who do I seek? There's no one here with more strength than I have myself.

Then he saw a head he recognized. It was his father, kneeling in the night, singing the wordless song of the Great Embrace. How did his father come to be part of the Joyous? Was he too to be sucked of life? There on his outreached arms where his mouth pressed to his sleeve was the stain of white ooze, the residue of his lost lir. And there by his side was Seeker's mother, the lir trickling from her lips, too.

"Mama! No!"

His doubts vaporized in a sudden flash of fury. Gulping power as a drowning man gasps for air, he seized the savanter by the temples and overwhelmed his defenses with the sheer force of his rage. No thought, no hesitation: only the needed kill.

"No!" screeched Manlir, writhing in his grip. "You don't know what you're doing!"

"Die!" cried Seeker, crushing, suffocating. "Die!"

"Noman! Brother! Help me!"

"Noman wants you dead!"

"Don't—make—me—"

The words came choking from the savanter's mouth. His eyes were starting from his head in the intensity of his struggle to survive. But Seeker's rage did not abate. All his being was now concentrated on the kill.

"Die!" he cried. "Die!"

All at once he felt Manlir's resistance give way.

"My life is all life," the savanter whispered. "Not even you can kill all life. I will never die."

His lips twisted in a strange little smile. Then he opened his mouth and white ooze began to stream from between his lips. It slithered down his chin to fall in heavy drops on the ground between them. Seeker released his grasp. Manlir gave a choking gasp and a great gush of ooze came bubbling out. On and on it came, the lir pouring from within him, puddling in an ever-growing pool at his feet. A heavy vapor rose from the pool, which gave off a rich, sweet sickly smell.

Seeker looked on in horror. He had never seen a man expel his own lir before. It was suicide. There was no need for him to intervene. He saw the life fading in the savanter's eyes as the lir drained out of him. Then his head lolled, his body slumped, and he crumpled to the stained ground.

Round them the people of the Joyous were now emerging from their swaying trance. The humming song faltered and fell silent. The linked hands fell away as the people looked about them in confusion. Line after line disengaged, and the great merged network of lir broke up into a crowd of individuals once more.

Seeker looked down at the savanter, now forever young in death. It was the Joy Boy who lay before him, his head on one side, his cheek to the cream-drenched earth. His mouth was open. Out through his parted lips trickled the last of his lir. And so finally the flow ceased.

Then Seeker heard a deep sound, so deep that it was almost no sound at all, and he felt a shuddering in the ground on which he knelt. Seized by fear he looked again at the face of the dead savanter and leaned down close to feel if he was still breathing after all. But there was nothing. Manlir was gone.

Seeker rose slowly from his knees. On all sides the people of the Joyous were getting to their feet too, and asking each other what had happened to them, and if they had been made into gods as they had been promised.

"Where's the Beloved?" they said. "What are we to do now?"

Seeker turned and walked slowly away. He wanted only to be far from this place, far from the killing, far from the sickly smell of spilled lir.

Behind him he heard the cries as the waking people discovered the dead body in the mist.

"The Beloved is dead!"

Let others do what must be done, he thought. My work is over now.

Unnoticed by the increasingly agitated crowd, he passed among them and crossed the bridge over the river.

A small group was still gathered where the Wildman lay, the friend he had killed to do what had been asked of him. As Seeker approached, one of them rose from her kneeling position to scream at him.

"Murderer! You killed him! Murderer!"

It was Caressa, her handsome face contorted in grief and rage. Beside her, still crouched low by the dead body of his friend, knelt Morning Star. She looked up and saw Seeker, and her face too was streaked with tears.

"Killer!" screamed Caressa. "All you can do is kill! You kill all beauty, all hope, all love!"

Seeker came close to his dead friend. He looked down at his beautiful face, and heard in memory his ringing cry.

Heya! Do you love me?

Yes, Wildman. I love you. Take my life for yours. I don't need it any more.

"Let me hold him."

"Don't touch him! Get away from him!"

Caressa beat at him with her fists, punching in her frenzy as hard as she was able, but Seeker seemed not to notice. He forced his way past her, and stooping down, he took up the Wildman's dead body in his arms. As he did so, Morning Star followed him with silent grieving eyes.

Seeker held the dead body in a full embrace, his arms round the Wildman's back, his brow pressed to the Wildman's brow. In this way, eyes closed, body trembling with the intensity of his effort, he streamed the lir in him into his dead friend.

Live, Wildman! Take my life and live!

As the lir flowed out of him, he weakened and found it harder to support the Wildman's weight. But as the lir entered his friend, so the muscles began to stir. At first, without breath or heartbeat, the legs and arms of the dead man jerked and twitched, responding to quickening nervous impulses. Then there came a hoarse groan from the dead man's throat, and with a series of spasmodic choking noises, he began to breathe. Seeker kept tight hold of him and poured out his own life's lir and felt the sudden thump as the Wildman's heart began to beat. The legs stiffened beneath him and took his own weight, just as Seeker was finding the burden too great. The limp arms reached out and clasped Seeker as he was clasped. So as the lir flowed on and Seeker weakened, the Wildman began to support him in his turn.

Now the Wildman's eyes were open, and understanding was returning to his waking mind.

"Seeker," he said. "My friend."

"Forgive me," said Seeker.

He felt his legs give way beneath him. He felt the Wildman hold him, saving him from falling.

"We stand together," said the Wildman, "against the world."

Seeker folded in his arms, and his head fell forward on the Wildman's chest. He had given so much of his own life that he had too little left for himself. As his eyes closed, his last sight was of Morning Star looking on, the tears streaming down her cheeks.

⚕ 19 ⚕

Go to the True Nom

RAISED VOICES SOME WAY OFF. THE FLICKER OF BRIGHT light. Sunlight falling through a gap in the tent cloth. The cloth flapping in the breeze.

Seeker was alone in a bed of rugs. He heaved himself up into a sitting position and looked out towards the clamor. A noisy meeting was under way by the bridge. He saw Caressa and Sabin and the Orlan captains, and the Wildman and his spiker chiefs. He saw Morning Star standing apart from them all, her eyes on the Wildman, listening in silence. Beyond the bridge the immense crowd that had called itself the Joyous was broken up into smaller groups, and from every group came the sound of agitated voices.

I killed my friend, said Seeker to himself, and I gave him back my own life. Why am I not dead?

Now more than anything he longed to be alone. Once they knew he was awake they would all come pushing round him, blaming and pleading, looking to him for answers he did not have.

Nothing more for me to do here, he thought, watching Morning Star. Better that I go.

He rose unsteadily to his feet and stood still for a few moments, breathing slow deep breaths. He felt giddy, but he did not fall. The raised voices of the chiefs came to him through the tent walls. They were disputing over status.

"This is spiker land!" he heard the Wildman say. "None of your yabba-yabba can take that away!"

So the Wildman was himself again. And Morning Star had eyes only for him, as always. No need to stay and watch.

He untied the tent cloth at the back and eased himself out. The bright light of day made him blink. For a moment he felt too weak to walk, but he stood still and gathered his strength, and the moment passed.

He set off steadily, not looking back. Shortly he was over the brow of the hill and out of sight of the crowd. He strode on, trying to empty his mind of all the confusions of the day gone by. He made for the high road, hoping to find again the door in the wall and the Garden beyond. He wanted to be released from his powers now. He wanted to throw himself down before the All and Only and ask to be given his own life back.

Then, as he strode along, he heard once again the low deep boom that had sounded as Manlir had died. It was a little louder this time, though still more a vibration in the ground than a true sound. It sounded like the land echo of thunder in the sky, but there were no clouds.

Then came a sharper sound: the rapid click of hoof-beats ahead. Out of the roadside wood burst a riderless Caspian, running wild. He knew the horse at once from his markings: it was Kell.

"Kell!" he cried. "Where's Echo?"

As if in answer, Kell turned and trotted back into the trees. Seeker followed. There was a track through the wood, but no sign of Echo. Thinking she might have fallen and be lying injured nearby, he called to her.

"Echo! It's me—Seeker!"

There was no answer. But then he heard a rustle in the branches, and looking up, he caught a sudden rapid movement between the dry summer leaves.

"Echo? Is that you?"

"You think you've killed him, don't you?"

The voice was mocking and shrill. There, clinging to a high branch, was Echo—her eyes wild and staring.

"You can't kill him!" she taunted. "Manny's coming to get you!"

With that, she swung away with astonishing agility, from one high branch to another, and turning back to look down on Seeker, she called again, in the same harsh high mocking voice.

"Manny's coming to kill you!"

She sprang away, leaping from branch to branch, until she was high up in one of the highest of the tall trees. Here she came to a sudden stop, and crouching in the crook of a branch, she bowed her head to hide her face. Seeker followed to the foot of the high tree.

"Echo!" he called to her. "It's Seeker, your friend. I want to help you."

She raised her head then and looked at him with her beautiful eyes. She smiled a sad smile and spoke to him in her own voice.

"Too late," she said. "Good-bye, friend Seeker. I have to go now."

She released her grip on the branch and kicked with her legs so that she vaulted away from the tree and began to fall. Her arms reached wide as she fell, and she turned in the air, making no effort to save herself, meaning to dash her brains out on the ground and so end her torment. But her outstretched hands brushed against clusters of leaves, and instinctively snatching herself closer to the trunk as she fell, she found the elastic support of the branches once more, and so sprang back unharmed.

"No-o-o!" she cried. "Let me die!"

At once the other, harsher voice answered from her own mouth.

"We want to live! We want to live forever!"

Seeker watched in horror and pity as Echo flew back up the ladder of the trees and tried once more to throw herself to her death. Again she caught herself, and again she cried out in her wretchedness.

"Let me die!"

But even as she called with her own voice, the other within her was pushing to the fore, taunting Seeker on the ground below.

"Seeker's the one who's going to die! Can't escape Manny now!"

She was away again, swinging fast through the trees, gaining height as she went. Far off now, she dived once again from the treetops like a hawk on its prey, dropping almost to the ground before swooping up, helplessly secure in the familiar branches, hunting for death, unable to die. He heard her cries recede into the distance as she bounded through the trees, and Kell trotted over the woodland path beneath.

Haunted by Echo's piteous voice, Seeker returned to the high road. What had she meant? Manlir was dead. He was sure of that. Why then did he feel such dread at her words?

Can't escape Manny now!

When he reached the road, he found a bullock cart drawn up by the verge, as if waiting for him. The driver was a lanky youth with protruding eyes and a smile on his face. In the open cart lay a litter covered by a white canopy.

The driver fixed his gaping face on Seeker and, giving a nod behind him, said, "He wants to speak with you."

A hand reached from within the white canopy and drew it aside. Seeker approached. There in the litter, robed in white like a corpse, lay Jango. His deep-set eyes gazed out at Seeker.

"Hurry, boy," he said. "You have very little time."

"Jango!" cried Seeker. "Are you hurt?"

"Not hurt, my friend. Just old."

He did seem older than before. Talking tired him. He

stopped to catch his breath, like one who talks while climbing a mountain.

"Why do I have little time?" said Seeker. "I've done what I was sent to do."

"Not all," said Jango. "Not yet."

"Manlir is dead!" He shouted it out to make it be true. "I killed him!"

"His body is dead."

"I don't understand—"

Jango held up one frail hand to silence him.

"Soon, soon. Do as I say." Again he paused to gain strength. "Touch me."

Seeker put out his hand. Jango took it in his and pressed it to his withered cheek. A faint smile formed on his face.

"Warm hand," he said. "Strong hand."

"Tell me. Was I not strong enough?"

"You were strong. Stronger than him. He knew you had the power to kill him. So he did what no man has ever done before. He released his living lir."

Seeker heard this with a return of dread.

"I saw it," he said.

"No man knows lir as he does," said Jango.

"So where is he now?"

"Everywhere."

"Everywhere!"

"There is lir in the earth," said Jango. "In the trees. In the rivers. In the clouds. In the oceans. But this great power that exists in all living matter has never before been united in a single will."

"Manlir's will!"

"No one has ever done this before. He has lost his self. But he has not died."

My life is all life. Seeker heard again the savanter's last choking words. *I will never die.*

"What can I do?" said Seeker.

"Go to the True Nom. Call on the strength of the All and Only."

"What True Nom?"

Jango's eyes closed, and in his exhaustion, he panted softly as he lay. Seeker knew of no True Nom, so he waited for Jango to regain his strength before he asked more. But when Jango opened his eyes once again, it was to ask him a question.

"Tell me, boy," he said. "Do you love the All and Only?"

"Yes," said Seeker.

"Think only of your love. Your faith must be strong. True faith is the only armor that Manlir cannot pierce. Do you hear me?"

"Yes," said Seeker.

But Jango gripped his hand tight, painfully tight, and said again with fierce intensity, "Do you hear me?"

"I do hear you," said Seeker.

"Faith, boy. In the end, faith!"

With that, he sank back and let his weary eyes close again.

"Which road am I to take?" asked Seeker.

"The road to the True Nom. We have been there before."

Seeker could only think he meant the door in the wall, through which he had found the shadowy trees and the glowing Garden.

"West," said the old man, his voice now faint. "Go west. He'll be ready soon. Go quickly . . ."

He spoke no more. He had slipped into sleep, his enfeebled energies drained by their exchange. Seeker looked up at the lanky youth in the driver's seat.

"Do you know where he means me to go?"

The youth shook his head.

"Where are you to take him?"

"West," said the driver. "Through the forest. On to the west."

Seeker stood irresolute. Then once more came the deep boom of sound that shook the earth. He looked up at the driver. The staring youth showed no sign that he had heard anything.

Am I the only one who hears it?

Now the boom was fading away. It had been longer this time, and nearer.

⚹ 20 ⚹

People Need Gods

"No more yabba-yabba!" cried the Wildman. "Stop your yabba-yabba, fool woman! You're on spiker land now."

"Go feed it to the pigs!" retorted Caressa.

"Orlans are outsiders!"

"Got any more pig swill in your bucket?"

"Orlans have no rights!"

"Oh, shouting now? I can shout, too."

They followed each other across the camp, yelling like ox jockeys at a market-day race.

"Orlans have no rights to rule in Radiance!"

"What's rights? You got rights in your pocket, Wildman?"

"I swear I'm going to squeeze the life out of you!"

"Do rights grow on trees?"

"Rights are what's right!"

"Here's what's right!" Caressa drew her short blade and jabbed it towards the startled Wildman. "Orlans got rights too, Wildman. And we keep them sharp."

"Don't mess with me, Princess!"

"Orlans don't kneel to spikers."

"The Wildman don't take orders from a woman."

"Why didn't you do us all a favor and stay dead?"

"Yabba–yabba–yabba—"

She smacked the Wildman's head. He seized her wrists and forced her arms down, pulling her face close to his as he did so. She glared at him, panting with anger.

"Now what? Bite my nose off?"

"You're as spiker as I am!"

"Look round you, Wildman! See those warriors in armor? They obey me. Me! And they're not the stinking bandits you call an army, I can promise you that!"

"Here's how it is, Princess," he hissed back. "I'm number one. My land. My people. I rule!"

"Not me, pretty boy."

Exasperated beyond endurance, the Wildman released Caressa's wrists and stamped away to his command tent, kicking the ground in anger as he went. Caressa swept back her luxuriant hair and retreated to the Orlan quarters, from where she could be heard shouting orders at her underlings. The lesser spiker chiefs and Orlan captains scowled at one another and strutted about with their weapons ostentatiously on show.

The great gathering was disintegrating. The promised Great Embrace had not come to pass. Bewildered and exhausted, the people were beginning to drift away.

A number of those who had counted themselves closest to the Joy Boy had come together to honor his body in death. Sorrowfully they dressed him in white and laid him on a litter beneath a white canopy. They found then that they were unable to agree on how to properly dispose of the body. The hill people had a tradition of burial, the people of the plains burned their dead on funeral pyres. The two groups were equally vociferous, and each outraged by the other's disrespect for the mortal remains of the Beloved.

"Bury him? Like a dog buries a bone?"

"You'd throw him on a fire like a bag of old clothes!"

It was the small band from the coastal region who proposed the compromise. Let the Beloved pass away as the fisher people passed away: on a small boat released into the great ocean. This proved acceptable to all. The mourners then set about commandeering a barge to carry the litter downriver to the sea.

Morning Star took no part in these discussions. Nor did she intervene in the squabbles between Caressa and the Wildman. What power did she have now to unite people? Instead she went in search of her mother and father and found them among a large group from their village, preparing to set out on the long walk back.

"It's a bad business, Star," said Arkaty. "And I guess we look like fools."

"He made fools of us all, Papa. And he would have done worse if he hadn't been stopped."

"But it's not all sorry." He gave her a small sweet smile. "Never danced like that before."

Mercy, her mother, could not smile. "I feel so tired," she said.

"So where do you go now, Star?" said Arkaty.

"I'm going to find him."

They didn't need to ask who she meant.

Nearby a loud quarrel broke out between Shab and an Orlan captain. Morning Star heard the Orlan's taunts and Shab's heated rejoinders and thought how recently they had all been dancing together.

"If you find him," said Mercy, "come back and tell us."

"I will, Mama."

"I'd like to know there's—" She hesitated, not knowing what words to use. Then, with a little shrug, "More than I know."

"The All and Only," said Morning Star.

"Something, at least. If there's nothing, I don't know that I can go on."

"There's something, Mama. I'll find it, and come back and tell you."

All at once the nearby quarrel exploded into violence. Shab drew a spike, there came a flurry of blows, and the Orlan fell to the ground. Men on all sides began to shout and draw their swords.

"You want more?" cried Shab, brandishing his spike. "I've got more!"

But an ominous silence had fallen over the crowd. The Orlan was dead.

The Orlans picked up their slain comrade and carried him back to their camp. Caressa listened to what they had to say. Then she mounted her Caspian, and with Sabin by her side, she rode to the Wildman and spoke to him not as his friend and lover, but as the Jahan of Jahans.

"A life for a life," she said. "Bring me the body of the killer by dawn, or I call the Orlan nation to war."

With that, she rode away.

The Wildman sat up late into the night, brooding by the fire. Here Morning Star found him.

"I don't know what to do," he said. "Shab's a hothead fool, but I can't hand him over."

"No."

"Make us love each other again, Star. Like you did before."

"I would if I could," she said. "But I've lost the skill."

"Too much getting lost. I can't hold it together, Star."

"No one can."

"No one except Seeker."

She watched the silky smoke curl out from the burning timbers, a slow white plume now tinged with flame, now shot with flame, now leaping into flame.

"People need something to believe in," she said. "People need gods."

"Got to have a god worth believing in, then," said the Wildman. "Can't crawl about on our knees hoping a god will come along, like a chick with its beak open clucking for worms."

She smiled. "No."

"There'll be fighting tomorrow. Can't see any way to head it off."

"Caressa doesn't want to fight you. She's crazy about you."

"Caressa's not my problem. The Jahan of the Orlans—there's my problem."

"Tell your men not to fight."

"And let them take Shab? I do that, I'm finished."

"But it's all so stupid. It's all so unnecessary."

"Maybe so. But it's how it is."

"Let me think about it," she said. "I may be able to find a way out."

She left him there and went away by herself. As she passed quietly through the night crowds, Burny saw her from where he lay huddled with the other children. He jumped up and came after her.

"Lady," he said. "Wait for me."

"You should be asleep," said Morning Star.

"Been asleep," he replied. "Awake now."

She let him hold her hand as they walked.

"Where you going?"

"Nowhere. I'm just walking and thinking."

"Thinking what?"

"About gods."

"What gods?"

"Have you ever heard of the All and Only, Burny?"

"No."

"He's got lots of other names, too. The Wise Father. The Quiet Watcher. The Lost Child."

"The lost child? That's like me."

"Yes. Just like you."

"So maybe I'm a god."

"Do you think so?"

"Don't know," said Burny. "What do you have to do to be a god?"

"Well . . ." Morning Star was about to say that a god had to have great powers. But then she thought of it the other way round. "You don't have to do anything. People have to believe in you."

"And then what?"

"And then people do as you tell them."

"Why?"

"To please their god."

"Sounds easy," said Burny. "I'll be one of them if you like. One of them lost childs."

This conversation stayed with Morning Star long after Burny had returned, yawning, to his sleep huddle. It gave her an idea.

As dawn broke, the Orlans were seen to be mounted and ranked in battle array. The spikers gathered in their more disorganized fashion, but in far greater numbers. The Wildman, weary from a night with little sleep, walked forward to speak with Caressa. By his side was Shab.

"Heya, Princess." He gestured at the battle line. "No call for this."

"A life for a life, Wildman. That's the Orlan way."

She wasn't shouting any more. He didn't like that.

"Here's the man who did it. Say your piece, Shab."

"Got into a quarrel." Shab spoke in a low mumble, his

eyes fixed on the ground. "Way men do. Turned into a fight. Way it does. Never meant to kill. Sorry he's dead."

Caressa never once looked at Shab. Her eyes were on the Wildman.

"You handing this man over, Wildman?"

"What happens if I do?"

"Rope his ankles," said Sabin. "Hitch him to a horse. Drag him away."

Shab went white.

"Can't do that, Princess," said the Wildman.

"Then you pay the price."

The Wildman gazed up at her, and even as he was angered by her threats, he marvelled at her beauty. The rising sun was full on her face and glinting on her silver breastplate. She sat high and proud on Malook, the silver-handled whip in one hand, her army massed behind her.

"More beautiful than ever, Princess."

He caught a momentary flicker in her dark eyes, but she held her resolve.

"I am the Jahan of Jahans," she said.

So that was that. The Wildman understood the forces that drove her to this intransigence, because the same forces were at work on him. A leader never backs down in public. There was no way out.

Then, from the body of the spikers behind him, there came a long high howl. Morning Star appeared, her arms reached above her head, her eyes staring like a madwoman, howling as she came. It was a tormented haunted howl, like the death cry of a creature from some other world.

The men fell back, afraid. Caressa and the Wildman looked on in astonishment as Morning Star approached them, staring and howling.

"Star!" cried the Wildman.

She went to him, still howling, and gazing right through him, she struck him hard across the face. He staggered back. Then Morning Star swung round howling still and struck Shab, making him yell out with anger.

"Let me spike her, chief!"

"Leave her alone!" said the Wildman. "She's the spirit of the spikers!"

Still howling, Morning Star went to Malook's side, seized hold of Caressa's foot, and heaved and twisted. Caressa went tumbling to the ground.

"Rat child!" cried Caressa, jumping to her feet and raising her whip to strike.

Morning Star moved right up close, her face in Caressa's face, and screamed at her. Caressa backed away in dread.

"What does she want?"

Morning Star now began to turn round and round, and her howling slowly lessened in volume, and everyone there could see her staring eyes and knew that she was possessed. When at last she came to a stop and her screams ceased, there was a dead silence all round her.

She spoke then, in a voice that was strange and deep, as if some other being spoke through her.

"I dream the Lost Child," she said. "I dream the one who cries in the darkness. Wake from your sleep and hear the cries in the night."

The people in the crowd strained to hear her, and those further back called out, "What does she say?" The ones at the front told them to be quiet. "It's the little mother. She's in a trance. Don't wake her."

The Wildman took her hand. She let him hold it, showing no awareness that he was there.

"Tell me, Star. Do you have a message for us?"

"I am the All and Only," said Morning Star in that chilling deep voice. "I am the Reason and the Goal."

"What are we to do?"

"Build me a Garden, where I can live in peace."

Her words were passed back, echoing through the crowd, causing a sensation. "It's the god of the Noble Warriors come back to save us!" the people said.

"Where are we to do this?" said the Wildman.

"Follow me," said Morning Star. "Follow me."

Then she faltered and began to shake. She covered her face with her hands, and her head jerked from side to side. A low cry of pain escaped from her lips. And so at last she was still. She let her hands fall to her sides. Then she looked about her in fear, not knowing how she came to be here. Her voice was soft and low.

"Why do you all look at me?"

"You've had a dream," said the Wildman.

"Yes."

"You dreamed of the Lost Child."

"Yes. Did you dream it, too?"

She looked from the spikers to the Orlans.

"You were all in my dream. The Lost Child returned to watch over you all."

Caressa listened with suspicion.

"What has this hoodie dream to do with the Orlans?"

"I don't know," said Morning Star humbly. "All I know is that you were there. All the Orlans were there."

Caressa was far from convinced by this, but she could hear the excitement in the lines of Orlans behind her. She met the Wildman's eyes. Shab was forgotten.

"What do you say, Wildman?"

"I say we're going to build a new Garden."

"And if we don't?"

"We go back to killing each other."

Caressa nodded at that. She didn't believe in Morning Star's dream, but she was no fool. She could see that this bizarre intervention offered them all a way out of the deadly standoff. So she turned to her army and gave the order.

"Sheathe your swords! Break ranks! Let's all get ourselves some breakfast."

The armies dispersed, and the moment of crisis passed. The Wildman beckoned to Morning Star and they walked away together down the riverbank until they could speak without being overheard.

"So what was that all about, Star?"

"What do you mean?"

"That was an act, wasn't it?"

"Was it?"

"I've heard your dreams before, remember?"

"It worked, didn't it?"

"So no dream. No Lost Child."

"There could be."

"What's that supposed to mean?"

"You wouldn't understand."

"Try me."

She looked at him doubtfully, but what she saw in his face was not mockery—it was curiosity. This was the Wildman who had wanted to be a Noble Warrior, and had wanted to find peace. So she did her best to explain what she herself only half understood.

"I realized something in the night that changed my ideas about gods. It's about the way round things go. With most things, you see something, like you see the river. You dive in, you feel the cool water, you know it's real, so you believe it's there. I thought it was like that with gods. You go to the Garden, you feel the power of the All and Only, you believe the god's there. But maybe it's the other way round. Maybe it starts with believing, and then the god comes."

"So we build a new Garden and the All and Only comes and lives in it."

"Maybe."

"And maybe not."

"That's what we'll find out."

"How are we going to find out?"

"We're going to build the Garden, all of us, all the spikers, all the Orlans, because people need gods. If you have nothing to believe in, you have nowhere to go."

The Wildman studied her face in silence. She did not smile.

"You're quite something, aren't you, Star? Smooth as a feather, sharp as a claw."

The slap of a sail in the wind drew their eyes to the river. A barge was just getting under way, sitting low in the water, its deck crowded with mourners. In their midst, beneath a white canopy, lay the body of the Joy Boy, now beginning his last slow journey to the distant sea.

"You going to do it?" said Morning Star.

"Just tell me where," replied the Wildman.

⊰ 21 ⊱

A Bell Rings

SEEKER FOLLOWED THE ROAD WEST. AS HE WENT, HE felt a deep rumble in the land and smelled a sweet heavy smell on the air. Whether these were true sensations or the product of his fear he could not tell. But it seemed to him that Manlir was following him, watching him, readying his revenge. But why then did he wait?

Ahead lay the great forest; and beyond the forest, the land of crags and tines that marked the limits of his known world. He was retracing his own route, the track he had followed with such urgency and single-mindedness when he had been a hunter. Now he was racing against time to reach an unknown destination, trusting a memory he did not know he possessed.

We have been there before, Jango had told him.

From time to time he encountered other travellers on the road, but they passed him by with no more than the usual greetings, and he did not accept their invitations to join them. He travelled faster alone.

At a point where the road passed once more between trees, he heard the sound of a distant bell. It was a tinny clanging sound that he knew he had heard before. He stopped, and was at once so overwhelmed by memories that tears came to his eyes.

It was the sound of the school bell on Anacrea. In his mind's eye, as clearly as if he was in the school yard again, he saw the children returning to their classroom at the end of morning break. There, already at his desk, gazing out of the window, sat the lonely pale-faced boy he had once been.

He looked into the trees to see who had rung the bell. The ringing had ceased. He heard running footsteps. A man came bounding out of the trees, a thin man with a bald head and sunken eyes. He was waving and calling.

"Come and look!" he cried.

Seeker saw with a shock that it was Narrow Path. The high brow and the gaunt features were unchanged, but it was clear that he no longer recognized him. The sharp intelligence of those deep-set eyes had been replaced with a childish eagerness. Seeker knew at once that he had been cleansed.

"A puzzle!" Narrow Path cried. "A mystery! Come and look!"

Seeker felt a surge of anger at the Community that had ordered so terrible a punishment, and guilt because the punishment should have been his. Narrow Path had freed him from his prison in the Nom and had paid the price.

Now he was tugging on his arm, drawing him away from the road. Seeker let himself be led into the trees.

Narrow Path came to a stop before a tree. Pointing, smiling, wrinkling his bald brow, he showed Seeker a coat that hung from one of the branches.

"That's a good coat," he said. "A fine coat. I'd like to have a coat like that, for the nights."

Seeker felt a wave of pity.

"Do you sleep in the open?"

"Where else would I sleep?" replied Narrow Path. "I have no home."

"You had a home once."

But Narrow Path was only interested in the coat.

"I could wrap it round me and lie down on the soft grass and I'd sleep like a baby."

"Then take it."

"But it's not mine. Someone left it hanging on this tree. I've been watching it since yesterday. No one's come back to get it. Don't you think that's strange?"

"I think you should take it," said Seeker, wanting him to be happy. "It's doing no good to anyone hanging here."

"Oh, no." Narrow Path shook his head several times. "I can't take it. It's not mine. If he were to give it to me, that would be different." He looked wistfully at the coat. "But I can't just take it."

All through this absurd exchange Seeker was remembering the old Narrow Path, and was overwhelmed by sadness.

"It's not your coat, is it?" said Narrow Path.

Seeker looked away.

"Yes. It's my coat. I left it there for you."

"For me! You're giving the coat to me?"

"Yes."

"For me!" A smile of simple joy filled Narrow Path's face. "It's just what I want."

A cloud of doubt swept away the smile.

"But why would you give me such a good coat?"

"Because I knew you once. You did me a good turn."

"Did I?"

It was enough. Narrow Path's curiosity did not extend to this shared past. The coat filled his mind. Carefully, reverently, he took it down from the tree.

"It's so heavy!"

Seeker wondered as he watched him if the cleansing process could be reversed. His power was very great. If he could give life back to the Wildman, why should he not be able to give Narrow Path back his memory of his own past?

"You don't know who you are, do you?" he said.

Narrow Path was trying the coat on now, feeling his thin arms into the sleeves.

"Your name is Narrow Path. You were a Noble Warrior."

"There!" he said, drawing the lapels close. "I thought it might be too big, but the length is just right."

"Don't you want to know who you are?"

He stared at Seeker.

"Why would I want to know who I am? I want to know where I'm to find my next meal, and how I'm to pay for it. I want to know if strangers on the road will harm me. But as for who I am—I don't see what there is to know. Here I am, and that's all there is to be said about that."

"Yes," said Seeker. "You're right."

"What's this?" Narrow Path shook the coat. "There's something heavy in here. Why!"—he pulled out a gold coin—"It's gold!"

"Better still," said Seeker.

"But who does it belong to?"

"The owner of the coat."

"And who's that?"

"You."

"Me!" Once again his face lit up. "I have a coat! And I have gold for food! There's nothing else I need. What a lucky day for me!"

He hugged the coat round him, turning from side to side.

"I shall tell my friend. He'll be so happy! And you shall meet him, so that he can thank you, too."

"No need. I must be on my way."

There came again the sound of the bell. Narrow Path smiled to hear it.

"There! My friend is calling me."

"It's your friend, ringing that bell?"

"Yes, yes. That's his way of calling me. Sometimes I get lost, you see."

"Then I would like to meet your friend after all."

Narrow Path's face lit up with joy.

"Come," he said. "My two best friends will meet."

He led Seeker through the trees. Not far from the road, by the side of a deep fast-flowing stream, there was a woodsman's hut, a small shelter built of brushwood. Before its doorless entrance stood a little old man with a bell in his hand.

It was the school meek from Anacrea.

"Gift!" cried Seeker. "It's you!"

The meek nodded his head and smiled.

"I heard you were on the road," he said.

"Look!" cried Narrow Path, spinning in his heavy coat to make the tails fly out. "He's given me a coat!"

"Heard from who?" said Seeker.

"From the other meeks."

"There's gold in the coat!" Narrow Path held his gold coin up for Gift to see. "We won't go hungry again!"

"We've not gone hungry yet, my friend," said Gift.

"Nor we have. But I shall get out the gold even so and count it."

He went inside the hut.

Seeker saw the way in which Gift was looking at him, as if he was searching to learn something.

"So what brings you here, Gift?"

"My friend." The meek nodded at the hut. "He needs a companion for now."

"You didn't choose to join in the great gathering, with my father?"

"No. But I hope to serve your father again soon."

"You think he'll open another school?"

"If the All and Only so wills."

Narrow Path poked his head out of the hut.

"Is your name, by any chance," he asked, "Seeker after Truth?"

"Yes," said Seeker.

"There!" Narrow Path was pleased. "My friend has spoken so much about you. You are the one who is to save us all. And you have given me this fine coat."

He disappeared again.

Gift had turned away and was fiddling about by the smoldering remains of a fire.

"Gift," said Seeker. "What is this?"

"Just the talk among the meeks."

"I'm the one who is to save us all?"

"Who knows, master?"

"You know, it seems."

He heard a new voice speak then.

Surely you know it's you who will save me.

He looked round, startled. But of course the voice was inside his own head, as it had been long ago.

"We mustn't keep you, master," said Gift. "There's so little time."

"You're right. I must go. Thank you for your kindness to this poor man. He doesn't deserve such punishment."

"And yet he's as happy as any man I know."

Seeker left him then and headed back through the trees towards the high road. As he went he thought over all that Gift had said, and he became more and more puzzled at the extent of his knowledge. Then he recalled how Gift had said, "There's so little time"—the very words Jango had used. On a sudden impulse, he turned and strode back through the trees.

He found Gift now crouched over the fire, fanning its embers back to life.

"I've been very stupid, haven't I?" he said.

"How have you been stupid, master?"

"You're not just a school servant. What are you?"

"I'm a meek."

"Then who are the meeks?"

Gift went on fanning the embers. A flame flickered briefly and died.

"We are the servants of the servants of the All and Only."

"I remember you with a broom, sweeping leaves in the school yard."

"We are sweepers, yes. And pan scourers. And water carriers. And fire lighters."

The embers burst now into full flame. Gift fed the new fire with kindling.

"Why do you do such humble tasks?" asked Seeker.

"It's our service to the All and Only. We each of us have our tasks. You too, Seeker."

Your life is an experiment in search of the truth.

The voice spoke in Seeker's head. A sudden suspicion dawned. "Did you hear the voice I just heard?"

"In a way."

"Was it your voice?"

The old meek looked up at him and smiled. "In a way."

"You put the voice into my head!"

"I did that time, yes."

"How?"

"Oh, that's part of our training. It's not hard."

"Whose training?"

"The meeks."

Seeker gave him a long intent look.

"Do it again."

Surely you know that where your way lies, the door is always open.

It was startling, uncanny. The words sounded in his own head like a thought spoken out loud.

"Was it you all along? Putting voices into my head?"

"Not me. Other meeks."

Seeker thought back to the first day he had heard the voice, when he had thrown himself down in his sadness before the Garden. Yes, there had been a meek somewhere behind him. He recalled the rustle of the broom as he swept.

"I thought the voice came from the Lost Child. It was a child's voice."

"How you hear the voice is up to you."

"But all the other times—"

"We're never far away. But it's better that we go unnoticed. We do the work that makes us invisible."

Seeker now blushed in shame at the memory of every meek he had ever met. He had paid them no attention. He had considered them to be of no account.

"I never knew."

"You didn't need to know. You have your task. We have ours."

"Tell me, Gift, truly. Are you Nomana, too?"

"No. We're meeks. We have a different mission from the Noble Warriors'. Though we all work to the same end."

"What end is that?"

"A kind of healing."

Seeker shook his head, ashamed and amazed.

"I never knew," he said again.

"I think you knew," said Gift. "But you have forgotten. You have more memories than you know."

"How, Gift? Make me understand. Am I older than I know?"

Narrow Path now came out of the hut, his cupped hands brimming with gold coins.

"There are hundreds!" he cried. "More than I can ever count!" Then his face fell. "I shall be robbed!" He turned in sudden anxiety to Gift. "How can we keep our gold from the robbers? *He* may be a robber."

This was directed at Seeker. Narrow Path clutched his gold to his chest as if Seeker might take it from him then and there.

"Throw it in the stream," said Gift. "The robbers will never find it there."

"Throw it in the stream! Of course!"

Narrow Path hurried to the stream bank and began to throw the shining coins, one by one, into the water.

"Go, master," said Gift to Seeker. "Find the True Nom."

Splash! splash! went the golden coins as they sank down into the water. Gift nodded at Seeker, and Seeker knew that the meek had no more to tell him.

He went on his way.

As he reached the high road, he saw a flock of passing birds and heard their harsh cries. They were seagulls, far inland. Then, deeper than the cries of the birds, he heard the boom at the heart of the land.

My enemy is everywhere. I am no longer the hunter, I am the prey.

So let him find me.

"Here I am!" he cried aloud. "Why do you wait? Here I am!"

THE FOURTH STAGE
OF THE
EXPERIMENT

PROOF

*I am alive and not alive. I play my part in this
long experiment without knowing what it is I do. This
is a trial of all men through the trial of one man.*

*If he loses himself and finds the beauty round him;
if he comes face-to-face with the All and Only at last; if
he holds me in his arms and I see in his eyes that he
has found the truth; then I will have my proof.*

⇥ 22 ⇤

Act As If You Believe

MORNING STAR RODE IN THE LEAD, ALONE. BEHIND HER rode the Wildman at the head of his army of foot soldiers. They marched along in groups and gaggles, no orderly force, but in high spirits and glad to be on the move. Behind the fighting men trailed their women and children, their beasts and chattels, to form a long dusty train moving across the plains.

Alongside the spikers and keeping pace with them rode Caressa Jahan and her Orlans. Smaller in number than the great spiker army, the Orlans kept to their ranks as they rode, proudly conscious that they were trained warriors. They too looked ahead to Morning Star, who was leading them to a new beginning.

Pico, loping along beside the Wildman, shaded his eyes against the glare of the sun and stared ahead.

"That's the lake," he said. "We're going to the lake."

"Could be," said the Wildman.

"We're going to Radiance."

"Could be."

"But chief, that's no place for a god. Radiance is a ghost city."

"You afraid of ghosts, Pico?"

The two armies marched into Radiance as the day was ending. At first sight the city seemed to be abandoned. Goats foraged in the gutters, and the doors of the houses hung open on smashed hinges. Roofs stripped of tiles exposed bare rafters. The water in the troughs at the crossings was stagnant and slimy.

Spikers and Orlans alike fell silent as they passed down the looted streets, shocked by the devastation. Here and there a scurry of movement behind broken windows revealed that there were people hiding in the houses, but whoever they were, they stayed out of sight. Wild yellow cats, casting long shadows as they prowled, turned their slit eyes on the newcomers and slunk slowly away.

Morning Star led the armies into the temple square. Here beneath the towering shadow of the temple rock, a marketplace had sprung up, where looters spread out their wares on cloths on the paved ground. The old stalls in the arcades were gone, smashed and burned in the fires that were to be seen everywhere. The dealers who now squatted beneath the arches had pitifully few goods on display: here a row of three drinking glasses, here a string of onions, here a single pair of shoes.

The people in the square fell back as the armies entered, and huddled round the arcades—staring and curious. The Wildman looked up at the high rock and pulled a face.

"Smells of death," he said.

Caressa rode up beside him. She pointed with her silver-handled whip at the temple, with its imposing gates.

"That where the king used to live?"

"Yes," said the Wildman. "The king and the priests."

"Then that'll do for me."

She rode towards the broad steps that led up to the temple gates. The Wildman went after her.

"Not so fast, Princess," he said. "Who says the Orlans get to live in the king's palace?"

"I say."

"And I say this is a spiker city now. And I say spikers rule."

"Not me, boy. No one gives me orders."

"I don't give orders, Princess. I do as I please."

Caressa dismounted and climbed the steps, gesturing to her men to follow her.

"Open these gates! Clear a way for the Jahan of Jahans!"

The Wildman too jumped off his horse and strode up the steps, shouting to his chiefs.

"Heya, bravas! Spikers to the top of the rock!"

Morning Star did not go with them. Her eyes had fallen on a small crowd huddled round a fire. There was a trestle table by the fire, on which were lined up many small clay pots. Two men stood at the table, crying their wares. Morning Star recognized them at once. They were Ease and Solace, the tribute traders who had seized her and sold her as a living sacrifice.

"Come with me," she said to the spikers nearest to her. "I'm going to need your help."

She crossed the square and heard the traders' cry.

"Treasured remains!" Ease was calling out, holding up a small clay pot. "Do you have a loved one murdered by the priests? Take home a relic of their sacrifice!"

"Respectfully raised from the lake," said Solace, raking with a fork in the glowing embers of the fire. "Purified by fire."

"The honored ashes of our beloved dead!" cried Ease. "Treasured remains! One gold shilling a jar!"

Morning Star pushed her way through the little crowd.

"Give me one of those," she said.

"Certainly, lady. You have a loved one who fell from the high rock? One shilling, lady."

Morning Star took one of the clay pots from the table, and holding it up for all to see, she let it fall to the ground. The pot shattered, spraying ashes onto the paving stones.

"Desecration!" exclaimed Ease.

"These men sold the living," Morning Star cried. "Now they sell the dead."

"Oh, you wicked woman!"

"Seize them!" said Morning Star to the spikers who had accompanied her. "Tie their hands!"

"For what? Is it a crime to honor the fallen?"

The spikers had the two traders by the arms and now proceeded to bind them with leather straps.

"You don't remember me," said Morning Star, "but I remember you. You tied me up, as you're tied up now, and you sold me to be thrown from the temple rock."

Beckoning the spikers to bring the captives after her, she strode across the square to the temple rock.

"Where are you taking us? What right do you have to do this to us?"

"You'll find out."

"Even if we've done wrong in the past," wheedled Ease, "you wouldn't want to lower yourself to our level, would you?"

Morning Star reached the base of the steps cut into the high rock and began to climb.

"No!" cried Ease. "Not the rock! I won't go up the rock!"

Morning Star stopped and turned to the spikers.

"These men are tribute traders. If they refuse to climb the rock, throw them to the ground and stamp them to death."

"I'm climbing," said Solace. "See, I'm climbing."

Morning Star continued up the steep steps, climbing flight after flight, and the spikers with their captives followed behind. Ease maintained a flow of whining speech all the way.

"Maybe we did make some mistakes in the time of the priests, lady, but if there were deaths, who was to blame for that? We never hurt a soul, not even your good self, your honesty compels you to admit that. Is it our fault if the priests were wicked and deluded? What a blessing it is that no one will ever inflict such cruelties again! Cruelty is a terrible thing, lady, as you know more than most. You know the horror and the wickedness of those monstrous sacrifices."

His words came more slowly as the exertion of the long climb began to take its toll, but he never ceased talking.

"What a blessing it is that power is now in the hands of those who have the most reason to be merciful. You being a lady, good lady, will have a natural tendency towards mercy. I know in my heart that where we were weak, you'll be strong. You'll show all the world what it is to have a noble heart."

As they reached the top of the rock, the spikers asked, "Where do you want them, little mother?"

"By the edge," said Morning Star. "Blindfold them."

"Little mother!" cried Ease. "He called you little mother! A mother doesn't hurt her children!"

"Why are we to be blindfolded?" said Solace, faint with terror.

The spikers tied cloths tightly round the tribute traders' eyes. When they were blindfolded, Morning Star ordered the spikers to walk them across the rock terrace.

"Mercy, little mother!" cried Ease.

"You shall have mercy," said Morning Star. "In my mercy I've blindfolded you. You can't see the drop. But I can see it." She stood on the western lip, where the tributes had been made to stand, and looked down. "It's a long, long way down to the water. You sold me to this death. Did you ever think what it would be like to fall from this rock?"

"Please, lady," said Ease, now sobbing. "Those were different times. We all make mistakes."

"Will your stomach melt as you fall? Will you be able to breathe with the wind whipping in your face?"

"I don't want to die!"

"And when you hit the water, do you die quickly, or do you lie broken in the water and drown?"

"No! No-o!"

Both of them were now convulsed with sobs of terror.

"Hold them by the edge!" ordered Morning Star. "Sacrifice them for all the innocent men and women they've sent to their deaths! Throw them down!"

They screamed as they fell, uttering terrible high-pitched cries of despair. But the edge over which they had been pushed was not the great drop down to the water. They fell no farther than one flight of the rock steps. There they lay, at the bottom of the steps, bruised and moaning.

"You should have made them take the big jump, little mother," said the spikers. "Scum like that don't deserve to live."

"I came close," said Morning Star. "So very close." She shuddered and moved away from the high cliff's edge. "Let them go now."

The shaken tribute traders were released from their bonds. Morning Star watched as they limped down the steps to the square below. Across the lake the sun was now setting, as it had been setting when she stood here a year ago, surrounded by the pomp and ritual of the court of Radiance.

Caressa and her men now emerged by the internal stairs onto the open terrace, followed by the Wildman and his spiker chiefs. They were still quarrelling.

"This is where I'll stand and greet my people," Caressa said. She went to the terrace wall and waved to the crowd in the square below. A cheer went up from the Orlans. "Jahan! Jahan!"

"This is where I'll stand," said the Wildman. "A spiker lord in a spiker city."

He too cried down to the men below.

"Heya! Do you lo-o-ove me?"

"Wildman!" they cried. "Wildman! Wildman!"

"Neither of you will stand here," said Morning Star. "This is where we will build the new Garden."

The Wildman and Caressa stared at her in disbelief.

"Here! In the temple!"

"On this rock."

"The temple's in ruins!" said Caressa. "The place is a dump!"

"What sort of god would want to live here?" said the Wildman.

"This is the place," said Morning Star. "This will be the home of the All and Only. I've seen it in my dream."

She walked away from them, back to the western lip. Caressa and the Wildman looked at each other.

"Is she crazy?" said Caressa.

"Could be," said the Wildman.

"Let me talk to her alone."

Caressa joined Morning Star. The descending sun was

close to the water now, turning the gleaming surface of the lake a deep coral pink.

"You can tell me the truth," said Caressa in a low voice. "This dream of yours. It fools a lot of people, but it doesn't fool me. So don't think I don't know."

"That's just what I think," said Morning Star, her eyes on the sun. "I think you don't know. I think you don't know anything. But I do know."

She spoke with a hard, clear assurance that Caressa had never heard from her before.

"The Garden will be built," she said. "The god will come. The people will believe. Even the Orlans will believe."

She turned her gaze on Caressa.

"The Orlans will believe because you will tell them to believe. You are the Jahan of Jahans."

Caressa was awed. The quiet, plain-faced girl was transformed. She had become sure and strong and magnificent.

"How can I tell them to believe?" she said. "I don't believe myself."

"Act as if you believe," said Morning Star.

The Wildman, grown impatient, now joined them.

"So now we're here," he said, "what do we do?"

Caressa turned to him.

"She says we're to build a home for the god up here," she said. "You believe in the hoodie god, Wildman?"

"Can't say I don't," said the Wildman slowly. "Can't say I do. Seems like I half believe."

Caressa looked at his golden skin, warmed by the light of the setting sun, and thought how beautiful he was.

"I'll do it if you will," she said.

"Heya, Princess. Why not?"

The sun sank at last beneath the horizon. The sky glowed with the fading sunset.

"Build it," said Morning Star, "and the Lost Child will return."

Over the days that followed, the two armies gradually restored order to the shattered city. The frightened people came out of hiding, and the bandit gangs that had ruled the streets were driven away. The six floors of the temple were cleared, swept, and cleaned, and teams of builders and gardeners set about transforming the summit of the rock. A wall rose up, built of rough-edged stones set in such a way that little chinks of light pierced the mortar in a thousand places. Barrels of soil were hauled to the top and tipped inside the wall. Young trees and bushes and grasses and flowers were planted. The tanks that had held the tributes were filled with water pumped up from the lake, and from the tanks a channel was cut to trickle water into the newly created garden. The work went on rapidly because all the laborers knew what they were building and were excited by it. They were making a home for a god.

Morning Star kept to herself over these days, because wherever she was recognized she was besieged by people calling on her for help. To escape the burden of prayers, she went out riding on Sky, and rode farther each day, taking the little-used tracks to the east. Sky asked her no questions and made no demands. The beautiful Caspian shared her solitude and her silence beneath the endless summer sky.

Then one day she returned to the city and found the people had been looking out for her.

"Little mother!" they cried joyfully. "We thought you'd left us!"

"Not yet," she said.

"The work is finished! The Garden is built!"

"Then we must keep vigil," said Morning Star. "The Lost Child will come to the Garden tonight."

⇥ 23 ⇤

The Return of the Lost Child

THEY BUILT A GREAT BONFIRE IN THE TEMPLE SQUARE, and the spikers and the Orlans and the people of the city crowded between the broken arcades to watch for the coming of the god. A half-moon rose in the sky, and by its light they gazed up at the new stone wall on the top of the temple rock, within which lay the new Garden. The wall had no doors or windows and was twice the height of a man. If the god was to enter the Garden, he would have to fall down from the sky like a star.

The waiting people were curious and excited but unsure how much to believe.

"How's any god to get in there?" said some.

"There's no god," said others. "They're telling us stories, same as the priests told us stories before."

Caressa heard the people talking among themselves,

and she became increasingly nervous as the night hours passed. She conferred with the Wildman.

"What if nothing happens? What do we do?"

"Star'll know what to do."

"Wildman, she's funny in the head. You only have to look at her."

"So maybe she knows things we don't know."

"And maybe she's making fools of us both."

Morning Star was not in the crowd in the temple square. Quite where she was no one knew.

Midnight came and went, and some of the people left, no longer believing any god would come. The rest huddled together and slept round the glowing bonfire.

"This is stupid," said Caressa. "I'm tired and nothing's going to happen. Let's sleep."

"You sleep if you want," said the Wildman. "I'll call you if something happens."

Then something did happen. There came the sounds of a faraway voice singing and the tread of many feet. Those who were awake round the fire prodded their sleeping companions.

"Wake up! Someone's coming!"

A flickering column of lanterns wound its way down the street and into the square, and with it came the song, high and clear.

> "Mother who made us
> Father who guides us
> Child who needs us
> Light of our days and peace of our nights . . ."

The lantern-bearers formed an escort. In their midst, lit by their swaying lights, walked Morning Star, head held high, eyes fixed on the temple rock, singing. The crowd woke and watched, filled once more with eager anticipation.

"It's the little mother," they told each other. "The child will come now."

Morning Star crossed the square and made her way up the many flights of steps that clung to the side of the great rock, singing all the way.

> *"We wake in your shadow*
> *We walk in your footsteps*
> *We sleep in your arms . . ."*

The Wildman watched her climb, with bright eyes.

"Heya," he said softly to Caressa. "Star won't let us down."

> *"Lead us to the Garden*
> *To rest in the Garden*
> *To live in the Garden*
> *With you . . ."*

Now the people in the square could see her emerge onto the top level of the rock, lit by the ring of lanterns, silhouetted against the moonlit sky. She stood before the stone wall that was to be the new Garden, and there her song came to an end. Like everyone else in the city that night, she too now waited for the coming of the Lost Child.

The sight filled the crowd with a new intensity of anticipation.

"You see," they told each other. "The god'll come now."

"How will we know?"

"You just know. That's how it is with gods."

Candle sellers moved through the crowd, crying their wares. "Light a candle to greet the god!"

"What do I want a candle for?"

"Shine a light for the Lost Child to find his way!"

Once one person had bought a candle and lit it, others began to think it must be the thing to do, and soon the square was a sea of candle flames. Everyone was now awake and eagerly staring up at the high Garden.

"Must be soon now," they told one another, seeing the faint twinkle of the morning star on the dawn horizon. Tired though they were, none slept. All wanted to see the coming of the god.

Caressa felt the tension acutely.

"Wildman," she whispered. "What do we do? The sun'll come up, there'll be no god, and what do we do?"

"I got a feeling about this one, Princess. I feel like it's going to work out."

"Then it needs to be soon. Look east."

Many eyes were looking east. The ridge of mountains was now rimmed with pale light. A rumor sprang up and ran through the crowd that the god would come with the sunrise. Some watched the glow on the horizon; others kept their eyes fixed on the stone wall high on the temple rock, eager to be the first to spot the moment the god entered the Garden.

"There! I saw something! I think I saw—"

A young woman in the crowd pointed, stammering in her excitement.

"What? Where?"

The sun broke over the mountains. People looked from the sudden dazzle of light to the temple rock. The rays of the rising sun pierced the cracks between the stones and lit up the Garden like a lantern.

Morning Star suddenly let out an unearthly cry. The sound caused a sensation. All eyes reached up to gaze on the dazzle of the Garden.

"I see it! I see it!"

Many more now thought they saw movement in the Garden. The excitement infected all those round them.

"See! Something moving!"

"Where?"

"I see it! I see it!"

"It's a little child! Oh, the dear one!"

"There! I see it!"

The whole crowd was in a ferment now. Those who had seen nothing to start with now supposed they too saw movement—a figure, a child—and seeing, weeping with joy, they believed.

"The god has come! The child will protect us!"

"I never thought I'd live to see this day!"

"Now all our troubles are over!"

Caressa looked from the temple rock to the Wildman and back to the temple rock.

"I don't see it, Wildman. What do you see?"

"I see what they see," said the Wildman.

Caressa looked round at the ecstatic crowd and shook her head in admiration.

"Act as if you believe, and they'll believe."

The big gate of Cheerful Giver's old house stood open, and the courtyard inside was littered with leaves and the remains of fires, but Morning Star remembered it well. She crossed to the cellar steps and went down into the dark space below. She stood there, letting her eyes adjust to the light that fell through the grated air hole. She had been tethered here and had expected to die. But for all the terror of those days, she found herself envying her younger self. She still had her colors then. She still had her dream of becoming a Noble Warrior. She still had her faith in the god of the Garden.

Now what was left?

She had watched the joyful crowd from the top of the temple rock and felt only sadness. It clung to her like a blanket of darkness. Everything had happened as she had said it would, but there was nothing there. The people believed because they wanted to believe. They had passed the night waiting and watching for the god to come, and so the god had come. She felt no superiority over them. How could she? She too had once believed in the god, and with as little reason. The very eagerness with which this crowd now embraced belief told her that there was no god, only the hunger for a god. She shared their hunger, but could not share their faith. Seeker would understand.

"Where are you, Seeker?"

She spoke aloud, knowing there was no one to hear.

"Find me. Help me. I'm in prison, here in the darkness."

This time of course no voice came to her from the grating. So she climbed back up out of the cellar into the bright light of the courtyard. And there was the Wildman.

"Been looking all over for you," he said.

"I've been keeping away," said Morning Star. "I'm not good company these days."

"What is it, Star? You should be proud. You made it all happen."

"For everyone else, maybe. Not for me."

They sat down side by side on the step that led up to the house's main door. The sunlight glittered on the Wildman's bracelets.

"You're going to go look for him, aren't you?"

"Yes."

"Think that'll help?"

"No."

They grinned at each other.

"Things keep on changing, Star. Never know what's coming."

"You got what you want, Wildman?"

"Some. Not all."

"What's left to want?"

"Oh, you know. Me and Caressa, we don't seem to be able to sit quiet. She's a bitch with a bark, that one."

"You never were any good at sitting quiet."

"Maybe not. But I'll tell you what, Star. There's one thing I can't get out of my head. First thing I ever heard from a hoodie: 'Seek your own peace,' he said."

"Still looking for peace?"

"Don't know that I'm looking. No, I'd say I've just about given up."

"Maybe you found it."

"Not a chance. Not with Caressa and her yabba-yabba in my face all day."

One of the Wildman's men came into the courtyard looking for him.

"Go away," said the Wildman.

The spiker retreated to the street outside.

"Always someone pestering me."

"Maybe you found your peace," Morning Star said again. "Maybe you just don't know it. Peace isn't the same thing as quietness."

"So what is it?"

"Being right with yourself. Being who you really are. Living the life you were made to live."

"Heya, Star! Where'd you learn that?"

"I don't know. I just thought it."

"So have you found your peace?"

"No. Not yet. But I think you have, Wildman. I think when you're fighting with Caressa, you're at peace."

The Wildman let out a great laugh.

"That crazy woman! She'll give me no peace for as long as I live!"

Morning Star looked at his golden laughing face and remembered how she had loved him with such intensity that it hurt her just to look at him. It didn't hurt now. Not one bit.

"I do love you, Wildman," she said.

⊰ 24 ⊱

Look with Your Own Eyes

THE GREAT FOREST WAS BEHIND SEEKER NOW, AND THE
flatlands, and he was following the winding road that
climbed the western hills. The sun was in his eyes and the
wind was at his back and he was moving fast. The shivering of the land was with him all the time now, the deep
boom sounding behind him every few minutes, always a
little closer with each reverberation. He felt he was being
herded as a shepherd sets his dogs to herd his sheep, letting them show their teeth but never permitting them to
attack. His enemy was guiding him to his destination, for
a purpose he did not yet understand.

Manlir meant him to find the True Nom.

Now as he came over the ridge, a view opened up before him that made him stop and stare. It was the valley
of the Scar, lit by the descending western sun. He had

come this way before, travelling eastward, hunting the fleeing savanters.

So I've come back.

He looked down on the harsh glory of the desert valley, with its towering stone spires that stood like sentinels
down its dusty way, and the high jagged crag of the Scar.
It was a pitiless landscape, but it was magnificent. The warm
wind blew on his back, urging him on. And carried on
the wind, relentless, inescapable, the sound of the one who
drove him, the deep beat of a distant drum, the tread of
an army's marching feet.

He descended the hillside and strode on between the
high tines. Now that he was among them, they clustered
before him like the trunks of trees in some giant winter forest. He passed from inky shadow to golden sunlight and
back again, as the sun sank towards the Scar. He moved fast,
loping now over the dry land, feeling the wind on his back,
racing for the same goal, seeker and hunter. Surely now they
were close. He scanned the valley as he ran, looking for a
doorway, certain now that he was very close. But all he saw
were the stripes of light and dark, and the dazzling sun ahead.

He slowed to a walk so that he could look about him
with closer attention. It must be near, it must be here, he
sensed it so strongly: the door into the True Nom. But
there were no buildings, no walls, no doors. Only this leaf-
less forest of stone, these guardian columns through which
he was passing.

He looked up. The sky above him was a soft blue, a
muted ever-deepening blue as the calm sky yielded slowly

to night. He looked down again, at the sunlit columns of stone.

Why do I feel I know this place so well?

The elusive memory teased the edges of his mind for a few moments longer. Then as he gave up the search, it flickered into view.

Of course.

All this time he had been looking for the entrance to the True Nom—but he was in it. He had entered it an hour and more ago. This was the Cloister Court, this entire pillared valley. Surely he was inside the True Nom and was approaching its heart, which could only be the great crag called the Scar.

He fixed his eyes on the dark mass, now silhouetted against the sunset sky. He walked on until he reached the rim of its shadow, and there he came to a stop. If this was the heart of the True Nom, the Garden within was well guarded indeed. The towering cliff of rock was a far more formidable obstacle than a high silver fence. But he remembered the last time he had been here. When the sun had set, for a few short moments the Scar revealed its many portals.

The deep boom sounded all round him. He turned to look, as if Manlir might rise up in the form of an old man, or in the form of the Joy Boy, and confront him at last. But he saw no one—only the changing colors of the sky reflected on the high stone tines, and the distant hills beyond.

"Where are you?" he called. "Why do you wait?"

But he knew now what they were both waiting for. They were waiting for sunset, with its gold and scarlet key.

The shadow of the Scar crept over him, bringing with

it cooler air. He looked back at that forbidding height and
saw the red sun touch its rim. He held his gaze steadily on
the rock face, and drew deep slow breaths. Then the disc
of the sun slipped down behind the rim of rock, and the
Scar began to glow. Light burst through the mighty rock
face, turning the monolith into a burning pyre. As the setting sun descended unseen, the Scar was pierced and jewelled and starred with brilliance. A lance of light, hurled
from the crag, sliced across the land to Seeker's feet. The
rays of the sun came streaming through a slot briefly illuminated in the Scar: a slot like a doorway.

He walked towards it, slowly at first, then faster, then
at a run. He clambered up and found that the high fissure
was wide enough for him to pass through. Its base sloped
upwards, a bed of loose scree on which he scrambled as
he hurried to climb. Up and up, eyes squinting into the
dazzle of sunlight, until the enclosing walls on either side
fell away. He found himself standing on a high narrow
ledge looking down into a great hollow. The hollow was
dense with trees and shrubs and grasses. Beyond the trees
was the gleam of water.

I'm in the Garden.

But not quite in. The ledge on which he stood was
high above the hollow, and there was no path down. The
light was changing every moment as the sun set. Already
the far side of the Garden was in shadow. Then he heard
the sound of his pursuer behind him, the beat sounding
faster now: *boom-boom-boom*. Seeker did not hesitate. He
launched himself off the ledge as if it were no more than
a grassy hill before him.

He fell, and rolled, covering his head with his arms as he went; and as he rolled, he heard the sound of crashing and thought that his enemy was falling after him. But when he came to rest and looked about him, he found he was alone.

Shaken but unhurt, he rose to his feet. There before him was a verdant wilderness, far bigger and deeper and more mysterious than it had looked from above. It was in shadow now, lit only by the diffused glow of the sky. This tender twilight made the scene all the more beautiful in Seeker's eyes—vast and secret, a fitting refuge for a Wounded Warrior, a Lost Child.

He made his way into the trees, pushing through deep undergrowth, looking round him as he went. He saw no living creature. He thought he heard a sound behind, but when he stopped and looked, there was nothing.

He came after a while to the water. It was a large pool; more than a pool, a lake. It glowed with light, its clear water bubbling where an underground stream rose up to feed it. The rippled water shivered the reflections of the overhanging trees. He stood by its verge and knelt down and cupped his hands to drink. The water was cold. He splashed his face and neck, burned by the long walk in the sun. Then rising to his feet again, he saw that the lake was crossed by a low bridge, an unrailed timber track raised a few inches above the water's surface. This bridge, barely wide enough for one person to walk, disappeared into the shadows on the far side. There, surely, he would come to the end of his journey.

It struck Seeker then that the sounds that had followed him ever since the end of the Great Embrace were now silenced. Manlir had not entered the Garden after him. Or if he had come, he had come quietly.

He followed the lake's margin to the start of the bridge. He tested the planks with one foot. The surface was slippery, but the structure supported his weight. He crossed the bridge slowly, steadily, reaching fearfully with his eyes before him. The lake was very wide, wider than he had supposed, and the bridge was longer. For a time he was alone in a silvery world, held between water and sky. Then the far shore came into view. There among the trees a shelter waited for him, a natural bower formed by overarching branches.

In the bower stood a chair.

Seeker strained to see through the shadows. For a little while he could not tell what he saw. It seemed to him that the chair was empty, but he must come closer to be certain. He scanned the surrounding trees as best as he could in the gathering darkness, but he saw no sign of life. As far as he could tell, he was alone.

Then he heard a sound behind him: the soft fall of bare feet on the timbers of the bridge. He turned and saw the figure of an old man coming slowly towards him, moving with the aid of a stick, crossing the black strip between the softly glowing panes of still water.

"Jango?"

The old man raised his stick in answer. His frail voice called out to Seeker over the water.

"Do you see?"

"No," said Seeker, his own voice sounding loud in the stillness. "I see nothing."

"Look again. Have faith. Look again."

Seeker looked again, but still he could see nothing. A sudden terrible dread seized him.

I don't want to look. I don't want to know.

"Do you see?" repeated Jango.

"No," Seeker replied. "It's too dark."

He was very near the end of the bridge now. He tried to continue, but his legs would not move. The heavy dread weighed him down, held him back. He had come to a halt twenty paces or so from the clearing in the trees. Here he waited for the old man to join him.

"Seeker," said Jango, coming up to him and gripping his arm, "you must be strong. You must go on. You must hold to your faith." His voice trembled with urgency. "Manlir is waiting for you."

"I can't," said Seeker helplessly. "I don't know why, but I can't."

"Why should you fear to see the All and Only? Isn't this the moment you've longed for all your life?"

"Yes! But what if—"

"Don't say the words!" cut in Jango sharply. "Don't think the thought! Look at me."

Seeker turned his back on the dark clearing in the trees and faced the old man. Jango's eyes burned with a fierce energy. He laid down his stick on the bridge and raised his arms.

"I had hoped not to have to do this," Jango said. "But I see that I must."

Seeker understood that he was to come into the old man's embrace. He stepped forward. Jango put his bony hands on his shoulders and gazed deep into his eyes.

"Do you see me?"

"Yes. I see you."

"Who am I?"

"You are Jango."

"That is one of my names. Look deeper."

Seeker looked closely at the old man's weathered face, lit by the last glow of the setting sun. As he did so, it seemed to him that he recognized him from long ago. He resembled someone he had once known well. But he could not tell who.

"Have we known each other in some earlier time?" he said.

"Indeed we have. Look deeper."

Seeker gazed for another long moment at that old and gentle face, searching for clues. Jango closed his eyes, and then opened them again. Seeker blinked too, in instinctive response. As soon as he did so, he had his answer.

"Of course! I know you!"

"So you do."

"But how—how is it possible?"

Jango held him with his steady gaze. Seeker, looking at him now in fearful amazement, could say no more.

I know you. I am you.

This never-known always-familiar face before him was himself grown old.

Now Jango took him in his thin and trembling arms, and Seeker held him close, and it was the strangest sensation.

It was apartness and oneness together. It was the sublime comfort of total love, and yet he was alone.

As they embraced, Seeker felt the old man dissolve in his arms, and he sank into him and was him. Now he was Jango, embracing his younger self.

I am more than I know.

Then, like two dancers holding each other close, turning together, he was Seeker once more, and the old man was gazing at him with long-cherished love.

"Look with my eyes, Seeker. Look into the Garden."

Seeker turned then and looked again into the clearing. The deep shadow tricked his gaze, and for a little while he could not tell what he saw.

"Have faith," said Jango. "See with the eyes of faith."

Seeker looked among the trees into the bower where the chair was placed, and all at once a wave of joy rose in his heart, and his eyes filled with tears.

"I see!" he whispered.

The All and Only was before him, beckoning him forward.

"Go to him."

Trembling now, weeping with joy, Seeker crossed what remained of the bridge and stepped onto the shore. Jango came after him. There before the overpowering presence, Seeker fell to his knees and felt himself warmed by transcendent love.

"Command me," he said.

From behind him came a deep close boom of sound.

Seeker leaped to his feet and turned to face the lake. The sound filled the world. There could be no mistaking now: Manlir had entered the Garden. But Seeker knew his faith was strong. He was ready.

Boom! So deep and strong that surely the waters of the lake must shiver to hear it. But nothing moved. Jango was watching him, leaning on his stick. Then his old eyes too turned to stare across the lake.

A figure was coming into view on the bridge, far away. Too far to detect any details, but he was in the form of a man, and he moved with a slow grace that could only be born of great strength.

Seeker calmed his mind, ready to strike.

"Let him come," he said.

The deep boom sounded nearer: not the footsteps of the approaching stranger, but the power that rolled before him. Prompted by some inner instinct, Seeker stepped back onto the bridge. There on that blade of darkness he would meet his enemy, and so the final combat would be fought at last.

As the stranger approached, Seeker advanced to meet him. There was little light left in the sky now, and such light as there was, reflecting on the lake, threw all else into silhouette. So it was two dark forms who converged upon each other, to the slow boom of the sounding land.

Is it me he comes to destroy, thought Seeker, or is it the All and Only? Is this the Assassin of the legend, whose day must surely come? If so, I am no more than an obstacle in his way. But he will find I'm not so easy to pass.

Now the stranger was close. Seeker stilled his mind for combat. Instinctively taking his ground, he adopted the stance known as the Tranquil Alert. His arms loose at his sides, he let his eyes defocus so that he could catch any and all movement. The stranger too, seeing him halt, came to a stop. All round him, the rolling boom of sound filled the air.

Then the stranger spoke, his soft dry voice sounding clear through the echoing night.

"Look with your own eyes, Seeker."

Seeker's whole body stiffened in surprise. He knew that voice.

"Noman?"

"Manlir is waiting. Look again."

Seeker turned to look. The darkness between the trees was deeper now. But he had already seen what was to be seen.

"I have seen the All and Only."

"Go closer. Look again."

"I have looked."

Noman's voice cried out, sharp as a knife.

"See with your own eyes!"

At this, the dread that Seeker had felt before returned with redoubled force. He did not want to turn round. He did not want to look again.

"I have looked," he said. "I have faith. I have the strength in me now of the All and Only. I'm ready."

"Seeker!" The old voice drilled into his brain. "Seeker! Jango faced this test before you, and he failed. The only lasting strength is truth. Look with your own eyes!"

So Seeker turned once more and forced his heavy limbs to take the first step. Step by slow step, as if dragging himself through sand, he made his way back across the bridge.

There was Jango, waving at him, mouthing something that he did not hear. There was the dark clearing between the trees on the shore. There was the shadowy outline of the chair.

Seeker stepped onto the shore. Once again, he came to a stop. The dread was so strong in him now that his whole body shook.

What is there to fear? he asked himself. I've seen the truth once already.

No, he answered. I saw then through Jango's eyes. Now I must see with my own eyes.

Shivering uncontrollably, he forced himself to approach the shadowed chair. He heard the crackle of dry leaves beneath his feet. He moved clumsily, as if half asleep, heavy with dread.

Now as he looked, as he forced his weary eyes to strain into the darkness, he saw that there was indeed a figure seated in the chair: the figure of a man.

He strode nearer, his heart beating, his heaviness falling away. The man in the chair gazed towards him and raised one hand in a familiar gesture.

"Seeker," he said. "My son. I'm proud of you."

"Father?"

Seeker stopped in consternation. How could it be his father? But there was the familiar high smooth brow, there the steady blue eyes. His father was smiling at him, as he had always longed to see him smile: with a look of love and pride.

"Father! Why are you here?"

"Isn't this what you want?" said his father.

Then as Seeker stared, his father's features began to melt and change. Now before him in the chair sat his brother Blaze.

"Blaze!"

"Hallo, little brother. I've been watching you. You're good!"

"Watching me?"

"Skim stones. I saw that last one. Three jumps!"

"But you never saw, Blaze. I could never do it right while you were watching."

"Well, I've seen now. That's what you want, isn't it?"

Then Blaze's features changed too, and he shrank down in the chair until Seeker saw crouching before him the aged body of the Elder.

"So, Seeker," he said. "You turn out to be strong after all. All the rest of us have failed. Only you have true strength."

"How can I believe that, Elder?"

"Why not believe it, child? It's what you want to believe."

Seeker felt then a sinking in his heart. He looked away in shame. He put one hand to his face to cover his eyes. When he looked again, the chair—the chair that had given him all his childish longings—the chair was empty.

⊰ 25 ⊱

The Assassin

IT WAS A COMMON WOODEN CHAIR WITH A CURVED
back and arms, the kind that stands at the head of the table
in every modest household. It had no upholstery on the
seat, no carvings on the back. Seeker touched it and felt
the smooth grain of the wood. It was just a chair.

So what had he seen before, when he had looked
through Jango's eyes?

I saw what Jango wanted to see. Then I saw what I
wanted to see.

And now? All there is before me is an empty chair.

On a sudden impulse, he turned and lowered himself
into the chair. He heard Jango cry out.

"No!"

But he was seated now. It was done. He was in the
very chair that he had believed held the All and Only.

He heard the shivery boom of his enemy—from the

night sky above him and from the ground beneath him, from the trees behind and the lake ahead.

"Let him come," he said. "All he'll find here is me."

He felt the rising of a wind blowing off the lake. It blew in his face, ruffling his hair, making his eyes water. He tried to raise one hand to brush his cheek but found his hand was fixed to the arm of the chair. The wind blew stronger, buffeting him as he sat. He tried to get up. All movement had become impossible. No bonds held him down, but he could not leave the chair. Now the wind was so strong it hurt his face. He twisted from side to side and pulled on his arms and legs, but he was caught.

Ahead the black line of the bridge stretched away across the lake, and the lake reached from horizon to horizon. The wind whipped the dark waters, forming ridges and waves that hissed against the near shore. Over it all boomed the ceaseless beat of his waiting enemy, so near but never revealed, before whom he was now helpless.

Seeker struggled to free himself with all his might. As he did so he shouted his defiance.

"Here I am! Do your worst!"

Then, from the far rim of the lake, there came a new sound and with it a fleeting movement, a play of light over the water. A rustling murmuring like the fall of blown leaves, like the wind in dry grass, swept softly towards him. Flickering crests rose in the water that might have been waves but were not waves. As they came closer, he saw that they were formed of fine filaments, cobwebs carried on the wind, tumbling and snaking over the lake. Each strand glowed with its own faint luminescence, forming as

they were blown along ever thicker skeins and braids of
light.

The windswept threads now covered the lake, as more
and more streamed over the distant ridge and down to the
water. The nearest strands reached the shore and came
rustling over the ground towards him. The murmuring
took form; he began to catch words and phrases, at first too
tangled, one with another, to be coherent, but through the
low hum came again and again two clear words: *Help me.*

Now the whispering threads were twining round his
feet and the legs of the chair. They were so fine, so light,
that he could barely feel their touch. But all the time more
came, and more, gathering round him like blown cobwebs, gradually coating his feet and shins. He caught their
sounds now, as the soft words pressed closer to him.

Help me! he heard. *Hear me! Give me! Love me! Save me!*

"Get away!" he cried, trying to kick with his feet. But
he could not free himself. Only his head could twist and
turn. He looked round for help, but he was alone.

The glowing webs of sound continued to flow towards
him and to heap up round him, clinging ever tighter with
the sheer mass of their numbers. Their murmuring filled
the air.

*Ease my pain! End my loneliness! Give me hope! Show me
mercy! Forgive my weakness! Punish my enemies! Watch over
those I love! Watch over me! Don't let me suffer! Don't let me
die! Let me live forever!*

Each fine filament was a prayer. All the prayers offered
to the All and Only by all those in need were swarming
over the water to cluster round the one who had taken his

seat in the chair. The threads were crawling over the mound that had already formed round his legs, and now he felt them twining round his arms and clutching at his chest.

In his terror he cried out.

"I'm not your god! I can do nothing!"

But the strands continued to pile up round him, layer on layer cocooning his helpless body, reaching now as high as his neck. Soon they would be curling round his face, choking his mouth and nostrils, stopping his breath.

"Get away!" he cried. "Do you want to kill me?"

But he knew as he cried that his words meant nothing. The miserable souls who uttered these prayers knew nothing of him. In their need they prayed, and their prayers flew forth, and he was imprisoned in the place where their prayers came to rest. He was being buried by prayers.

So this was what it felt like to be god: crushed by unmeetable needs, burdened by the deadweight of helpless misery, silenced by the great gagging mass of unanswerable prayers.

Now the webs were winding round his chin and reaching for his lips. He shook his head, but they clung on tight.

"Save me!" he cried.

Then he laughed aloud. It was a joke, a bitter joke: the one to whom all others prayed for help crying out to be saved. Where was his saviour? Who was he calling?

Surely you know that it's you who will save me.

He turned his head, twisting upwards in a vain attempt

to escape the mass of writhing threads. He threw his gaze up into the empty night sky above. There he saw, high overhead, a slowly circling falcon. He watched it as it flew, wings outstretched, hanging in the air so effortlessly, faintly rimmed by light from the dying west. Too high and too dark to read its markings, but he knew from the shape, from the edge-feathers of its wings and tail, that it was a peregrine. He knew the great hawks well. His brother, Blaze, had taught him to watch them, long ago. They were hunters who struck from above, from so high up that their prey could never even imagine their existence. They hunted by sight. It was late for a peregrine to be out. "They only see you if you move," Blaze had said to him—making him shiver. Seeker the boy had looked up fearfully then, wondering if there were other, higher hawks, entirely beyond the reach of his eyes, waiting to swoop down on him: unseen gods of punishment and death.

Now as he looked up, he remembered and his mind, reaching out of his imprisoned body, joined the circling falcon and looked down with the bird's keen eyes. Below him he saw lake and shore, verge and woodland, and it was a hunting ground—nothing more. This True Nom, this place of power and mystery, was to the falcon no more than a breeding ground for its prey.

My world is many worlds.

His gaze then swooped like a falcon down the night sky, through the branches of the trees to the world of grasses and roots, where mice and shrews lived their little lives all unaware. And there, tall among the grasses, stood a single blue flower. His eyes came to rest on it, lit by the silvery light of the web of prayers, and he greeted it like an old friend. He knew this flower well. He understood its beauty. It was itself, the only way it could be.

As he thought this thought, a tumble of further thoughts followed, faster than he could grasp them: how the falcon's world and the world of the mice and the shrews and the cornflower intersected in a bolt of death from the sky; how his world and the world of those whose desperate prayers clutched at him were different too, all of them, and yet shared the same land and sky. Like blindfolded prisoners they shuffled about in their private darks, bumping into each other, not knowing who or what they had struck.

We are all connected.

This was a massive thought. He felt himself grow, reaching out into the trees and over the water and up into the night sky.

He saw then with astonishment what had always been there to see, what was so laughably obvious: the way all the elements of the world work together and could not exist without one another. The mountains need the plains, and the lakes need the hills. The river could not be a river without its riverbanks, and the high road would not be a road without the fields and forests through which it cuts its way. The shore needs an ocean, and the ocean needs a horizon, and the horizon needs a sky.

The revelations exploded like fireworks in his mind. Every smallest thing is part of a greater whole. The greater things depend upon one another. Nothing is alone, nothing is without its function, nothing is without meaning.

And seeing this, and knowing this, makes the world beautiful beyond imagining.

I am more than I know. I am all that I know. I am all there is.

Could it be so? If it was true—

He realized then that the whispering strands that had been smothering him were falling silent. As if only the sound they made had given them substance; as they ceased to murmur, so they dwindled and faded and were gone. The whole creeping web that had covered the lake was melting into the night. He found he could move again.

He rose from the chair.

There before him in the night was Jango, staring at him with anguished eyes.

"What do you see?" he called.

Seeker knew what Jango needed to hear. But everything was changed now. He could only speak the truth.

"I see nothing," he said.

Jango sank to his knees and clutched his breast as if wounded.

"Assassin!" he cried.

So be it, thought Seeker. I'm not the god of the Garden. I'm the one who sees there is no god. I'm the Assassin.

He stepped away from the chair. He went past the sorrowing Jango. He went to Noman, on the lakeshore.

"What you have seen," said Noman, "I saw long ago. I was the Assassin then. You are the Assassin now."

He raised his arms. Seeker came to him. Noman put his hands on Seeker's shoulders and gazed into his eyes.

"Do you see me?"

"Yes. I see you."

"Who am I?"

"You are Noman."

"Look deeper."

Seeker met that bottomless gaze and he understood all of it at last.

I know you. I am you.

"You are Noman. You are Jango. You are me."

Then Noman drew him into a close embrace in his aged arms.

"Have I not always been with you?"

Apart and united, loved and alone, Seeker sank into Noman and was him. He saw through his eyes and thought his thoughts. He saw his own young face and found that he was weeping and wondered why he wept. He saw Noman's face, and it too was stained with tears. He kissed the old man's paper-thin cheek, and one of them spoke to the other, saying, "So the experiment has succeeded at last. We're ready now."

Then Seeker let his mind open like a door, and through it he fell into a sea of memories. This spiralling embrace was Seeker and Jango and Noman, it was all three at once, melting in and out of each other, a single mind dizzy with youth and age, with pity and wonder and love. He had lived for two hundred years, and lived now in this infinite moment in every one of those years at once. He was a baby at the breast and a warlord at the head of a conquering army and a crazy old man sitting on a stick waiting by an empty road. He was a lonely boy in a classroom and he was a lover in his lover's arms and he was a philosopher who dreamed of making a better world.

Swooping like a falcon down the years, plunging through never-known always-present memories, he stood once more on the summit of the island of Anacrea, before the screen that protected the Garden. He was Noman the omnipotent warlord. He commanded his warriors to tear down the screen. Alone, he entered the sacred wilderness. He found the Garden empty. He stayed in that godless wilderness for a day and a night. By the time he left, he knew the truth: it was he, in his own greed for knowledge, who had killed the god.

I am Noman. I am the Assassin.

Turn and turn again in this dance of the ages, and he was Jango, patient in faith, come to find what he needed too much to find; come to kneel, weeping tears of joy, before the All and Only; come to seek the truth, and to fail to see it.

I am Jango. I am the believer.

Turn and turn again, and he was Seeker crossing the line of darkness between the reaches of light towards an empty chair in an empty Garden; come to seek the truth, and to find it; come to bear the burden of that emptiness.

I am Seeker. I am the Assassin come again.

Too much knowledge kills the gods.

And what does the Assassin do then? He gives the world back what he has killed, and pays the price with his silence.

First I chose knowledge. Now I choose faith.

Wall up the Garden. Seal the doors. Set warriors to

protect the approaches. Act as if you believe. The people need gods.

How many centuries does it take to soothe the fear in men's hearts? This is the great experiment. Have we made mistakes? Of course. But the experiment is not over yet. We have a brother.

Our brother is the one we love more than any other, the one we wish to be, our elder and wiser. Our brother was the first to understand the life that beats in all things, the first to feel its limitless power. And now he is the first to be intoxicated by life, to be addicted to life, to conceive the possibility that he can live forever.

My life is all life. I will never die.

Believing he is all life, he is willing to let others die that he may live. This is his madness. This is why he is the last enemy.

Manlir our brother hears and mocks our experiment, speaking from a far memory. He speaks in bitterness and in truth.

"You give the people an everlasting childhood. Is that your way of loving mankind?"

And Seeker, remembering, hears himself speak, hears Noman's answer.

"I give them faith."

We have given them guides and called them the Noble Warriors. We have armed them with power, but not too much. We have given them an enemy, so that they remain vigilant.

And yes, there are casualties along the way. When the necessary enemy grows too strong, there must be an intervention. The plan allows for that. There must be a new defender of the faith, there must be deaths, there must be sacrifices. There must be renewal. When the opportunity presents itself, the Community must be torn up by its roots and left to find its own way back to new life, new vigor, new faith. Men can heal themselves. We have planted living corn.

Another remembered voice in the sea of memories: the voice of the Elder.

"I will let the Nom be destroyed," he says, his heart heavy. "But the brothers and sisters must know that the Lost Child is still with us."

"All must go," we say. "They must be stripped and left with nothing. Then from nothing their faith will be born again."

"So I must be the traitor."

"You betray their present to ensure their future. There can be no greater act of love."

Oh, the vastness of our plan! Oh, its outrageous ambition, its passionate love for mankind, its fragility!

If I can make there be light instead of darkness, I can end the hurting of the world.

All moments merging into one moment. All voices become one voice.

I am Noman. Long ago I began this experiment. I watch over it as a loving father watches over his growing child.

I am Jango. I am the one who failed. I am the keeper of the key to the door that is always open. I am the guide who waits by the roadside for my chance to come again.

And I am Seeker. My life is an experiment in search of the truth.

Noman released Seeker from his embrace.

"You're ready now," he said.

"Will you be with me?"

"How can I not be? I am you."

"Then, let it begin."

⊰ 26 ⊱

Duel

IT WAS FULL NIGHT WHEN SEEKER DESCENDED FROM the Scar and stepped onto the floor of the valley. In this moment there was no wind, no sound from the deep ground—only a far dark stillness.

Manlir was waiting. He felt him in the silence.

He began to walk. On either side rose the tall needles of rock that guarded the valley of the Scar. Ahead the line of hills. Beyond the hills lay the great plain, and the forest, and the fertile fields, and the river that flowed to the sea. Seeker knew that the final combat was near, but he did not know where it would take place. He waited for his enemy to declare himself.

"Here I am!" he cried into the night.

A sudden mighty crack split the sky. The ground bulged beneath his feet. The tine of rock before him toppled and came crashing down, smashing into fragments so close to him that he felt the sting of its flying shards. Out of the rattle of shattering rock rose a cackle of laughter. The ground heaved again. All down the valley the tines shivered and began to fall.

Seeker ran, springing this way and that to avoid each new rockfall, racing to outrun the rippling ground as it devastated the valley. As he reached the hill path he turned to see the last of the columns crumble and smash behind him, and there sounded again that mocking laugh. The whole valley heaved and shook. The great Scar itself rose up as if lifted by a sleeping giant, and then with a roar like thunder, it sank down again. As it sank it broke apart, the whole massive crag crazed like a glass bowl, shivered into fragments, and fell into itself in a cloud of dust. Seeker was far away; its destruction was no threat to him, nor was it meant to be. It was a show of power.

Now Manlir began his game in earnest. A ripple of movement in the valley swelled and accelerated. Seeker saw the land rise up towards him as a wave rolls in to the shore. He retreated before it, racing up the hillside, and from the hilltop hurled himself out into midair. As he did so, the hill swelled up beneath him and burst and sank down again.

He fell to earth in the valley below, landing on feet and hands, lithe as a cat, and ran on. As he ran, the hills rose and fell like the coverlet on a bed shaken by giant unseen hands; but always behind him, driving him onwards.

He wants me to live, Seeker thought as he ran. He wants me to feel his power, but he needs to keep me alive.

Down the last hillside, out onto the plain. Waves of

earthquake followed him, opening up sudden fissures before his feet. He dodged and leaped, this way and that,
hurdling the crevasses, working his way towards the forest.

Now at his feet he heard a scurrying sound and saw
that the ground was alive with rats. They came out of the
cracks in their thousands, maddened by terror. His bare
feet trod on writhing fur as he ran.

Still the land cracked and heaved, and now slithering
out of the gaping ground came snakes, their bronze bodies whipping over the turbulent earth, also crazed by fear.
But now, close by, the greater darkness of the Glimmen
offered its refuge. Seeker dived between the trees, and his
enemy followed, always just behind him.

The great trees of the Glimmen now fell as the tines
in the valley of the Scar had fallen, ripped up by their roots,
hurled across his path as if they were straws. The forest was
trampled like grass in his wake, and yet not one tree trunk
hit him as it fell, not one branch. The sound of the falling trees filled the night, every crash a thousand crashes
as branch shattered on branch. And over the agony of the
forest rose a sound like laughter, which was the sound of
power rejoicing in itself.

What is it he wants with me?

Out of the darkness now and into the fields, bucked by
the surging ground, riding the land waves like a skiff at
sea, the first light of dawn creeping over the mountains to
the east. He was covering the ground so fast and with such
bounding strides that his feet seemed barely to touch the
earth at all. Manlir who possessed all force, whose will
drove the force of the world, hurled him onwards, back

down the road he had travelled, back down the years of his life.

I can't do this alone.

Ahead now the pale gleam of the river, and Seeker was in his home country. As he ran he raised his head high and made the call. The long wordless cry sang out from him towards the distant great lake and the city of Radiance, towards the villages of the plains and the hills and the mountains.

"Nomana!"

The three syllables stretched out into a cry that rose high in the cold air of dawn and travelled for miles.

"Noo-maaa-naaa!"

He would be heard. The cry would be passed on. He had made the call.

As he reached the river, the rage of Manlir struck its slow waters and churned up a great wave. Without a moment's hesitation Seeker sprang into the heart of the wave and let it rise and roll, carrying him with it. It swelled with such force that on either side the riverbanks burst as it passed. High on the crest of the wave, Seeker let himself be swept downriver unharmed, as trees and rocks were lifted up and tossed aside in the roaring path of its destruction. Unlucky barges out on early river journeys were overtaken and flung into the air like toys, while Seeker, borne on the smooth crest, rose high above the flying debris.

As the sun rose he saw that he was approaching the river mouth, swept south so fast that a day's journey had gone by in minutes. And here at the end, as the river widened, the raging wave sank down and the racing of the water slowed, and he found himself swimming with steady strokes through slow currents to land.

He stepped out of the water onto a shelving beach he knew well. Once there had been an island in this river mouth. Once it had been his home.

Has he let me go? Or has he delivered me to the place he wants me?

Now on the open beach he saw a gathering of people, and in their midst a white-canopied litter. Nearby a second band of men were at work on a small boat that was hauled up in the shallow water. They were tying white streamers to the boat's mast and rigging. Seeker recognized the signs. They were preparing a sea funeral.

The silence and the stillness felt unreal after the shock and roar that had delivered him here. The mourners seemed unaware of the explosions in the land. But Manlir had not gone away. Seeker could sense him, waiting.

He needs me alive. He has brought me here. For what purpose?

He approached the group round the white litter. As he came near, a flurry of wind lifted the canopy and he saw the body within. It was the Joy Boy.

Suddenly Seeker understood: and understanding, he knew he must escape, now, at once, as quickly as he could. He sprang up the hillside, feeling a force rise up from the ground like a wind to pursue him. He raced to the lip of the high cliff and stood for a brief moment looking down on the ocean pounding below. As the ground on which he stood began to shake and crack, he launched himself from the cliff, arching out over the sea, and turned in a graceful curve to plummet, head down, hands outreached, body straight as an arrow, into the ocean.

One perfect dive.

At once, silence. He streamed into the green depths, slick as a fish, deep underwater, propelling himself down and down, and for one long moment all was light, all was quietness. Then below him the seabed heaved, and even as he turned to flee, the explosion burst round him.

The mourners on the shore looked on in astonishment as the sea erupted, hurling a giant spout of water into the air. In that gush they saw tumbling and turning the figure of a flailing man.

Seeker turned in midair, and in one giddy moment saw far over the land, saw the figures racing for the coast, before he slammed back into the water. Now in the blinding turmoil, knowing he could not escape, knowing help was on its way, he drove himself towards the source of the power. There in the deep water he found the heart of the force and let it seize him and spin him round and carry him away.

The watchers on the shore saw a churning on the surface of the sea as if a typhoon were raging towards the horizon, gouging a trough in the bright water as it went. Beneath the seething surface, Seeker drew the force ever closer towards him, no longer resisting.

Funny thing, strength. You can drink it in.

He met his enemy now, and clasped him in his arms. Angered, the raging underwater whirlwind broke surface once more, hurling Seeker up on a plume of spiralling foam. But Seeker did not release his grip. He was now locked to the one who sought to possess him, and his enemy, drawing on the power of the ocean, multiplied again and again the force of his blows. Turning and diving, thrashing the depths like a sea monster, the giant will that was Manlir threw the ocean up into mountains and let the mountains crash down again, and still Seeker did not yield.

Seeker knew now that they were well matched. He was too strong to be overpowered, not strong enough to escape.

The ocean beneath him heaved, rising up to form a towering peak of water that climbed as high as the clouds, an awesome display of power over the elements. Raised up on this sea mountain Seeker turned his gaze to the land, and there he saw his salvation.

"Nomana!"

They had come in answer to his call. They came in their hundreds, striding to the cliff top from which he had dived, forming an ever-growing line along the horizon, lit by the rays of the rising sun.

"Noble Warriors!" cried Seeker. "Be with me now!"

As the sea mountain subsided, carrying him back down to the thrashing surface, he saw his brothers and sisters reach out their hands towards him and he felt their lir enter him. As he was sucked into the depths once more, he could feel their lir still piercing the green water, like rays of sunlight, flooding him with power. He turned and turned in the spiralling combat, wrapping his growing strength round his enemy, containing him now, absorbing him now, dominating him at last.

You pursued me for my power. Now receive my power.

One last desperate spasm of resistance lifted Seeker out into the air, and down again into shallow water. Then it was over.

He rose and walked slowly out onto the shore. The mourners fell back, afraid. Seeker turned to greet the Noble Warriors standing on the cliff top. He raised his weary arms in the Nomana salute. Their arms went up in answer.

He spoke to the mourners by the litter. "Take off the canopy."

Frightened hands fumbled to undo the straps. There in the dawn light lay the body of the one they called the Beloved. Seeker bent over the litter and took the dead man in his arms. He held him close and gently fed back into him the life force he had prematurely released. As the mourners looked on, a miracle took place.

First there came a slight twitch of the dead man's fingers. Then his lips parted, and he was heard to utter a sigh. Then his eyes opened. The Joy Boy had come back to life.

He looked at Seeker for a long moment, and those round him, astonished, hardly able to believe their eyes, kept utter silence. Then he spoke.

"Why?"

His voice was faint, thin, fragile as glass.

"Your journey is not yet over," said Seeker.

The Joy Boy raised one trembling hand and touched Seeker on the cheek.

"Must I go all the way?"

"We must both go all the way."

Seeker lowered him gently to the ground. The Joy Boy then parted from Seeker's embrace and stood alone. He turned to the band of mourners. Awed and fearful, they fell to their knees. "Beloved!" they cried.

He smiled at them. He looked across the beach to the boat with the white streamers. "Is the boat ready?" he said.

"Beloved! Don't leave us!"

He shook his head and did not reply. Instead he turned to Seeker. "Promise me you won't let the knowledge die."

"I promise," said Seeker.

The Joy Boy set off alone over the shingle towards the boat. As he went he released his borrowed youth and turned before the eyes of the watchers into an old man. By the time he reached the boat, he was stooped, shrunken, half blind, barely able to stand. There, leaning on the boat's side, he turned back and raised one hand to beckon to Seeker.

Seeker opened his arms wide. Out from where he stood there stepped a second old man, who was Noman. He turned and touched Seeker's cheek as the Joy Boy had done, and on his ancient familiar face Seeker saw the coming of a serene surrender. The old warlord was entering his time of peace at last.

He smiled at Seeker and turned his face towards the seashore.

"Wait for me, brother."

He too then made his slow way to the waiting boat. There the two brothers helped each other to climb in. There they lay down in each other's arms, in their final rest.

Seeker joined his outstretched hands together and streamed his lir towards them. The boat creaked on the shingle, then shuddered and slipped into the water. The wind caught its sail and filled it and drove it out into the open sea.

⊰ 27 ⊱

Something Good and Strong

SEEKER ENTERED THE LONG HALL WITH ITS CRACKED mirrors and sat in the empty armchair, as he had done before. In the mirror before him he saw only himself, alone. He watched and he waited and time passed.

He saw the beams of sunlight falling through the long windows swing slowly by, picking out the knots and cracks in the old floorboards. He saw the cobwebs caught in the passing sunlight glow and then fade into the shadows again. He saw his hand on the arm of the chair, and the veins on the back of his hand.

Then at last he heard footsteps approaching, fast and light. Someone entering the house. The one he was waiting for hesitated in the entrance hall and then came on into the long room.

It was Echo Kittle.

She walked between the mirrors to where he sat, her slender form reflected in the broken glass. She came to a stop before him and met his gaze with those wide gray eyes.

"You know what I want," said Echo.

"Yes," he said. "I know."

"Just one last kindness."

She dropped down onto her knees before him.

"It's me who asks you, not the other one. But do it quickly, before she comes back. I can't bear to live like this. Set me free."

"I will," he said. "But not like this."

"She came from you. I kissed you as you slept. I'm well paid for my stolen kiss, don't you think?"

A spasm passed through her as she spoke. It began as a sad smile but then, for a moment, contorted her lovely face into something harder and older.

"I said I was bad inside. Do you remember? Now it's true."

"It's not you that's bad," said Seeker. "It's the one that's inside you."

"We're joined now," said Echo. "She'll never leave me." Tears filled her eyes. "She's told me so. She likes being me."

Her face contorted again, and her voice changed.

"You can't kill me, Seeker."

Now he was hearing the harsh mocking tones he had heard in the Haven, when the savanter had said to him, "You have strength, boy, but no love."

"If you kill me you kill the pretty one. And you don't want that."

Then Echo's true expression and voice returned.

"Do it, Seeker," she said. "Kill us both. Don't leave me like this. End the badness in me."

Seeker gazed at her, so lovely and so afraid. He had a promise to keep. He reached out his hands to take her hands.

"Stand up," he said. "Look at me in the mirror."

Echo did as he asked, turning to his reflection in the broken glass.

"I'm speaking to the other one in you now."

There in the mirror where Echo had stood, in Echo's clothes, weeping Echo's tears, was a shrivelled old woman.

"What do you want with me?" said the savanter.

"What do you want with her?" said Seeker.

"Her youth. Her beauty."

"For what?"

The old woman gave a dry little laugh.

"'For what?' he asks. Do you know what it is to grow old? Do you know what it is to see your own death approaching? I want to live, Seeker. I want to be forever young."

"And then?" said Seeker.

"Then? Then?" The old woman's voice became high and shrill. "There is no then. There's only life!"

"What of your mission?"

"Our mission is life! Noman charged us to seek truth without limits. We are to grow in knowledge forever. We are to challenge the stupid faith of the Noble Warriors."

"What you say is true. All warriors need a worthy enemy. Our swords grow rusty. You are the necessary enemy."

"Ah! You understand at last."

"But now you want to live forever. That was no part of Noman's plan."

"Knowledge has its own life. We have gained so much knowledge. Must it now die with us?"

Seeker considered this in silence for a few moments.

"Tell me your name," he said at last.

"Names come and go. Today I am Echo."

"No, tell me. When you set out on your journey, when everything was still new. You had a name then."

He spoke with an unexpected gentleness. The savanter too softened her tone.

"When everything was still new . . . Yes, I remember it. Enjoy it, boy. It doesn't last. Is this a trick to weaken me?"

"No. I too seek the truth."

"I had a name then." She gave her dry laugh. "I was called Hope. We live long enough to see our names mock us."

"Have you no more hope?"

"My dear boy. You have seen what hope I have. I live on through others."

I too live on through others, Seeker thought, and others through me. The power of the Noble Warriors comes from the Community, living and dead, reaching back into the past.

Leave even one alive and it will all begin again.

If the seeds he planted so long ago show that they can renew themselves without him, the farmer will know that he has planted living corn.

"You don't need to fear that I'll kill you," he said.

"Oh, you won't do that," said the savanter. "You'd never kill the pretty one."

"Nor would I kill you. You still have work to do. The savanters, like the Noble Warriors, must be renewed."

"Oh, clever, clever." But the old lady no longer sounded bitter. She sounded interested.

"I won't kill you," he went on, "but your separate existence must come to an end. You must give your life to Echo. She will live on for you. The lord of wisdom will not die. She will be called Echo."

"And why should I do this thing?"

"You have no choice. If you live divided within her, the torment will tear her apart. You know what I say is true. You knew it when you entered her. The old must die for the new to be born."

Now the old lady began to weep her own tears.

"Manny promised us we'd be forever young."

"Manlir is dead. You are the last."

"The things we learned!"

"You're the memory of the savanters, Hope. You're the link in the undying chain. Through you the wisdom passes to the next generation."

"The next generation . . . How I've hated them."

"But no more. You don't hate Echo. You love her."

"Why should that be?"

"Because you feel the pulse of her life like a child in your womb. This is your eternal life. There is no other."

The savanter wept as she looked at Seeker from the broken mirror.

"You ask me to let myself die, after all these years."

"You know you want it."

"If only Manny were here. He'd tell me what to do."

"He'd tell you to go further than you've ever gone before. He'd tell you to go all the way. There are no limits to your pursuit of wisdom."

"Oh, clever, clever."

"Choose the surprise."

The old lady's withered cheeks cracked into a smile.

"You're good," she said.

"And I'm right. And you know it. It's gone on long enough."

"Choose the surprise." She chuckled to herself. "Well, well. The girl's in for a surprise of her own."

"Do you need my help?"

"Certainly not." The savanter drew herself up in proud dignity. "I am capable of making my own exit."

With that she raised her bony hands to her withered face and covered it up. She stood like this for a few moments, as if hiding herself from fear or shame. Then she lowered her hands. There was Echo's young and lovely face staring out of the glass at Seeker.

He turned to her to look at Echo directly. She was blinking, unsure what had happened to her.

"How do you feel now?"

"I don't know. Strange. Has she gone?"

"Yes. She's gone."

"But it's not the same. I'm not the same."

"You'll never be the same again. You carry her life within you. Her long past, her memories, her deep knowledge."

"Why? What for?"

"Do you remember how you told me once you'd do something good and strong?"

"Yes."

"This is how it begins."

Echo looked frightened.

"Why me?"

"Because for you there's always more to want. You chose this when you leaned too far out of the tree to touch the first Caspians. You chose this when you followed me out of the Glimmen. You've chosen it with every decision you've ever made."

"So I have."

"Look in the mirror," said Seeker. "What do you see?"

Echo looked. There was her familiar face that others said was beautiful. There, her gray eyes. And in those eyes a new awakening.

There has to be more.

She began to breathe more rapidly, and a shiver ran through her body. She felt she was waking, but not from sleep: this was a waking from childhood; a coming out of a small dark room in which she had understood nothing to a new world of immense and brilliant space. Only the beginning, only the first step. But the adventure lay before her now, the seeking and the finding, the slow mighty building of the edifice of knowledge. She saw then how for all the rest of her life she would grow and multiply and embrace all things.

"You're to be a lord of wisdom, Echo. For you there'll be no limits."

She was stroking the little finger of her left hand. She blushed a little as she saw and remembered. But it felt different now. The badness in her remained, but no longer as a source of shame. She had cared too much for herself, and still did, but not because she was wicked. It was only a rawness in her, and a kind of restlessness that she knew she would never lose. She needed it, this worm of dissatisfaction that gnawed at her core, because this new world had so much to offer, and she did not mean to come to rest.

"Oh, Seeker!" she said, her eyes glowing. "I feel—I don't know what I feel!"

There were no words to express it, this overwhelming sensation of having crested a hilltop to find before her, like a giant landscape in the sun, her life to come, exciting, powerful, and mysterious.

"Go home," he said to her. "Say good-bye to your family and friends. Take nothing but the clothes you wear. And set out and find your life."

"And you?"

"I mean to do the same."

"Will I see you again?"

"I can't tell."

She took his hand in hers and held it.

"I wanted you to love me, Seeker. I wanted you like I wanted Kell: to have for myself. But I can't have you, can I? People can't have people."

"You wanted me to love you," he said. "But you never loved me."

He spoke without accusation in his voice. As she heard it, she knew it was true.

"No, I didn't. How strange."

"You don't love anyone."

"Is that bad?"

"Not everyone is a lover. Not everyone has to be completed by someone else."

"I'll just go on being me."

She had always known it, all her life.

I'm an explorer. I go alone.

"We're only just at the beginning," she said. "We're still young. I wonder when we'll meet again, and how we'll have changed. Imagine being old, and remembering today, and how I held your hand and said to you—"

She stopped, smiling at the absurdity of what she was saying.

"Said what?"

"I haven't said it yet. I was remembering it before the memory had happened."

She let go of his hand.

"You're the finest person I've ever known."

She turned and walked away down the long room between the mirrors to the open door.

⚹ 28 ⚹

Rain Falls on the Garden

MORNING STAR CAME AFTER A WHILE TO THE SEA OF grass. In one place to the side of the road the grass had been trampled into a narrow track. She turned off the road and followed the track, the waving grasses brushing her shoulders on either side as she went. The track led her to a small white clapboard house with a pale blue door.

The sun was high in the sky and burning hot. The interior of the house, glimpsed through the grass-fringed windows, was cool and empty and white. She knocked on the faded blue panels of the door. No one answered. She tried the handle and the door opened. She went into the house, seeking its shade.

"Anyone here?"

No need to call loud, it was a small house. The occupants would hear her come in even if she hadn't called. But no one appeared from the side rooms. She was alone.

The plain white-walled room pleased her. There was a blue cornflower in a glass on the table, which she took as a sign of welcome. She explored the house, and the more she saw, the better she liked it. It seemed to her that small though it was, there was just the right amount of room for everything. A main room for cooking and eating and talking. A bedroom just big enough for its bed. A washroom with a long brick-lined trench for washing clothes and dishes and people.

Outside a back door that opened from the washroom there was a small yard, a rectangle of bare earth cleared of the tall grass. Here there grew a single bay tree, shading with its broad waxy leaves a stack of stove wood and a well with a timber lid. Beside the well lay a tin dipper on a cord. She lifted the lid and dropped the dipper and heard it slap into water not far below. The water was sweet and cool on her dry lips.

She sat in the main room, with her cup of water in her hands and her bare brown feet stretched out before her, and let her eyes close. For the first time since the disintegration of the Joyous she felt something like a quietness of the spirit. These had been bitter days for Morning Star. One by one the pillars that had held up her world had broken and fallen away. The Nom was destroyed. Her passion for the Wildman had passed like a dream. She had lost her colors. The Joy Boy was dead. Seeker was gone. And most heartbreaking of all, she had watched a great gathering of people acclaim the coming of a god she had herself invented.

It was hard after so much loss to be so alone. But at least here in this plain house she could rest. She would go on her way again later. She would find Seeker later. For now, she let her head grow heavy and her breaths come slow, and the heat of noon passed overhead without touching her.

She woke and opened her eyes and there was Seeker, sitting in the chair by the stove. For a moment it seemed so natural that he should be by her side that she smiled and said, "There you are."

It was as if he had gone out earlier and had returned, as if this was where he belonged. Then, waking more fully, she let her smile turn to a laugh, and laughed at herself.

"I don't know what's happening to me," she said. "Where did you come from? What are you doing here?"

"I live here," he said, smiling back.

He looked so like the old Seeker, with his friendly face and his worried eyes, that all her recent fears of him slipped away.

"I came in for the shade," she said. "There's a well. There's sweet water there."

"I know."

"I don't believe you live here. You never said anything about it."

"See that cupboard." He pointed to the cupboard on the wall by the stove. "Look inside. There's a tin of oatcakes there. And a half-eaten jar of honey. Look in the bedroom. Hanging on the back of the door there's a belt with a bone buckle."

"So you've had a look around."

"Why should I make up things like that?"

"I don't know why. I don't know anything about you any more. You've gone somewhere so far away I can't follow you there."

"But you can read my colors."

"No. I lost my colors."

"You lost your colors! How did you do that?"

She gave a small shrug.

"It was too much. I couldn't go on living like that." She remembered then how the world had looked just before she fell. "There was a waterfall. It was very beautiful."

"A waterfall?"

He was looking at her with such an odd expression. She wondered why she had said that about the waterfall. It can't have meant anything to him.

"So you're telling me this is your house?"

"It's Jango's house," he said.

"Who's Jango?"

"A sort of a friend. He's old. He lives here with his wife."

"Is she old, too?"

"Yes. I'd say they're about the same age. They're very close."

Seeker looked at her in that new odd way of his and spoke the words Jango had spoken to him.

"My dearest friend, my life's companion, my comfort in old age, and my one and only love."

"The old man said that about his wife?"

"Yes."

"I suppose they'll come back soon. I hope they won't mind finding us here, sitting in their chairs."

"No, they won't mind."

Morning Star looked round the simple room.

"Don't you envy them?" she said.

"Not exactly," said Seeker.

"Oh, I do. To have one person to love, and to know they love you."

"One person above all others."

"Yes, I know. It's not the Nomana way. But all that's over now."

She looked away from his intent and curious gaze, feeling a wave of sadness pass through her.

"Do you say that because the Nom's been destroyed?" he said.

"That, and everything."

She didn't want to explain more, ashamed of what she had done in Radiance.

"Do you remember, Star?" he said. "Do you remember how you felt when you first came to Anacrea? When you wanted to join the Noble Warriors?"

"Of course I remember."

"Do you remember hiding by a wall in the night, and crying, and me finding you?"

"You were crying, too."

"You had a little bundle in your hand."

"I have it still."

She reached into her pocket and took out the plait of wool her father had given her when she had left to go to Anacrea.

"It's to remind me of home."

"And do you remember," said Seeker, "when we were on the road to Radiance, how we slept out in the open one night, and we both prayed, and the Wildman couldn't believe we meant it?"

"Dazzle me and flood me," said Morning Star, remembering his words then.

He nodded, pleased.

"No more memories, Seeker. They make me want to cry."

"Why, Star?"

"Because—because I wish I believed now what I believed then."

"Just because the Nom was destroyed," he said, "it doesn't mean there can't be another Nom, somewhere else."

"That's what makes me so sad. There can be as many as you want."

After that she knew she had to tell him, and she found that she wanted to make her confession.

"There is another Nom, right now, in Radiance. I told them to build it, and now everyone believes the Lost Child has returned." She spoke quickly, wanting to get her shameful tale over with. "But I just made it all up, so they'd stop fighting each other."

He was smiling at her as he heard her.

"And they believed you?"

"Yes."

"You must have done a good job."

"But Seeker, don't you see? It's all fake. There's nothing

there. Just the mystery, and the promises, and the wanting to believe. There's nothing in the Garden. Not just there. In our old Nom, too. In any Nom anywhere."

He didn't seem shocked. She herself was shocked to hear her new convictions spoken aloud, and also relieved.

"So there's no Lost Child anywhere? No All and Only?" he said.

"No," she said. "Nothing."

"Nothing is dependable," said Seeker. "Nothing lasts."

"I don't know what that means."

"Does it make you angry, Star? To have been so deceived?"

"Not angry, no. I don't think I've been deceived. I think I've deceived myself."

"Because you wanted so much to believe in the All and Only?"

"Yes."

"So did I," said Seeker. "Strange to feel so much longing for something that doesn't exist."

"That's because even though it doesn't exist, we can imagine what it would be if it did."

"That's true," said Seeker. "And that's strange, too. We can imagine something that we've never known. What can the imagining consist of?"

"It's what you said. A longing."

"Like wanting love?"

"Very like wanting love," said Morning Star. "Oh, Seeker, it's so good talking with you again. No one else understands the way you do."

"So imagining god is like wanting love." Seeker was

following his own train of thought, his eyes lingering on the blue cornflower. "But love does exist, even if we don't have it. We were loved when we were children. We know what it would feel like to be loved again. Maybe it's like that with god. We believed in god when we were children, didn't we?"

"But now we've grown older we know the Garden is empty. It was all a lie."

"And love is a lie?"

"No, no. That's different. At least, I hope it's different."

"You're willing to go on looking for love?"

"Oh, yes."

"Then why not go on looking for god, too?"

Morning Star realized then that these questions he kept putting to her were tugging her in a particular direction. There was something he knew that he wanted her to discover, too.

"Just tell me, Seeker. If you've got a way to make me believe again, just do it."

He was silent for a few moments. Then speaking slowly, frowning as he spoke, he began to tell her.

"Strange things have been happening to me," he said. "Not everything has come clear yet. But I'm perfectly sure that the All and Only is real."

"Even though the Garden is empty?"

"The Garden is not empty. The All and Only is there, in the Garden. And here, in this house. And outside, in the wide world. The All and Only is always and everywhere. Why do we have so many names for our god? Because our god is not limited to one place, or one person,

or one nature. How could god be limited? It's not our
god, it's ourselves that are limited. Our minds can't contain the immensity of god. So we build a Nom, we fence
a Garden, we say the god is in there, and we're comforted.
That's not a lie, Star. It's just a very small part of the truth.
And when we discover that there's no radiant being in the
Garden, that's not the end of god. It's the end of our little
idea of a little god. It's the beginning of the discovery of
the true infinite and eternal god."

As Morning Star listened to Seeker she felt the stirring
within herself of a new and fragile hope. She half understood him and half felt him—felt that intense conviction
that charged every word he spoke.

"Do you think it's so, Seeker?"

"I know it's so."

"How do you know?"

"I went in search of the True Nom. I found it, and
I didn't know it. I know it now. It's all round us, Star.
The whole world is our True Nom. We pass through the
Shadow Court every evening at twilight. We enter the
Night Court as darkness falls and we look up at the stars.
We find our way every new day through the columned
cloisters of our lives. And there waiting for us, whenever
we choose to see it, is the Garden."

"But where? What Garden?"

"Come. Let me show you."

He got up, taking the cornflower from the glass as he
rose. He opened the door and went outside into the long
grass. He led her into the waving sea, and there they stood
in the afternoon sunlight looking round them at the shim-

mer of fronds, and the trees beyond, and the distant heat-hazed hills. He gave her the blue flower.

"Look at it as if you've never seen it before."

She looked.

"It's beautiful. Such a perfect blue."

Seeker then broke off a stalk of grass and held it out to her.

"Look at this, then. No blue here."

She looked at the stalk, and the feathery fronds that grew from its top.

"See how it's made? See how every part comes out of another part. See how the branches grow from the stalk, the spikes from the branches, the fine hairs from the spikes. It hasn't been built. It's unfolded from itself. Do you see?"

Under his eager pressing she did begin to see.

"Every part of the grass is right and inevitable. Do you see? And every part of the flower. Don't you think that's beautiful?"

"Yes," said Morning Star. "That is beautiful."

"Now look up. Look over all the grass growing round us. We're in a sea of beauty."

"Yes, we are."

"Now look wider. Look as far as your eyes can see. We're in a universe of beauty."

"Yes," said Morning Star, catching his excitement. "Yes."

"I don't know how to say it better than that. Beauty isn't pretty shapes, or pretty colors. It's the life in all things, being rightly lived. Our whole world is the Garden, if we can only see it."

"I do see it, Seeker. A little."

"Remember the Nomana Catechism?" He spoke the familiar words. "So will the All and Only never come?"

She replied with the response from the Catechism.

"The All and Only is with you now."

"Will I ever see the All and Only face-to-face?"

"You will," she responded, smiling.

"When?"

"When you are a god."

"That's it, Star!" He clapped his hands, laughing aloud in his delight. "All the time I've lived with so much power, and people have wanted to treat me like a god, and I've driven them away, I've told them, No, I'm not a god. Of course I'm a god! And you, too! We call our god the All and Only, don't we? And aren't we too part of the All? The world is our Garden, and we're the gods!"

She smiled to see him. He made her so happy, he was so true and good and bursting with the excitement of his thoughts.

"You make a better god than me, Seeker."

"No, but you do see it, don't you, Star?"

"I see it. But it's hard. It's like finding that your father and mother don't know any more than you do. I think I liked it better when I believed there was something beyond anything I knew, living in secret in the Garden. Even though it terrified me."

She remembered then how she had been unable to go close to the silver fence in the Nom, how she had felt the power streaming towards her and had known it would overwhelm her.

"It did terrify me," she said. "I did feel something."

"You felt the power," said Seeker. "Each of us feels it in our own way. I saw a figure of a man rimmed in dazzling light."

"And there was nothing there?"

"I was there. I saw what I put there. I saw myself. Just as you felt yourself. The terror you felt was real terror, but it was the terror that was already in you."

"It's gone now. Gone with my colors."

"Do you miss your colors?"

"I thought I didn't, but I do. I keep looking at people, expecting to know what they're feeling, and I don't. It's like being blind."

"So you don't know what I'm feeling?"

"Only from what you tell me."

"Well, then. I'll tell you. I've seen my whole life from beginning to end. How would you feel if that was you?"

"I'd hate it. It would feel like my life was over."

"I do hate it. I've done all that I was asked to do. Now I want to go back. I want to be surprised by my own life again."

"Is there a way?"

"Just the one way." He looked up at the cloudless sky. "I'm going to make it rain."

"Rain! But it hasn't rained for months."

"This will be my own rain."

She guessed then what he meant to do.

"No, Seeker! Not that!"

"Just enough to be young again."

"I don't want to have anything to do with it. I won't come with you. I won't watch."

"I'm not going anywhere, Star. It's going to happen right here."

He reached his hands over his head in the Nomana fashion, touching together his two forefingers and pointing them high into the cloudless sky. He looked up between his arms to his touching fingers and beyond. He drew a deep breath, and Morning Star saw his entire body start to tremble. Then he gave a low groan, and every muscle rippled upwards, and out from the tips of his fingers shot a stream of pure energy. It poured out of him up into the high blue sky, and as it streamed, it formed a turbulence in the air that thickened into mist, and then into racing clouds. The strands of cloud spiralled in the sky, and swelled and darkened, and built pile on pile into great towering thunderheads, rolling one above the other. A shadow like twilight fell over the land.

A violent flash split the gloom, followed by a crack of thunder so loud it shook the land beneath their feet. For one long heart-stopping moment all was still. Then the rain fell.

It came down in sheets, as if an ocean had spilled its shores among the clouds. Hard and heavy, hissing through the air, rain hammered the dry summer grass flat to the ground all round where they stood. The rain drenched them to the skin within seconds of beginning to fall.

The lightning flashed again and again, and the thunder boomed, and the rain poured relentlessly from the darkened sky. Seeker spread his arms wide and turned his face to the downpour and began to hum a low steady note. Morning Star found she was humming too, and she too exposed herself to the warm rain. It stung her skin and drove all thoughts from her mind. She began to turn slowly round and round with her arms extended, as they had danced in the Joyous. She saw Seeker spinning in the same way and heard him humming that low sound. The rain slicked her hair to her head and her clothes to her body so that she felt stripped bare, but she didn't care. The storm embraced her; she had no choice but to be drenched and deafened and blinded, and as the rain stripped her, so she let go of the little she had left and felt her hopes and fears stream away into the seething ground.

Seeker was crying out now in pain, his eyes closed, his mouth gaping. He was spinning in the rain, tormented by the storm. His cries were drowned by the downpour, his pain blanketed by rain. He had made the storm and now it was unmaking him.

The rain that cleansed him and stripped him took away even the pain at last. He was turning more slowly now. The storm was passing. The cloud mountains were breaking up. A lone ray of sunlight fell across the land, striking a clump of trees on the far hills, and the water-charged leaves sparkled and shone in the distance.

Morning Star lowered her arms and pushed the sodden hair from her eyes. The rain swept away like a curtain, and warm sunlight fell all round. The soaked land steamed. She looked at Seeker to see how he had changed, and cried out loud in her surprise.

All round him shimmered a faint blue glow.

Her colors had returned.

He saw her gazing at him and smiled at her.

"I'm not so different, am I?"

"I'm not sure," she said.

"It's done. It's over. I've no more power than you now."

"But you've not forgotten everything you ever knew?"

"No. I remember everything."

"Who am I?"

"You're Morning Star."

"What do you know about me?"

"You're my friend."

"Of course I am."

"And there's something else. But I seem to have forgotten what."

He gazed at her, wrinkling his brow, puzzled by the fading memory. He saw the blue flower she still held in one hand, now drenched and drooping. He turned to look back at the white house, as if seeking the answer there. Then his features smoothed into one of his rueful smiles.

"There. Whatever it was, it's gone."

But his colors were changing as he looked at her. She could read every shade of his feelings. What had begun as the pale blue of youthful hope was turning a deep soft red. Morning Star saw it and knew what it meant.

"One day I'd like to come back here," she said. "I'd like to live in this house."

"Me, too."

"We could live in it together."

"We will," said Seeker. Then, wondering why he had said such a thing: "That is, I mean, I'd like to."

"When we're older."

"Yes. That's what I meant."

He was looking at her so sweetly, his anxious eyes ready to turn away at the smallest rejection.

"You think we'll be together when we're older?" he said.

"Yes," said Morning Star. "I do think so."

It was easy for her to speak this way, because she knew what Seeker was feeling.

"I do love you, Seeker," she said.

"Do you?"

He sounded stupid with surprise.

"Yes, I do."

"But—that's all I want," he said.

"I know."

Morning Star bowed her head. A slow warmth was stealing through her body. This was more than joy. It was rightness. It was the life in all things being rightly lived.

"You really truly mean it?" he asked her, still not daring to believe it could be so.

"Yes. Really truly."

"Then that's just—enough."

She looked up. The happiness was growing with every passing moment. It dazzled her and flooded her.

Seeker was beaming at her like a fool. He took her in his arms and held her close and still, cheek to rain-soaked cheek. Words formed in his mind, words from long ago or from some time yet to come; words that he did not speak aloud, because there was no longer any need.

My one and only love.

⊰ 29 ⊱

Farewell

THE WILDMAN RODE DOWN THE RIVER PATH, HIS golden hair streaming, urging his Caspian to ever greater speed.

"Go, Sky, go!"

He was racing Caressa on Malook. He could hear her close behind him, but he did not look back. The Wildman had become a fine rider, but he knew Malook was the stronger horse.

"Go, Sky! Don't let me lose!"

"Hey, Malook! Hey, hey!" cried Caressa, almost in his ear.

They reached the reed beds neck and neck. Lacking a clear finishing post both reached their hands in the air to claim victory.

"Mine!"

"Mine!"

"Not a fair start," complained Caressa, panting. "You took off first."

"Never said it was fair," retorted the Wildman. "Just said I won."

"Cheat!"

"Loser!"

The hard fast ride had done wonders for their spirits. Both were glowing with exhilaration. For all their insults they were grinning at each other like monkeys.

"Good to get away," said the Wildman.

"Heya!" cried Caressa, realizing for the first time that they were alone. "Let's never go back!"

"Know where we are, Princess?"

"Don't know. Don't need to know."

"We're in the reeds."

"What's in the reeds that I should care?"

"Jump down. I'll show you."

They dismounted, and leaving their Caspians to graze untethered, they pushed their way into the tall clicking reeds.

"Water ahead," said the Wildman. "You mind getting your legs wet?"

"You mind getting your face smacked?"

Shortly they were wading through knee-deep river water. A shape loomed before them. The Wildman strode on between the reeds and struck the high timber sides softly with his hands.

"She's still here," he said. "Waiting for me."

It was the *Lazy Lady,* the riverboat that had carried him on so many raids in the old days.

"I remember this!" exclaimed Caressa. "This is your pirate boat!"

The Wildman hauled himself up onto the deck, and Caressa followed. A litter of dead leaves lay over the pale boards, and birds had nested in the rigging, but to the Wildman's eyes she was all she had ever been.

"She's good," he said. "She'd slip away as sweetly as ever if I let her off the leash."

Caressa stood in the prow and looked through the screen of reeds to the open river.

"You getting itchy feet, Wildman?"

"You know me, Princess."

She returned to him and punched his right shoulder with the heel of one hand. Then she punched his left shoulder.

"What's that for?"

"So you don't forget. You don't go anywhere without me."

"Maybe you don't want to go."

"Maybe I do."

They looked at each other and saw there the same sudden longing. Then, at the same time, they both burst into laughter.

"What about the Jahan of Jahans?"

"Do I have to tell you?"

"Whoa, Princess! You bored with it already?"

"How's it feel being the spiker warlord, pretty boy?"

"Well, I'll tell you," said the Wildman. "Winning is good. Coming out on top of everyone else is good."

"You never came out on top of me."

"But after, when the winning's done, that's when I start to itch."

"Why's that?"

"Don't ask me, Princess. I know what I feel. I don't need to know why."

"I'll tell you why." She shook back her long black hair and touched his golden cheek with the fingers of one hand. "Because you're young."

"Could be."

"And me, I'm young, too. Too young for tomorrow to be the same as today."

"That's right, Princess."

"I still want to go places I've never been. I still want to do things I've never done. I want to live free as long as I can. There'll be time enough for settling down later. But when that day comes, I want to be sure to have some memories to light my fire."

The Wildman gazed on her with admiration.

"You just said it all, Princess."

When Seeker and Morning Star reached the city of Radiance, the streets were empty. It was like Radiance in the old days of the priests. They turned into the street that led to the temple square. At the far end they saw a crowd of people. The crowd was strangely silent.

"What are they doing?"

"Waiting for something." Morning Star could read their colors, even at this distance. "They're excited."

The closer they got, the bigger they saw the crowd to be. As they entered the square itself, they found they were faced by a tight-packed throng that filled the arcaded space to overflowing. And all of them, men, women, and children, were gazing towards them in utter silence.

A fanfare sounded: three rising notes from a horn. At once a great cheer burst forth. The people smiled and waved and cheered, moving back as they did so, opening up a broad path that ran across the square to the lakeside. Seeker and Morning Star blushed the same red at the same time.

"It's for us!"

They set off across the square, down a path strewn with fresh flowers, nodding and smiling for the cheering people as they went. At the far end, side by side on two raised chairs, sat Caressa and the Wildman. Behind them, standing on two barges rocking gently on the calm waters of the lake, a chorus of men and women dressed in white robes broke into song.

> *"Our saviour! Our saviour!*
> *Our thanks we gladly give!*
> *Return to us! Return to us!*
> *Through you alone we live!"*

It was the old choir of Radiance. Seeker and Morning Star recognized the song. Just as before, a high soprano voice now rang out above the rest.

"Receive our tribu-u-ute!"

Morning Star whispered to Seeker.

"They don't know any other tunes."

The cheering now broke out again as they came to a stop at the platform. Caressa greeted them with a grin.

"How's this for a party?"

The Wildman jumped up and cried to the crowd.

"Let's feast!"

Bands of men came streaming out of the arcades carrying tables and lanterns, and within a short time, as the light faded in the sky, the square was transformed into an open-air dining hall. A large fire was laid and lit. Cooks came filing into the square with pots of stew and baskets of cornbread. Flagons of wine were lined up on every table. Musicians took the place of the choir on the barges. As music played over the lake, the people settled down to party.

Seeker and Morning Star, the guests of honor, were seated at the raised table with the Wildman and Caressa. Here too came Seeker's mother and father, and Morning Star's mother and father. Sabin Jahan was at the high table, as was Shab, to Morning Star's amusement. His old resentments seemed to have melted away, and he was in excellent humor.

"That Joy Boy talked a lot of sense," he confided to Morning Star. "No fun being miserable. So now I just laugh."

And laugh he did, at everything.

Three small figures emerged from the milling crowd, their faces greasy with food.

"Where did you go, lady? You never said good-bye."

It was Libbet and Burny and Deedy.

"That's because I knew I was coming back."

"Should have said good-bye," said Burny reproachfully. "Deedy cried. She's a boggy baby."

"Am not!" said Deedy, pinching Burny's leg.

"Yow! Deedy pinched me!"

He ran into the arms of Morning Star's mother, Mercy.

"I've been looking after them," said Mercy, meeting Morning Star's surprised look. "They stay with us now."

"And go to the new school," said Arkaty.

"I hate school!" said Burny. "You have to sit down. You have to sit down for *hours* and *hours!*"

Morning Star thanked her mother with her eyes, knowing the children would not have thought to thank her themselves.

"We reckoned you'd not be staying with us for long," said Arkaty. "There's others need you more than us."

"But I'll always come back, Papa."

"As to coming back," he said with a smile, "let that fall as it may."

"See, Papa." She took out of her pocket the braid of lamb's wool he had given her long ago. "I don't forget."

Seeker was hearing from his father about the school he had recently started in the city.

"It's much like the old school," he said, "except that I'm not as young as I was. Though here's a strange thing." He threw his son a wry look. "The children never seem to grow any older."

"And has Gift come with you, Father, to help look after the school?"

"Yes, he has. I'm glad you remember old Gift. He doesn't say much, but the school wouldn't be the same without him."

Caressa was talking quietly with Sabin, who listened and nodded his head. The Wildman walked round the table to place himself between Seeker and Morning Star. His arms round each of them, he squatted down and spoke to them in a low voice.

"No one knows this yet," he said. "Caressa and I are going away. At first light."

"Where are you going?" said Seeker.

"Downriver on the *Lazy Lady*. Far away. Farther than I've ever been before."

"The river doesn't go that far."

"Who said we stop where the river ends?"

He saw the look on Seeker's face when he said that, and he grinned. Before either of them could reply, Caressa signalled to the Wildman that she was ready. He rose and joined her. It had all been planned.

Caressa jumped up to stand on the high table, her silver-handled whip in her hand. The Wildman beat on the tabletop with his fists, and called for silence.

"You tell them, Princess!"

The voices and laughter in the square faded to an expectant hush. All looked up at Caressa, beautiful in the firelight.

"My fellow Orlans!" she cried. "I call you all to witness."

She raised the whip high for all to see.

"I have been proud to lead the Orlan nation. We are now at peace, and my work is done. I hand the whip of the Orlans to Sabin, son of Amroth."

Sabin jumped up onto the table beside her. Caressa gave him the whip. He took it and held it up high.

"I am Sabin!" he called out. "Jahan of Jahans!"

For a moment there was a stunned silence. Then the Orlans in the crowd began to beat out their approval. They were not wearing armor or carrying swords, so they beat with their mugs on the tables and their boots on the flagstones. Sabin looked from face to cheering face, and he heard the thundering beat, and he reached out his arms as if to embrace them all.

The Wildman then joined him on the high table.

"If she goes," he cried, pointing at Caressa, "I go!"

"No!" the spikers shouted back. "Don't go!"

"You want me to stay?"

"Stay! Stay!" they cried.

"Heya! Do you lo-o-ove me?"

"Wildman! Wildman! Wildman!"

"Too bad! I'm going!"

He raised his arms high above his head and laughed a great laugh.

"But I'll be back!"

He was so fine, so glorious, so free. What could they do but laugh with him?

Then Shab was up on the high table.

"Spikers!" he cried. "When did we ever have a chance like this before? This is our city! We can live well here! Who needs a warlord? We can rule ourselves!"

The Wildman threw an arm round Shab, and pointing at him with his other hand, he offered him to the throng.

"Heya for Shab! Shab the magnificent!"

And Shab put his arms round the Wildman in his turn, and he laughed and laughed.

Later in that long night, Seeker and Morning Star climbed to the top of the temple rock and stood there by the new Garden, looking out over the city and the lake.

"You want to go with them, Star?"

"I don't know. I think maybe I do. Though I don't know where."

Seeker heard the distant call of seagulls and caught the faint tang of salt on the wind.

"To other lands."

"You know the way?"

"You go to the farthest place you know. And then you keep on going."

"Oh, well then," said Morning Star, "I'll come."

They sailed at dawn. They meant to slip away unnoticed, but all down the riverbanks there were people standing, waving, sending them on their way. They passed the fields of sunflowers, now tended once more, the great amber heads turning to greet the rising sun. They passed the corn plantations, where the cobs were fattening on the stalks. They glided silently by the shanties of Spikertown, empty now that the spikers had moved into the city. They passed the General Store, and the old man on the porch raised his cap in salute, and they saluted back. They passed the jetty where Morning Star had stood and waited for the river-boat to Anacrea, back in the days when all she had wanted in life was to become a Noble Warrior. And so they sailed down the bends of the ever-widening river until they came in sight of the sea. It was evening now, and the water was still. There where once the island of Anacrea had stood, capped by the castle-monastery of the Nom, was an unbroken sheet of trembling gold, reflecting the light from the western sky.

They moored in the river mouth for the night. As the sun rose the next day, they set sail for the open sea, and other lands.